DEATH
OF A
Mermaid

A Callie McKinley Outer Banks Mystery

DEATH
OF A
Mermaid

A Callie McKinley Outer Banks Mystery

by

Wendy Howell Mills

Coastal Carolina Press, Wilmington, NC 28403
www.coastalcarolinapress.org

First edition 2002
Printed in Canada.

10 9 8 7 6 5 4 3 2

Whole copy return only.

Mills, Wendy Howell, 1973-
   Death of a Mermaid: a Callie McKinley Outer Banks Mystery/
Wendy Howell Mills.
   p. cm.
ISBN 1-928556-38-8
   1. Restaurants—Fiction. 2. Restaurateurs—Fiction. 3. North
Carolina—Fiction. 4. Outer Banks (N.C.)—Fiction. 5. Women
dectectives—North Carolina—Outer Banks—Fiction. I. Title.

PS3613.I57 D43 2002
813'.6—dc21
                                                         2002073748

Cover Art by Paula Knorr
Cover Design by Maximum Design & Advertising
Interior Design by D.A. Gallagher

For the women in my life:
May we all find that rainbow.

Acknowledgments

When I first started writing, everybody told me to write what I know. So I did. What I didn't realize was that writing what you know still requires research. Thank you to the following people for their contributions— any errors in these pages are strictly my own: Steve Clinard and Kevin Brinkley of the Nags Head Police Department; Dr. Tosha Dupras of the University of Central Florida; the nice lady at the Old Dominion University reference section; Katie from Sea Breeze Florist. A sincere thank you goes to Alan Ross and my editor Nikki Smith for their invaluable help with the manuscript in its infant stages. Finally, I have relied on David Stick's extensive collection of Outer Banks histories; without them I would have been as lost as a ship in the Graveyard of the Atlantic.

Prologue

She swam in the night to keep herself sane.

Hate kept him sane.

He stood in darkness at the edge of the creek, the fronds of a weeping willow touching his cheek. He saw her, as he knew he would. Her lovely, narrow head sliced through the light-studded water, in and out of the shadows as she returned to the pier.

During those moments in the water she was untouchable, a goddess in her solitude, sufficient unto herself. It was the one thing in her life that was hers alone.

He understood this and hated it all the more. He hated it more than the image of her lying in bed with another man. He wanted her completely, and this was the one thing she always managed to keep from him.

No more.

He watched her climb onto the dock, standing naked with one hip canted as she wrung muddy water from her dark hair. A cascade of shimmering droplets flew in the moonlight. She was a beautiful mermaid, caught as she made her transformation back to life as an ordinary human.

He had loved her since she was a schoolgirl, had loved her in her shapeless teenage uncertainty, had loved her in her nameless angst as she struggled to become a woman, as she longed for the safety of childhood. As he watched her walk down the aisle he had known she was his and his alone. How could she doubt that?

She had brought him to this moment. It was her fault that he stood on this edge of warmthless love and the endless, boundless hate that beckoned him.

First had been the love: Her slim, childish body so at odds with her voluptuous mouth; the sleek lines of her head underneath the masses of dark silky hair; the way she laughed in joy, her head thrown back to expose the neat line of her jaw; the soft skin pulled tight over her high, arched cheekbones.

Then there was the hate, that pulsing hot twin of love, somehow so much more satisfying in its intensity: Those full lips twisted in disgust as she gave him another meaningless smile; the cool looks from those lustrous eyes as she chose to forget all that they had shared; the years he had loved her; the passion between them.

Hate was so much more satisfying.

He felt thick and sluggish with power. It was in him, it had always been there. As a child he knew he could be anything, do anything. A movie star? An astronaut? It had all been in his grasp. He had taken what he wanted back then. His best friend's toy he had taken without qualm. If he wanted a girl, she was his. His father had shown him what it was like to wield absolute power, and he learned his lessons well in a flurry of heavy fists, in the sounds of his mother's screams.

With one longing look at the water, she turned to the house—and saw him.

He recognized the moment when her gaze met his, and saw the dawning terror in her eyes.

He knew then what he wanted to do. Oh, he had known when he came here what would transpire between the two of them this evening. The knife felt light and eager in his hand. Now he saw the one way he could keep her for himself forever, to never lose the memory of those eyes, her lips, the angle of the cheekbones . . .

He stepped forward as she began to scream.

Five Years Later

One
Insane Asylum

Splat!

There's nothing quite like the sound of a good filet mignon hitting the floor—especially a rare one.

"Oh my God!" Margie wailed, and there was a collective intake of breath as every patron in the restaurant prayed that the steak on the floor was not *their* steak.

"Oh my goodness," said an older lady, wiping at the splattering of blood and juice across the front of her dress.

Margie fled into the back with the empty plate, leaving the steak lying on the floor with its accompaniment of mashed sweet potatoes and tender asparagus.

"Next," I said as I made my way through the tables towards the stranded steak, "we will be performing a juggling act with full water glasses. Stay tuned."

The guests laughed and applauded and went back to their muted conversations. On a foggy Outer Banks night when the ocean view out the fifth floor windows is almost nil, people take their entertainment where they can.

"Are you okay?" I asked the lady as she wiped at her dress.

"Oh yes, I'm fine," she said. "It was a juicy steak, wasn't it? I asked for it rare, and I do believe they got it just right. My iron's low you see, and what's needed is a nice bloody steak to bring it right back up again."

We both stared at the nice bloody steak oozing on the floor.

"Let me get you a wet rag to clean your dress, and of course we want to pay for your dry cleaning bill, or a new dress if that's needed," I said. "We'll get a new steak right out."

"That's very kind of you, but I believe a quick trip to the lady's room will fix me right up. You tell that sweet young girl not to worry a bit." She got to her feet and limped purposefully towards the restroom, and I breathed a sigh of relief. Thank God for an understanding, reasonable customer. In this day and age I was lucky she wasn't threatening to sue for emotional trauma.

I went into the back wait station where Kate was assembling a broom and dust pan for the cleanup and directing one of the other waits to get a mop.

"I can't find Margie, but I told Chef we need another steak," she said over her shoulder as she went back into the dining room. "It's not like Margie at all, is it? I wonder where she went. Is the lady going to be all right?"

"She's a doll," I assured my second-in-command, and went through the swinging doors into the kitchen.

"As if I don't have enough problems," Chef was yelling at the top of his lungs when I came in. "I have *peanut butter sandwiches* to make, two hundred of them, and I don't have time to be duplicating every entrée that goes to the restaurant!"

"It's just the one," I said, but he couldn't hear me over the rattling dish machine and shouting. Lee the dishwasher was reciting Shakespeare, as usual, in a hip-hop rhyme.

"What, no one knows how to clean a pot around here? Am I the only one who knows how to clean—" *crash* "—a—" *crash* "—pot?" Leah Hawkins, the banquet chef, smashed the heavy pot against the side of the metal sink. "Lord Jesus!"

I shook my head, feeling bemused as I went to the kitchen window where Chef stood staring at me.

"Can you explain to me why it is so difficult for a wait person to carry a plate to a table without dropping it?" he asked. "I have peanut butter sandwiches to make!"

"Ah, your expensive chef education is coming in handy," I said. "That's why you're mad, admit it. You resent having to make peanut butter sandwiches for that kiddy banquet tomorrow. You know perfectly well that Margie has never dropped anything before. Have you seen her?"

"No. She's probably checked herself into an insane asylum, which is what all of us who choose to work in this business ought to do," he said, and slid a plate into the window. "There's your rare steak. Again. See if you can get it safely to the table, will you?"

"I'll do my best," I assured him.

After I took the plate to the table and made sure the guest was okay (she was, especially after I told her the steak was on the house), I went in search of Margie. I found her in the back storeroom, sitting on the floor beside a box of rigatoni pasta. She was staring blankly at the wall.

"Margie? Is everything all right?"

"I'm sorry, Callie," she said without looking up. "I've never done anything like that before. Is the lady okay?"

"She's fine. She wanted me to tell you not to worry, that she's just fine."

"Oh Jesus, I think I'm losing it. I was walking out to her table and the guy at forty-three said my name. I thought it was *him* and it freaked me out. I spun around and the food went flying right off the plate. I don't know what happened." She plucked at the edge of her apron and stared at me helplessly.

"What's going on, Margie? You've been distracted for the last couple of weeks. Do you want to talk about it?" Now wasn't the perfect time for this conversation. Margie had six tables out in the restaurant, but something in her face told me not to rush her. Something was very wrong.

She said nothing, bowing her head so her dark, curly ponytail covered the side of her face. She was twenty-three and pretty in a fresh-faced athletic way.

I met Margie five months ago when I took the job as manager of the Seahorse Café in the Holiday House Hotel. In that time, she had proven herself to be an exemplary employee, always cheerful and polite, a wonderful waitress, and never late for work.

"You said a guest said your name and you thought it was him. Who is 'him'?" I prodded.

"He won't leave me alone," she said in a low voice. "I thought he was nice at first, but now he just won't leave me alone."

"Who? Doug?" Doug was the clean-cut young man Margie had been seeing this summer. He worked in the hotel as a houseman, and ever since she broke up with him he'd been walking around looking like someone had kicked him in the stomach.

"I don't know what to do. I don't think I can take it anymore," Margie continued as if she hadn't heard me.

"Tell me what's going on," I said. "Tell me who you're talking about and maybe I can help."

"Callie!" I heard Chef roar from the kitchen. "Margie! What, is this the night of the invisible wait staff? Should I expect the plates to waft themselves out of the window all on their own? Where the heck did everyone go?"

Margie got to her feet. "Jeez, I forgot about my other tables. How could I forget about them? Thank you for listening, Callie. Don't mind me, I've just got a lot on my mind."

She went out of the storeroom and I watched her

go. Maybe I was wrong, but all I felt was relief that she was going back to work.

We got busy right after that, and I didn't have a chance to think about Margie or anything else as the line at the door lengthened. Margie made no more mistakes that night, and if she wasn't as cheerful as usual, she was quick and professional and no one complained. It was only later, as I came back up the service elevator after two hours at my desk, that I remembered that I was going to talk to her when she got off. The wait staff was long gone by now, however.

I was debating whether to just go home or to go to Sharkey's as I passed through the deserted kitchen. It was almost eleven, and I was ready to get away from the Holiday House. Even though I was tired, I wasn't ready to go home and stare at my bedroom ceiling. Maybe I *would* go to Sharkey's.

The kitchen was quiet except for the hum of freezers and refrigerators and the clank-clank of the dish machine. Someone must have left it running by accident.

I went around the edge of the dish room and stopped cold. Oh Lord. It couldn't be.

I closed my eyes and opened them again. It was still there.

A skull.

The eyeholes gleamed at me as water trickled down the brownish plates of the skull. The jawbone was sitting separate from the skull itself, a macabre Cheshire grin.

It was a skull, I could see that; I'd seen them before in museums and in movies. What I had a problem with was *where* it was: on top of a pile of jumbled silverware in a plastic dishwasher rack.

Two
Skulls And Mermaids

"So, Callie, I heard you found another dead body."

Susan peered at me, her thick glasses reflecting tiny alligators from the neon beer sign over Sharkey's front door.

"Like I meant to! Besides, this was a skull, not a body."

"In the dishwasher," Susan said.

"Yes, in the dishwasher."

Sharkey's at one-thirty in the morning in the middle of October was not a hub of activity. Up front, local musician Steve Laten was breaking down his equipment after an easy night of entertainment. Susan, who looked enough like Aunt Bee for people to ask if she knew Andy Griffith, sat in her special chair at the end of the bar smoking her mile-long cigarette and drinking Jim Beam. Random remnants of Outer Banks life filled in the rest of the bar stools, mostly men drinking and talking about fishing.

"I'm beginning to wonder if you don't arrange these dead bodies for our entertainment," Kyle Tyler, the owner of Sharkey's said as he slid onto the stool beside me. "Nothing much happened on the Outer Banks until you got here."

Kyle was tall, about thirty-five, and wearing bleach-stained old jeans and a Sharkey's T-shirt. A baseball cap shadowed his dark blue eyes, and he chewed idly on a straw as he looked at me.

"Didn't you know? I arrange the dead bodies *just* for your entertainment, Pooh."

"Don't think I don't appreciate it." As usual, he ignored my use of his childhood nickname. One of his cousins had told me about it a couple of weeks ago and I'd been using it unmercifully ever since.

Susan laughed in delight. "If I didn't know better, I'd think ya'll were an old married couple." She settled back in her chair, a comfortable director's chair with "Susan" emblazoned across the back in curlicue letters. "So give. Tell us about the skull."

"There's not much to it," I said, scooting my stool back so I could see both of them. Melissa, the pretty blond bartender, refilled my Tanqueray and tonic and leaned on the bar to hear the story. Steve Laten finished breaking down his equipment and wandered over to listen.

It's fall. We take our kicks when and where we can.

"So I walk in the kitchen," I began. "I heard the dish machine running, and I went over to check it out. A plastic dish rack was just coming out of the machine, and all I saw at first was silverware. Then I saw it. The skull."

"Was it clean?" Elizabeth had wandered up, looking sexy in a tight miniskirt and a hat with peacock feathers sticking out at wild angles.

"Of course it was clean, Elizabeth!" Susan snapped at her best friend, who despite her outfit, was pushing eighty and could out-drink all of us.

"I was just wondering," Elizabeth said in a hurt voice.

"It was very clean," I said with a straight face. "I was a little surprised, of course."

"What do you mean? Haven't you ever seen a skull in a dish machine before?" Kyle asked.

"*Anyway,* like I was saying, then Lee the dishwasher came over, and when I asked him about it, he said his dog dug it out of the dune behind the hotel. He wanted to clean it up and put it on his TV at home, and he was mad when I insisted on calling the police. He kept talking about possession being nine-tenths of the law, and since he found it . . ."

"Finders keepers, losers weepers," Steve commented, and nodded when Melissa asked if he wanted another drink. "Is Lee the little dude who's always quoting Shakespeare—badly?"

"That's him."

"I want to know what the police said," Susan demanded.

"Well, not much, actually," I said. "Two ambulances, a fire truck, three patrol cars, and about a dozen volunteer firemen came up when I called. Then Dale Grain showed up—" I winced, remembering the look the Nags Head detective gave me when he saw the skull "—and put the skull in an evidence bag. They took the dish machine apart, and then they started asking questions. They took poor Lee to the police station; I guess they think maybe he had something to do with it, I don't know."

The front door opened and everyone turned to see who came in, but it was only more fishermen. Melissa went to wait on them.

"But what did they *say?*" Susan was the acknowledged queen of the beach grapevine, the gossip mill that worked faster than any newspaper. Since the Outer Banks didn't have a local TV channel and the newspapers came out only two or three times a week, you found yourself relying on the grapevine, as exaggerated and inaccurate as it sometimes was.

"Well, apparently it's not all that uncommon to find bones in this part of the state. There're a lot of American Indian burials in this area. They got Lee to show them where he found the skull and cordoned off the dune. They're taking it to the medical examiner's office in Greenville to be processed, and they should know pretty quickly if it's an Indian burial or something more recent."

"I doubt they come across skulls in dish machines very often. Now if it had been a skull driving drunk . . . ," Kyle said.

We all laughed. The police on the Outer Banks were notorious for giving out DWIs, and as the beach didn't have much in the way of violent crime, it sometimes seemed like that was *all* the Outer Banks police did.

"No, they seemed pretty much on top of things," I

said, though I was still smarting from the sarcastic questions Dale Grain asked me. "If it's a recent death, then naturally Lee looks pretty suspicious, so they're already questioning him."

"Anybody who would put a skull though a dish machine would look pretty suspicious in my opinion," Susan said.

"So where is the rest of the body?" Steve asked.

I shrugged. "They were searching the dune for the rest of the body when I left, but I don't think they'd found anything yet. We'll know more in a couple of days, once a medical examiner has gone over the skull. It'll be interesting to see who it belonged to."

From the other end of the bar, I heard a name that chilled my blood.

Laurie McKinley. My real name.

My face must have shown my distress, because both Kyle and Susan looked down at the other end of the bar. Two of the fishermen were pointing at me.

"Callie, dear," Susan said, "I think you have been recognized."

I was astonished at how apprehensive I felt. It was all over; it happened two years ago and several thousand miles away. I had been hiding for so long, it was difficult to remind myself that I didn't have to hide anymore. Several people on the Outer Banks—Kyle and Susan included—knew my real identity, but it was a jealously guarded secret and I was grateful to them for that.

My closest friends knowing my secret was one thing, having complete strangers recognize me was another.

One of the fishermen, grizzled and grinning, came over to me.

"You're that chick, right?" he said. "Laurie McKinley, the girl who saved Henry Gray's son. That's you, right?"

His breath could have knocked over the Wright Brothers National Memorial, a sixty-foot-high block of granite on top of Kill Devil Hill.

"Who you kidding?" Kyle said easily. "Callie here doesn't look anything like Laurie McKinley. I've seen pictures of Laurie McKinley, and she's a lot prettier for starters. I read in a magazine that she was living down in Florida trying to stay away from all the creeps who keep hassling her."

"Nah," Susan said. "Callie doesn't look anything like Laurie McKinley." She shook her head and blew smoke into his face.

The man swayed in his rubber boots. "Sure as heck looks like her," he mumbled, and went back to his buddy.

"Prettier than me?" I said, looking up at Kyle and trying not to laugh.

"That's my story and I'm sticking to it."

"Thank you," I said to Susan and Kyle, and fought back the insane urge to cry. What a day . . .

The conversation wandered back to the skull after a

while, but finally the speculations got too outrageous, even for Susan. The talk moved to more immediate subjects: the spurt of tour plane crashes; the local who walked into Sharkey's with a live turkey under his coat; the rumor of a witch coven operating in Nags Head Woods; and the opening of another bar.

I had been hoping to run into Margie. She often came by Sharkey's, but it didn't look like she was going to show. I wanted to talk to her about what happened tonight, but it would have to wait until tomorrow.

After my fifth yawn, I decided to call it a night. Maybe I would be tired enough to fall asleep right away.

I hoped so.

The next morning I grabbed a coat and whistled Jake outside. Ice dashed out with us, which he had been doing more often as he got used to his surroundings. Now the three of us sauntered down the quiet sandy road and climbed over the dune to face the ocean.

I was still cross-eyed and sleepy at just seven in the morning. As far as I was concerned, it might as well be the middle of the night. At least I felt *awake* in the middle of the night.

The beach was deserted, the yellow sand stretching undisturbed in both directions, the ocean lapping busily at the shore. Jake began his morning rounds and I sat on the side of the dune and watched him. At just under a year, he was seventy pounds of puppyish brown Lab and Heinz 57 Mutt. He looked back at me and wagged his tail before pouncing on a patch of rancid seaweed.

"I hate cheery morning people," I said. Ice, wrinkling his nose and squinting his golden eyes in the heavy salt breeze, tended to agree.

The sun had cleared the horizon and was spreading long rays of golden glitter across the quiet ocean. It was early October and the weather was still beautiful—cool at night, with the sun-kissed air warming as the sun climbed over the horizon.

"Whatcha think, Ice?" I asked, sipping from my coffee mug and feeling the caffeine jolt my system back to life. Ice ignored me, turning his head to sniff the wind.

"About what, you ask?" I continued. "Why, anything. You need to learn to be more flexible. We can have a conversation every now and again, you know."

Ice made it clear that he thought I was out of my mind and continued sniffing at the air, his long white tail lashing the sand.

I laughed, thinking of my grandfather Sam, the man who raised me. He used to always say: "Whatcha think? About anything!" to me when I was little.

I pulled a Marlboro Light out of my pocket and lit it.

"Don't look at me like that," I told Ice. "I wanted

one for the ride home last night so I stopped and got a pack."

Ice thought I was insane, but then he knew that already.

I inhaled the cigarette and drank my coffee. A pod of dolphins was porpoising out beyond the breakers, shiny gray backs sliding through the water as they searched for their breakfast. Jake saw them and barked, racing through the shallows as he tried to keep pace with them.

"Crazy dog," I commented. Now that I was starting to wake up, I didn't feel half bad. I was sleeping better the last several months, the sound of the surf and the fresh sea air working wonders. I only had the nightmare every once in a while. Last night, I didn't even dream about the skull in the dish machine.

I stretched, felt the pulling sensation in my stomach, and cringed instinctively. There was no pain anymore, just the pulling. I drew up my shirt and stared at the purple crater on my right side just under my rib cage. Almost two years later, it was still healing. The surgeons told me I could get plastic surgery if I wanted to get rid of the scar, but I just wanted to forget about it. I didn't think I could face another visit to the hospital.

Jake returned to me, dripping wet, sandy, and happy. Of course, he waited until he was beside me before he shook. Ice hissed at him and took off over the dune.

As I got up, I caught a glimpse of something in the

ocean. Jake and I followed Ice up the dune, and I looked back when we reached the top.

I could have sworn I saw a woman swimming way out beyond the surf among the dolphins.

Three
I Hate Cheery Morning People

I could hear her bellowing when I came through the employee entrance and I swear the walls were shaking.

I went into the office, nodding at Jerry Matthews, the restaurant chef. He was muttering under his breath.

"Crawfish Etouffee? That'll use up that crawfish . . ."

"How was your day off, Jerry?"

"What day off? I spent the whole day working on the new menu." Jerry was cherubic and pink-faced, and his long toffee-colored hair flowed around his shoulders. "By the way, Lily is looking for you," he said without looking up.

"Why am I not surprised?" I asked, and started down the hall.

The bellowing had stopped. The hall was ominously silent as I passed the various offices and paused at the closed door. A plaque read:

Lily Thomas
General Manager

I knocked with care.

"Come in already," a voice snapped, and I opened the door.

Lily Thomas swiveled her leather chair around and inspected me like a bug found in a garden salad. A mustard-yellow dress was wrapped around her large frame and a peacock blue and yellow scarf tied back her riotous copper curls.

"Hi," I said, seating myself across from her. "What, did someone pee in your cornflakes?"

"I think I liked it better when you were scared of me." She scowled.

Lily *did* scare me at first. She was incapable of speaking in anything less than a roar, and had a habit of staring at you with flat green eyes as if she were contemplating vivisection. It could be a little intimidating. I learned, however, that she had a heart of gold and was really very sensitive about her large size. She was just very loud about expressing her sensitivity.

"If one more person calls me about that stupid skull I think I will commit murder," she said.

"Ah."

"The press has gotten hold of the story, and they're off and running with it. Don't talk to the press. Tell your staff that. I've already told the front desk. If we don't respond, maybe they'll leave it alone." She leaned back in the chair, the springs groaning in protest. "I wish you had just thrown the damn thing in the ocean." She glared at me.

"Sorry," I said, my tone not apologetic. "Have you heard anything from the police yet?"

"I called Dale Grain this morning," she said. "He

hasn't called me back yet. All I know is that they found some teeth and bits of the cervical bone in the dune and nothing else."

"Where's the rest of the body?" My mouth felt dry.

"You tell me." Lily grimaced. "For all we know, it was some pirate who died two hundred years ago, but I'm beginning to think the police know better. The press is having a ball with the story. Somebody let it slip that the dishwasher ran the skull through the dish machine, and they're suggesting all kinds of nutty things. Which reminds me, is that guy all there? I talked to him on the phone this morning and he kept reciting poetry at me. Why the hell was he washing the skull anyway?"

"Shakespeare," I corrected. "He was reciting Shakespeare. He wanted to—er, put the skull on his TV. I take it he's home from the police station?"

"I knew he was a nutcase," Lily muttered. "He's home, for now, but they still want to question him. He's freaking out. The police are already saying that at the very least he might be charged for defacing a burial site—at the very least, they said. What is that supposed to mean? Do they really think he would kill someone and then run the skull though the dish machine?"

I shrugged. It didn't strike me as that unbelievable.

"Let's pretend it never happened and maybe everyone else will pretend with us. That would be nice, wouldn't it?"

"Sure," I agreed.

As I left Lily's office I passed Stephen, a tall, roughly handsome man with a tool belt around his waist and a cup of coffee in his hand. He was sopping wet.

"Hi Callie," he said in his Southern drawl.

"Good morning," I said, trying to ignore the way his eyes were roaming. The fact that I found Stephen attractive made it worse. "What, you jump in the pool?"

"The whirlpool in 428 is jammed up," he said. "I was painting in there and Lily asked me to look at it. What're you doing tonight? Any plans?"

"You know better."

"You're divorced, right?" he asked. "That's why you're so down on guys?"

"Just because I won't go out with you, I'm down on all guys? Aren't you being a little conceited? Next you'll be asking if I'm gay."

Stephen laughed and scratched his neck. "Are you?"

I threw a mock punch at his shoulder.

"Doesn't hurt to try," he said.

He smiled and went down the hall. Lily hired Stephen to paint all the guest rooms, and he had been staying in the hotel for the last month. He asked me out daily, and I turned him down daily. The man just didn't give up.

I realized I was blushing.

Jerry was gone and the food and beverage office was empty. It was a rare occurrence to get the office to myself, and I had a lot of work to do with the new menus.

There was a note on top of my stack of To-Do's.

Callie-
I can't take it anymore. He won't leave me alone. I have to go away for a while. I'm sorry for doing this to you.
Margie

Wendy Howell Mills

Four
In The Name Of Love

It was eight o'clock before I got a chance to call Margie's house again.

After leaving a frantic message on her answering machine that afternoon, I scrambled to find a wait to fill her shift. We were already short-staffed, and though I found another wait, he was not nearly as good as Margie. The night was a disaster, with unhappy customers and wrong food orders. I had a headache.

I went down to the office and unlocked the door, sighing when I saw the unfinished new menus spread across my desk.

"Yuck," I said, and grimaced. We changed the menu twice a year, and I was working on getting the new fall/winter menu typed up and formatted. It was not a fun job.

I picked up the phone and called Margie's house again. This time a girl answered.

"No, Margie's not here," she said.

"Is this Valerie?" I asked. Valerie was Margie's room-mate, and though we had never met, we chatted on the frequent occasions I called.

I explained who I was and Valerie sounded relieved.

"Do you know where she went? I don't know what

to do. She packed up when she got home at two in the morning, took the dog."

"Did you ask her where she was going?" I leaned back in my chair and ran a hand through my hair.

"I was asleep. I just remember she was making a lot of noise, thumping things around. When I got up in the morning there were clothes and boxes of food all over the place. She left a note and asked me to take care of her finches." Valerie's voice, thin and childish, was rising as she spoke.

"Did the note say anything else?" I asked.

"She said she was sorry."

There was silence as I thought. "How many clothes did she take? Do you have any idea how long she was planning to be away?"

"Jeez, I don't know. It looked like she packed in a hurry. I know one thing, though. She took some of her sketches and art supplies. I'm not sure she's planning on *coming* back."

Valerie had disintegrated into sobs at that point, and I asked her to call me if she thought of anything else. She agreed and hung up. I sat with the phone in my hand, staring up at the picture of the wait staff at the last end-of-the-season party. I had found a box of hats up in banquet storage, and everyone at the party had been wearing one. Margie wore a Saint Patrick's Day green bowler hat, and she looked happy and relaxed as she posed for the picture with her arm around two other waits.

What the heck happened?

I thought back to the night before. Margie seemed upset, but I didn't think it was too serious. I planned to talk to her the next time I saw her. Now it was too late.

Where did she go when she left the hotel? She left before I found that stupid skull in the dish machine, which had been about eleven o'clock. Valerie said Margie didn't get home until after two. Something must have happened between the time she left the hotel and when she got home. I could not believe that Margie was planning to leave when I spoke to her last night. She was just too responsible. She had never been late, called in, or missed a shift in the five months I had been here. This was not like her at all.

Yet, I reflected, who's to say I really knew Margie? I didn't, really. For example, I didn't know she sketched. What else didn't I know about her?

I came at it from another angle. What *did* I know about Margie?

She was twenty-three. She had worked at the Holiday House for over two years. She grew up somewhere in western New Hampshire. She came to the Outer Banks the summer before her senior year of college and never went home. She sketched. She was quiet, responsible, and kind.

That was the sum total of what I knew about Margie Sanders.

I wished I could get into the accounting/personnel

office and pull Margie's file, but it was locked up tight for the night. I dialed the accounting extension and left a message on their voice mail requesting it first thing in the morning. I hung up the phone before I realized that tomorrow was Sunday. I would have to wait until Monday.

I had another thought and picked up the phone to call the front desk.

"Is Doug working tonight?" I asked.

"He's delivering some pillows to the fourth floor," Ray, the front desk manger told me.

I asked him to send Doug to my office when he got a chance. I was looking through a file containing recent employee applications when Doug appeared in my doorway.

He was out of breath from running. He wore shorts and a green Holiday House polo shirt with his nametag pinned over his heart. His blond hair was combed back with some type of gel, and his face looked smooth and polite.

"Do you know where Margie is?" I asked.

Doug looked surprised, and with reluctance, came into the office. "No. Why do you ask?"

I looked at him appraisingly.

He saw my look and flushed. "It's just strange that you would ask me out of the blue where Margie is. She broke up with me two weeks ago."

I nodded, seeing his point. "She didn't come to work today. Her roommate said she packed up and left last night. She left me a note, but I'm still kind of worried about her. Do you know any reason why she would leave like this or where she would go?"

Doug sank down into a chair, his lanky legs folded to fit into the small space under the desk.

"She worked last night, right? She didn't say anything?" he asked.

"No. That's why I was so surprised she left like this. She didn't say anything last night."

He ran a hand through his hair and seemed surprised to find it slicked back by gel. "I wonder if she's running from me?" he murmured, not talking to me at all.

"Why would you say that?" I asked. "Why would she run from you?"

"She was like a . . . a wild animal, a deer, I guess. She looked so beautiful, and I just wanted to love her. But when I got too close, off she went. We had the best time just driving around, camping down at the national campground in Hatteras, sitting on the beach naming the stars…" Doug looked up at me, his dark eyes grief-stricken, blotches of red on his high cheekbones. "I never told anyone that before."

I patted him on the hand. "You didn't talk to her last night, did you?"

He looked away. "No."

Why did I get the feeling he was lying to me?

"She's had something on her mind the last couple of weeks. Do you have any idea what's been bothering her?"

He shrugged. "She broke up with me. I'm the last person she would have told."

"Well," I said, "is there anything else you can think of that might help me figure out where Margie went?"

Doug's walkie-talkie crackled and Ray's tinny voice asked him to deliver some towels to room 415.

He got to his feet and headed for the door. "I think she might have been seeing someone else. We weren't exclusive you got to understand. That was fine with me; there're plenty of chicks out there, you know?" The momentary bravado faded. "There were a couple of times this summer when she said she had plans when I wanted to do something. She said they were just friends, but well . . . I wonder where in the heck she's got to?" His voice cracked as he stood at the door.

"She probably just went away for a while to think," I said. "I'm sure she's fine."

"You don't know her," Doug said, and left.

"You're right," I said, "I don't."

I sat for a moment, thinking. I remembered that Margie had dropped the steak last night because she was startled by someone saying her name. She said she thought it was "him." In the note she left me, she said that "he" wouldn't leave her alone. Who was the guy? Doug?

Something just did not sit right with me. I may not have known her very well, but I had worked closely with Margie for over five months. She was a good, conscientious person. I had no doubt about that.

Something had gone very wrong for her to pack up and leave like this. What happened Friday night? Why in the world didn't I pay more attention to what she was telling me?

I picked up the phone. When Valerie answered, her voice sounded drained and quiet, as if she'd had a good cry.

"Valerie, this is Callie again," I said. "I have a bad feeling about Margie. I'd like to come by tomorrow to talk to you."

Five
Testosterone Junkie

The Seahorse Café bar was dark and smoky and Lenny Marks was singing Willie Nelson's "Angel Flying too Close to the Ground." I paused by the edge of the bar to listen.

Lenny was thin and polished a burnished brown by the sun, which had lovingly touched each and every line on his weathered face. His dark hair was pulled back into a shoulder-length ponytail and was streaked with silver. He made you want to look two or three times to make sure it wasn't really Willie singing.

I slid onto a bar stool and nodded when Matt asked me if I wanted a drink.

"You gonna hire someone to replace Margie?" Matt's New York accent endeared him to our many northern visitors, despite the fact that he'd lived here for over twenty years.

"I called and arranged an interview with a server. We need someone else even if—when Margie comes back."

I sighed, wishing I could go see Margie's roommate tomorrow instead of Monday, but Valerie was working a double. Monday would have to be soon enough.

"Callie, how you doing, girl?" Leah asked as she

came out of the kitchen and saw me at the bar. She gazed at me from behind thick glasses as she pushed herself up onto a bar stool.

"Just listening to Lenny," I said. Leah seemed subdued tonight, which was unusual for her. She was known for her wild, cackling laughter and for periodically flashing her impressive breasts, none of which had changed since she'd been promoted from breakfast cook to banquet chef.

"Where is Margie?" she asked. She leaned forward, her plump face drawn with worry lines, her dark eyes concerned. "Do you know where she went?"

"No, I wish I did."

"She's a good girl, not like some people around here," she said, tapping my knee. "I'm worried about her."

"I am too. I'm sure she'll be fine."

"Something, Leah?" Matt asked.

"No, I got to get home to my old man. He'll start calling all his young bimbos if I leave him alone long enough." She snickered and patted my back.

"You better get home, then," I said, smiling, and she waved as she maneuvered herself off the bar stool and left. I watched her, her words cheering me for some reason.

Leah carried around an aura of irrepressible good cheer wherever she went. Lily had struggled to find someone to fill the banquet chef's position, and it was Chef who suggested promoting Leah, though she didn't have a lot of banquet experience. The food and beverage department had been strapped for money after this summer, and we couldn't afford to pay a professional chef the money he or she would expect for the position. Leah was more than coping with her new job, and I was very glad—for her and for us.

"Hi, Callie."

I turned around to see Stephen, still wearing his tool belt, white paint smeared across his shirt.

"Hi," I said, and he took that as an invitation to sit down beside me.

He ordered a Budweiser and tapped square, oil-stained fingers to Lenny's song.

"Tell me about yourself," he said.

I looked at him in surprise. Did he know who I really was? I took a deep breath. "I grew up in Virginia Beach, loved coming down here on vacations. I graduated from college with a history degree, took a job with a restaurant chain where I had been working through college, and moved to California. Then I moved here." There, that sounded innocuous enough. "How about you? You live in Raleigh, right?"

"I own my own painting company, but I lived here a couple years ago. I worked for a realty company doing maintenance on those big oceanfront cottages. Takes a lot of work to keep those babies looking nice, you know? I come to the beach a lot, even now that I live in Raleigh. This job is great. I get to stay at the beach and get paid for it. Hey, since you've had an actual conversation with me this time, maybe we could go for a bike ride tomorrow. Doesn't that sound like—"

"Callie-girl!" A voice reverberated through the bar and the sound wave threatened to knock off a man's toupee across the room.

I turned and saw Lily entering the restaurant. She was drunk, and I groaned. Lily had a tendency to get into arguments with people when she got drunk—stupid arguments, like what color the ocean really is, or why bleached blonds dye their hair. I had heard them both.

Kyle and one of the hotel guests, Charlie, were with her.

"What are you doing here?" I asked as they took seats at the bar.

"We were all at Sharkey's and Lily talked us into coming back here," Charlie said in his booming voice. "I was about ready to come back to the hotel anyhow. I'm still recovering from last night at Kelly's."

"Matt, I'm here," Lily called, and he sped over to make her drink. Lily was dressed in ivy green tonight, a sheet-sized garment wrapped around her voluptuous frame.

"Put them all on my tab," Charlie said to Matt. "Oh, hell, buy the whole bar a round while you're at it." He pushed aside a lock of the silky blond hair that lay across his bronzed forehead.

Charlie was big, loud, and tanned. *Tanning bed*, I thought. He had been staying in the hotel for the last several weeks while he looked for a vacation home. He owned a used car business, and judging from the way he spent money, it was a very successful business at that.

I turned to Kyle, who still hadn't said anything. "So what are you doing here?"

"Oh, I'm not allowed to leave my own bar now?"

"It looks like you're checking out the competition."

"He doesn't go out much," Lily said.

Kyle shrugged.

He smelled good.

I've always had a really good nose. For some reason I smell things other people don't. Tonight, Kyle was dressed in clean jeans and a green, long-sleeved button-down shirt, and he smelled particularly masculine. After-shave, soap, and a hint of just plain man wafted from him like a cologne. I tried to find something annoying about his appearance, but wasn't able to. Damn.

Beside me, Stephen coughed. "Who's this, Callie?" he asked.

Stephen smelled of paint and sweat.

Kyle stiffened at the possessive tone of his voice, and I glanced at Stephen in irritation. I felt like a teenybopper at a high school dance.

"Kyle, this is Stephen. He's here painting all of our guest rooms. Stephen, this is Kyle, the owner of Sharkey's." I made my voice neutral and the two men shook hands cautiously.

"I painted four rooms today," Stephen said. "Wooo. What a day."

"We served three hundred people today by the time I left," Kyle said with a straight face.

"The testosterone level in here just hit the roof, didn't it?" Lily commented.

"I'm just glad I'm married," Charlie said, and laughed. He turned to Lily and started telling her about a house he looked at with an elevator, two hot tubs, and a gazebo overlooking the ocean.

"I've got a new one for you." Kyle turned to me, his blue eyes amused. "Who is Reginald A. Fessenden?"

"Ah," I said, and grinned. I had been waiting for this one. "Reginald A. Fessenden. He made the first wireless broadcast of musical notes from Buxton to Roanoke Island in 1902. The Wright Brothers weren't the only ones who made history here on the Outer Banks."

"Very good," Kyle acknowledged. "Did you know he put a patent on a parking garage with ramps and hoists?"

"And the patent expired before we even needed parking garages. He was a man ahead of his time."

"I should have known. I'll get you with something you don't know, don't worry."

I thought about the pile of books on Outer Banks history I had purchased at Outer Banks Books over the past few months. This game had cost me some money, but the satisfaction I felt at seeing the expression on Kyle's face was worth every penny.

"Are you two still trying to one-up each other? First

it was World War Two history, now this. Haven't you heard that verbal foreplay is passé?" Lily pretended to yawn. "Bor-ing."

"Any foreplay is better than no foreplay," Charlie said, slurring his words a little as the tequila shot kicked in. He rolled up his sleeves and I saw a crude tattoo of a blue spider on his forearm. He saw me looking and grinned. "Isn't pretty, is it? I thought my mama was going to kill me when I came home with it."

Stephen stood up. "I'll see you later, Callie," he said, and threw some money on the bar.

Kyle looked after Stephen as he sauntered out the door. "I guess he absconded," he said with a deadpan expression. "I hope I didn't scare him off."

"He's a womanizer, anyway," Lily said. "Stay away from him, Callie. He's a good painter but he flirts too much."

"How's your Jeep running? The last time you left Sharkey's you were having a lot of trouble getting it to start," Kyle said.

"Right now it's making this waaa-waaa sound whenever I try to start it." I winced. "I love my Jeep, but it's always something."

"Battery or the starter, probably," Kyle commented. "What do you think, Charlie?"

"Yep. It could be either."

"Get Charlie to look at it, Callie," Lily said. "You'd do that, wouldn't you, Charlie?"

"What? Sure, sure. I'll take a look at it, Callie. Just

let me know when." His eyes were drooping, and he had his arm draped familiarly around the back of my bar stool.

"Oh, I almost forgot. Guess what? I talked to Dale Grain tonight; he's heard from the medical examiner about the skull. It belonged to a young woman who probably died less than ten years ago. Congratulations, Callie, you've landed us in the middle of a murder investigation. Dale's mad because he's stuck going though missing person reports." Lily turned back to the man on the other side of her. I stared at her in shock, but apparently that was the end of the subject. I turned to Kyle.

"That's all she told me, too. I tried to get more out of her, but I can't tell whether she's being close-mouthed, or whether she really doesn't know anything else and wants to look like she knows more than she does."

"I heard that," Lily said over her shoulder.

"Lily told me all about the excitement around here," Charlie said. "I wondered when I got back from Kelly's last night and saw all the police cars." He accepted his tab and signed his name to what I was sure was an exorbitant amount since Matt had been busy making everyone at the bar a drink at Charlie's expense. "I'll see you all tomorrow. My bed is calling and I still have to call my wife tonight."

We said good night, and when it was clear Lily wasn't going to say anything else about the skull, I gave up and changed the subject.

"I've never asked, Kyle. What did you do before you bought Sharkey's?" I thought how little I knew about Kyle. I was realizing how little I knew about the people around me. Was I self-centered, or did everyone have acquaintances they saw frequently and never really knew?

"I left for college for a couple of semesters, then just traveled around doing about everything. Fishing, restaurants, construction, you name it I did it. But I never could find a place I liked as much as here. So I came back."

"All those places and you decided to come back here."

"It gets to you. Makes other places just seem not quite real, though you know that this place is the one that's not quite real—but it is." He shook his head. "I'm not making sense. Either you get it or you don't."

"I think I get it," I said.

"Did you hear about the mermaid?" Kyle asked.

"A mermaid?" Lily turned around.

"Yep," said Kyle. "A mermaid. Several people have seen her swimming out beyond the surf, naked as a jaybird. She disappears without a splash when people call to her."

"Fins and all?" Lily asked.

"One guy said he saw fins, but he also claims that Colin Powell is his long-lost son."

"Mermaid of the Outer Banks," I murmured. "You know, I think I saw her this morning. I saw something in the ocean anyway, and I really thought it was a woman."

"Can't be any stranger than Batman," Lily said. "He haunted the Outer Banks a couple of years ago."

"Mask, cape, utility belt, and everything," Kyle said.

"Kyle had to throw him out of Sharkey's because he attacked some guy who made fun of his Batmobile," Lily said, laughing.

"His bicycle," Kyle added.

Lily asked about Margie and I shared what I knew while Kyle listened in silence.

"The poor thing." Lily's voice softened and she looked at the bottom of her glass. "I always liked Margie. I wish she could have come to one of us." She looked back up at me. "But this is the Outer Banks, and stuff like this happens all the time, as much as we don't like it. Are you sure Doug doesn't know where she is?"

I explained that I had talked to him, and finished up by saying, "I'm not sure he's telling me everything. We'll see."

"Doug is in love. People in love do stupid things. You keep on him and he'll tell you what he knows, or *I'll* talk to him."

Lily turned away and asked the man beside her why all people from New York were such jerks. The man, of course, was from New York. Lily can sure pick them.

"Do they?" Kyle asked. His voice was odd, and I had to scramble to catch up to his train of thought.

I looked at him. "I certainly have. You've never done anything stupid in the name of love?"

Kyle took a sip of his drink. "You know, I'm not sure I've ever been in love."

"Are you serious? You're what, in your thirties?"

"Oh forget it," he said. Then he asked me about how busy the restaurant was that night.

I didn't realize until later that he changed the subject without answering.

Men.

Six

Dead Angel

"**A**void Lily at all costs," Chef whispered to me as I arrived in the food and beverage office Monday morning. "I take it you haven't heard? I'll be praying for you." He brushed by me as he left.

Since Chef was given to flights of insanity, and I could sooner see him serving raw chicken than praying, I didn't pay him much attention.

I spent Sunday hiding out at my house, eating brownies and reading an Elizabeth Peters book. I had just finished working breakfast this morning and was feeling slaphappy. Have I mentioned I am *not* a morning person?

"Oh Jesus, I'd hide if I were you," Jerry said as he came into the office.

"What are you talking about?"

"It's Lily," he said, and his voice dropped to a whisper. "She's looking for you."

I stared at him a moment. I was aware that Lily still struck fear in the hearts of my co-workers, and to be honest I did feel a quiver. But just a quiver.

"Oh well," I said, and started rifling through the contents of my desk.

It was ten o'clock in the morning on a gray, wet

day. The weather made me feel tired and irritable.

It was always interesting how much junk accumulated on my desk when I left it unattended. People
just threw things on top of it—memos, notes, files,
brochures—and by the time I arrived the pile was
always thick and fat.

I flipped through the papers, separating them into
stacks. I squinted at the special sheet trying to decipher
Jerry's handwriting, and then laid it to one side. I came
to a memo from Chef about the new menu and spent
the next half hour at the computer changing "roasted
potatoes" to "red roasted potatoes."

Finally, I sighed and put that away. There was one
last folder on my desk.

Ah. Accounting was on the ball. It was Margie's file.

I opened it and looked through the accumulation
of over two years' employment: awards for employee
of the month; copies of positive comment cards; IRS
information; a wage increase when she was promoted
to head wait; her original application.

Two and a half years ago, Margie had filled out
the application in a rounded, childish hand. She
listed her high school and the college she had been
attending; she was majoring in English. She had
worked at several restaurants since she was sixteen,
but Smiley's Bar and Grill was the only one with a
phone number. She had listed two references and left
the space for "person to contact in an emergency"
blank. Usually college kids put down their parents as

their emergency contact. I wondered why Margie didn't.

I thought a minute and picked up the phone. I called the number that was listed under the first reference. Under "relationship to applicant" she had put "teacher."

"May I speak to Janet McClintock please?" I said when a woman answered the phone.

"Who?" The woman's voice sounded robust, but quavered a bit around the edges, betraying her age.

"Janet McClintock."

"You must have the wrong number."

I read out the number and the woman agreed it was right.

"I guess maybe she's moved," I said.

"I've had this telephone number for fifteen years," the woman said. "Good-bye."

I pressed the receiver down, waited a moment, and let it up. Dial tone.

I dialed the number listed under "Michael Denehey, doctor," the second reference. No one answered, but a machine picked up. A young, exuberant voice announced that the house belonged to a Mr. and Mrs. Brian Hiller.

Hmmm.

I put the phone down and thought. It was possible that there was a mix-up with the numbers, or that telephone numbers had changed in the two and half years since she listed them.

Still, it worried me. I was hoping to find someone

who would know Margie's parents. It was possible that she had mentioned something to them about where she was going. Maybe she simply went back home. I wondered why I was bothered so much by her disappearing act, but I couldn't get the memory of her face that night out of my head. There was a tinge of guilt as well, because if I had taken the time to find out what was wrong, maybe she wouldn't have left.

My phone rang and I picked it up.

"Callie? Is that you? Get your butt in here!"

Lily had found me.

"Great," I said, and got up to trot down to her office like a good little girl.

"Have you seen this?" Lily snapped as I came through the door. She threw a newspaper at me and I caught it before sitting down.

The headline read:

MURDER OF A MERMAID

"What in the world?" I said, re-reading the headline. I looked up at Lily.

"Keep reading," she said in a dangerously quiet voice.

I skimmed through the article and saw that some eager reporter put two and two together and got eighteen. A woman named Angel Knowling was murdered in Virginia five years ago while she swam nude in the creek in her backyard. She was young and pretty, and her husband Keith was the prime suspect, all of which made it a sensational case. The kicker though, was that the woman's head was never found.

The reporter surmised that the skull belonged to Angel Knowling. A police spokesman said they were looking into the possibility and were working with Virginia law enforcement.

I handed the paper back to Lily. "That's pretty horrible."

"Horrible? Horrible? Is that all you have to say? Some woman's head was buried in our dune and you think it's just horrible?"

"Catastrophic? Is that better? You knew about the skull last night. Why is it so much worse today?" I asked.

She threw the paper on her desk in disgust, her coppery curls bounding around her head like Medusa's snakes. "Today we know who the head may belong to, and I remember hearing about that grisly murder. Today, we have reporters calling and making reservations. This has already been picked up by one of the national magazines, one called *Nothing But the Truth*. They've booked a room for one of their reporters. I wouldn't be surprised if more follow. So *today* is a much worse day than *yesterday!*"

"It doesn't have to be such a bad thing," I said. "We get national exposure, we give interviews mentioning the great rates and wonderful views, and people book rooms just to see the hotel where the skull was found." I thought it sounded pretty good.

"The Pete's already called," Lily said.

The words dropped like shells in the deep, dark ocean.

"Goodness," I said. "How did he find out?"

The Pete, or Jefferson Peterson, was the owner of the hotel. He was a second-generation millionaire, and had bought the Holiday House Hotel on a whim. Whimsical would describe the way he oversaw his investment. He lived in Vail, and I was surprised he had found out about this so quickly.

"He has his spies," Lily said.

"Well, what did he say?"

"He asked what the heck I was doing, and if he had to come here to straighten this mess out, the little bugger. Like he knows a thing about running a hotel." She stared out her window at the rain sliding across the pavement.

"This looks like a horrid murder," I said. I picked up the paper and began to re-read the column.

"You don't remember it?" Lily sounded surprised.

Five years ago I had been happy and sun-tanned in Palo Alto, California, with no idea that I would ever leave my husband and come to the Outer Banks.

"I was in California," I said. "We had our own little murders to worry about."

"It was in the news a lot for a while. I guess it was just so sensational, a young woman murdered by her husband as she swam nude. Top that with the fact that no one knew why he would kill her, plus he took off with her head . . . it was pretty bad," Lily said. "The papers took to calling her the 'Murdered Mermaid,' which is pretty tacky, I think.

"Everybody said she was the sweetest thing, all dark fluffy hair and big eyes. Her husband was a schoolteacher and they lived in this pretty little cottage on the edge of a lake, or a creek, or some body of water. The neighbors said she loved to swim in that creek. They showed pictures of it in the paper, and of her beautiful flower garden. Nobody could believe her husband would do something like that, because everybody said they were the perfect couple—a little old-fashioned, but they were suited to each other. His fingerprints were all over the crime scene, and he disappeared that night. Come to find out later there had been a domestic disturbance call the month before she died. Her husband had smacked her around pretty good. Appearances can be deceiving, hmmm? They've never been able to find him, as far as I know. And that poor young thing, he stabbed her twenty-something times before he cut off her head. What a monster."

I was silent. What did the young woman think when she saw her beloved husband coming towards her with murder in his eyes? Had she known, or was it a complete surprise?

I looked away. It's hard finding out that someone you love isn't what he seems.

"I'm handling all the interviews myself," Lily said, shaking herself a little bit as if she was shrugging off the bad memories. "I'm just going to say that we have no idea why Keith Knowling would bury his wife's head here, if he did, and then dazzle them with my brilliance. I want you to reiterate to your staff that no one, I mean no one, talks to the press. I'm putting out a memo to that effect. Not that anyone really knows anything, but I don't want somebody running their mouth."

I stood up.

"Where do you think you're going?" Lily glared up at me.

"Was there anything else? I've got an appointment." In fact, I had two appointments. One was an interview with a prospective wait, the other was with Valerie, Margie's roommate, to try to find out where Margie had gone.

Lily stared at me and then waved a hand. "No, not really. Get out of here."

I went to the lobby and found my applicant waiting for me. Rob was short with blue eyes and flaming red hair.

"I hear you're in a bit of a spot," he said, lounging back on the couch in a flowing silk shirt.

"You could say that."

"Well, look no further; I'll rescue you. I'm your knight in shining armor."

Seven

The Hood

*A*fter I hired Rob—who may not have looked like a knight in shining armor, but he certainly looked like a pretty good wait—I headed out into the cool rain to make a dash for my Jeep. I followed the directions Valerie had given me and ended up in front of a small, white bungalow behind Belk in Kill Devil Hills.

The house was off Third Street, in an area affectionately known as the "Hood," though the unkempt rental cottages and young population had little resemblance to any "hood" I had ever known in California. Margie and Valerie's yard was overgrown, but there were boxes outside the windows that held a variety of flowers and herbs.

I made a dash for the carport and rang the doorbell.

A young woman, slender and tanned, with a big nose and a thin smile answered the door.

"Valerie?" I asked. "I'm Callie McKinley from the Holiday House Hotel."

"Oh yeah. That's right," she said. "Come in."

The door led into the living room, and I sat down on a gray corduroy couch. The room was filled with cast-off furniture, but plants and original paintings made it comfortable and homey. A flock of birds, yellow, white, and blue, twittered inside a cage in the corner of the room.

"Have you lived here long?" I asked Valerie.

She looked around as she seated herself in an old peach-colored armchair. "For a while, I guess. I met Margie at Quagmire's last summer. I was cocktailing and she used to come in with some people I knew. We started talking, and then we realized that both of us were looking for a place to live. We decided to find a house together. I like this house, though it's old as the hills."

"So you've only known Margie since this summer?" I asked, a little disappointed.

Valerie nodded. Her eyes were puffy and sleepy, and she wore boxers and a basketball jersey with no bra. It was clear I had woken her up.

"Have you heard anything from Margie?" I asked.

She shook her head and curled her feet up under her legs. "Not a thing."

"Do you think she may have gone back home to visit her parents?"

"Who knows? Margie never talked to her parents. I always thought it was kind of funny, because I talk to my Mom like every other day."

"What about her other friends? Could she be staying with one of them?"

"I called 'em all already. No one knows anything."

Valerie was trying her best to be cooperative, but she was not a very imaginative girl and her responses were not helpful. She also had a distracting habit of talking with her hand on her face, rubbing her eyes, patting her cheeks, or running a finger down her chin. I recognized the camouflaging movements from my stint with braces. She was embarrassed of her nose.

"Do you mind if I see her room?"

Valerie shrugged and got to her feet. "Sure."

I followed her down a dim hall towards the back of the house. We passed two open doors, a bathroom, and a messy bedroom, and then she led me into a tiny square room.

At work, Margie was a neat person, and it was obvious that she was no different at home. However, it was also obvious that she left in a hurry. Drawers were open, clothes were strewn over the bed, and toiletries spilled over the dresser. In one corner of the room a dead spotlight trained on an empty easel and deserted worktable.

I wandered over and looked at the easel, reminded yet again how little I knew about Margie.

There was a vase of roses on the battered dresser, and another vase of dying flowers sat in one of the windows.

Valerie went over, sat on the bed, and looked apathetically around the room.

"She was a good roommate, you know? Now I don't know what I'm going to do. I can't pay rent and bills on my own, and I don't know when she's going to come back. I can't believe she did this." Her hand wandered over her face as she talked.

I picked up some of the clothes on the bed: shorts, shirts, and jeans. Nothing unusual.

"Valerie, do you have any idea why Margie took off like that?"

"I don't know." She wiped at the corner of her eye. "She never talked to me all that much. I mean, she was nice and all, but she was real private about stuff. She'd hate it if she knew we were in here. She was always real picky about keeping her room private." She looked around, as if expecting Margie to show up and demand to know what we were doing in her room. If only she would!

"What about the night she left. Did you talk to her?"

"I was out late the night before and I was still kinda hungover, so when I got off work I just went straight to bed. I heard her come in around two in the morning, and then I heard her banging around and talking to someone, which was strange, because usually Margie was pretty considerate. When I woke up the next morning, there were boxes of food left out all over the kitchen and I saw the note."

"Can I see it?"

"Oh. Sure."

She left the room, and I took the opportunity to look through Margie's open dresser. In the top drawer were neatly arranged stacks of bank statements, electric, water, and phone bills, awards from work, and an appointment book. There was a shoebox full of pictures. I shuffled through them: a big golden lab;

various beach scenes; lighthouses; the Holiday House and the people who worked there; pictures of Doug.

I put the photos back and picked up her appointment book. I flipped through it, looking for Margie's parents, but the numbers were all local and most were names I recognized. There were several loose bits of paper in the back and three paychecks.

Waits are paid less than three bucks an hour, and their paychecks seldom add up to much, especially after taxes based on tips earned are taken out. It isn't unusual for a server to receive a zero-dollar check, or even end up owing taxes at the end of a pay period. Margie was no exception. It wasn't surprising that she stashed her paychecks in a drawer. It didn't seem worth the bother to cash them.

I heard Valerie returning and shut the drawer. She came into the room and handed me a piece of paper. As I took it, I realized that it had been ripped out of the yellow pages of the telephone book. In the margin was scrawled:

Valerie. Got to go. I'm sorry. Can you please watch my finches? Margie

"You're sure this is Margie's writing?"

She stared at me blankly. "Sure it is. Whose else would it be?"

"Can I keep this?"

She nodded, and I folded the page and put it in my purse.

"Do you mind if I look around?"

Valerie looked uneasy and began rubbing the side of her nose. "I don't know . . ."

"Valerie, I'm worried about Margie. She's been gone for two days and no one has heard from her. I think she may be in some kind of trouble."

"I guess it would be okay . . ."

Before she finished speaking, I went to the closet and opened the door: clothes and shoes, disorganized and jumbled. I looked under the bed. More shoes. I never realized what a shoe horse Margie was. I looked through the dresser again and then the nightstand by the bed. And that was it as far as searching the small room; nothing spectacular.

I looked around at a loss. Margie's walls were bare except for a few of her own paintings—pretty seascapes, with more than a hint of promise—and plaques for winning employee of the month. Other bare spots on the walls suggested she might have taken a few of her paintings with her.

Other than that, nothing. No personal letters from her parents or friends from school, no pictures of anybody except Outer Banks people. There was nothing to indicate where she came from, or where she might go if she felt the need to run.

I pointed at the two vases of flowers.

"Who sent those?"

"They came last week. A guy from the flower shop delivered them."

I went to the flowers and saw the note with the

Seaside Florist and Gift Shop logo, which was a popular local shop. Seaside Florist delivered the flowers we used in the restaurant. I slipped the card out of the envelope.

An investment in our future, the first card read. No signature.

The second card was just as anonymous. *Our love will last an eternity.*

"Are these from Doug?"

Valerie stared at me with that blank look that was beginning to annoy me. I felt like shaking her and shouting, "Wake up!" The poor girl would have just stared at me and wondered what in the world I was so mad about.

"Doug?" I asked again. "She was seeing him over this summer?"

"I don't know any Doug," Valerie said. "Margie was seeing someone?"

Eight
Rumors And Pictures

I shook my head in disbelief. "What? Margie never mentioned Doug to you?"

"I told you she was private," she said defensively.

It was hard to believe that two young women sharing a house would not sit up at night, giggling over boys and mutual friends. Then again, I couldn't see Margie giggling over anything. Even at twenty-three, she came across as much too mature for that. Though, I admit, I wouldn't mind having a close girlfriend to giggle with. I missed those childhood friendships where no subject was taboo and the conversations ranged from the banal to the extra-terrestrial.

"You said she was talking to someone Friday night, the night she left. Someone was here? Who was she talking to?"

"She was talking real low. I guess she was talking on the phone. The phone rang, now that I think about it. And some guy called yesterday for her. I told him she had been gone since Friday and he hung up."

"Okay, Valerie," I said. "Thanks for your help. I'm going to take these, too." I held up the cards from the flowers. "If Margie calls you, or if you think of anything else, please call me. I'm thinking about calling the police."

"Oh, you can't." Valerie looked alarmed. "Margie would kill you. She doesn't want anything to do with them. Someone broke in her car a while ago, and she wouldn't call the police."

"Why not?"

She rubbed her cheekbone. "She just doesn't like them. A lot of people are like that. Anyway, she left on her own, the cops aren't gonna care about that."

She was right, of course, but I didn't like it.

She saw me to the door and I went out into the misting rain to my car.

I pulled into Kmart and ran inside to pick up some pictures that had I dropped off to be developed over a week ago. Pictures in a bag beside me, I drove as fast as I could on the slick roads back towards the hotel. I was gone longer than I planned to be and I still had a lot to do today.

I passed the Wright Memorial, shrouded by mists, and Jockey's Ridge, the hundred-foot hill of sand on the Roanoke Sound. In the summer brave beginners, attached to hang-gliders, flung themselves down the soft incline of the sand dune. Most of them landed on their stomachs, sliding closer and closer to the busy Bypass. A fanciful castle, part of an old putt-putt course, peeked from under the blowing sand.

It was after twelve by the time I got back to the hotel. I pulled into a parking space next to an older blue Jeep with its hood up, a familiar sight since Stephen had arrived last month.

"Hi, Stephen," I said. I could hear the breakers rolling on shore behind the hotel, pounding the sand.

"Hey, Callie. Don't you just love Jeeps?" Stephen poked his head out from underneath the hood and grinned at me.

"Tell me about it."

As I came through the door into the kitchen, the first thing I saw was Chef's grim face. His gray hair was rumpled, and his mustache seemed to be drooping more than usual as he listened to someone talk. He saw me come in and looked at me with no expression.

When I saw who he was talking to, I understood.

Short, stocky, no-nonsense, the woman wore a gray wool dress, support hose, and a helmet of smooth salt-and-pepper hair. Her thick glasses shaded her eyes as she turned her head to inspect me.

She was good at it. That's what she was, the health inspector.

"I think you've met Callie McKinley, our restaurant manager," Chef said.

Ms. Jack peered at me and turned back to the clipboard.

"One point for the uncovered florescent lights, two for the cracked tile by the ice machine, two for the open dumpster lids, two and a half for the water temperature, one for the missing paper towels in the restroom, two for the flour not being labeled properly, and a half point for not having appropriate notice of clean plates. And that's being charitable." She stared up at Chef, and he looked down at her without speaking. I was proud of him. He didn't often hold back his true feelings like this.

I did some rapid figuring. Eighty-nine. She gave us a "B," darn her.

Every couple of months, the health inspector dropped by unannounced to grade the cleanliness of the restaurant. She wrote the grade on a certificate that had to be displayed in a prominent place for visitors to see. If the grade was low enough, she could shut the place down. The Seahorse Café hadn't scored anything less than a ninety-six the entire time I had been working there. An eighty-nine, a "B," was not good.

"I would advise you to get your act together. I'll come back—at my convenience, of course—and inspect you again," Ms. Jack said, filling out the form and peering at us over her glasses. "I certainly expect to see some improvement when I return for my regular inspection."

Ms. Jack finished her forms and handed them across to Chef.

"Good-bye," she said, and walked out, her low heels tapping a purposeful tattoo on the tiled floor.

"Ugh," Chef said in disgust. "That woman must be PMSing."

"Jesus Christ, Chef, do you have any idea how sexist

you sound? Things have been a little disorganized since this summer when we lost Noel, Mac, and Janet. Half the food and beverage gone in a month? Is it any wonder we've been having trouble? This is the first inspection we've had since then. We just need to get it together again," I said, striving for calm. It was a never-ending job keeping the big kitchen clean, and the lack of staff and the menu changeover was monopolizing our time. "Let's just sit down and make up a list of things we need to do before we call Ms. Jack to re-inspect us."

"Leah's going to be mad," Chef said. "I'm glad she wasn't here, or she might have flashed the health inspector."

Our eyes met and we couldn't resist laughing. Leah *was* going to be mad.

"Well, it could be worse. At least our food costs are back in line. It could be worse—we could have a 'B' *and* our food costs be out of whack."

"Callie, has anyone ever told you that you are cold comfort on a bitter, frigid day in northern Ontario?"

I grinned, happy to see Chef was taking this in stride. There was a time when something like this would have sent him over the edge. It took a whole lot of hard work to get our food costs back in line, and it was only Lily's unswerving faith in Chef's abilities that had given him the chance to straighten up his department after this summer's debacle. Lily could be very devoted when she considered you a friend—

but God forbid if you ever got on her bad side.

After a month of rehab this summer, Chef was staying away from the drugs and alcohol, but it wasn't easy for him. I took a good look at him, his gray hair winging back from his forehead and curling upwards on the ends, his handsome face lined with too much alcohol and cocaine, but filling out now. As a matter of fact, Chef was getting hefty since he'd been off the stuff.

He turned back to the fruit tray he had been working on when Ms. Jack interrupted him, and I opened the breakfast refrigerator and pulled out a few strips of cooked bacon. I put them in the microwave and put together bread, mayonnaise, lettuce, and tomato while I waited for the bacon to heat up.

I went and stood by Chef as he skillfully cut a watermelon into the shape of a basket.

"Do you know anything about Margie seeing someone besides Doug?"

"Nope. Not that I wouldn't have been interested if I didn't make it a sacred rule not to date the help. That goes for you too." He leered at me.

I ignored him. "Did she ever say anything to you about her parents?"

He put the knife down and started scooping out perfect melon balls. "I remember when she first came here. She was shy and I really didn't think she would last. No backbone, or so I thought. But she stayed, and she is the best wait we've got."

I smiled, appreciating the compliment of Margie, which was a rare occurrence for Chef.

"She got along with everyone, but she didn't have any close friends that I know of. She'd have a drink with us after her shift, but I don't remember talking to her about anything but work."

That was my own impression of Margie. The microwave beeped, and I built my sandwich and took it out to the bar to eat.

After I ate, I went downstairs and stopped by Lily's office, but the door was closed and I could hear her yelling. I beat a hasty retreat and went back to my office. I sat down at the desk and started editing the new menu, but my heart wasn't in it. I got out my function sheets and forecasts for the next week and started making the schedule. All that did was remind me that Margie was missing. I never realized how much I relied on her until now.

My gaze fell on a stack of pink message slips, and my heart thudded when I saw Margie's name. I picked up the slip and read it in disbelief.

Margie called.

October 17/10:35 am

I jumped up and almost ran down the hall to the front desk where Dowell—wide, placid, and friendly— was working. He held up one finger as I came through the door, finished his phone conversation, and hung up.

"Hi Callie, have you heard we've had detectives here

asking questions? And they're grilling Lee again at the police station. Do you think maybe he killed some girl and chopped off her head?"

"No, I don't think so. Did you take this?" I held out the message.

"Yep. She called this morning. I tried to transfer her to your voice mail but it was busy."

"Imagine that." I grimaced. We had installed a new voice mail system a month ago, and it still wasn't working right.

"Did she say where she was, when she's coming back, anything?"

Dowell looked confused by my questions, backed up until his fanny met the stool, and sat down.

"No, she just said she'd call you back. What's going on?"

I stared at him in disbelief. Dowell always knew everything that was going on in the hotel. "You mean you don't know? Margie's gone missing."

He looked defensive and rubbed a hand on his shirt. "I've been in Georgia, remember? I just got back yesterday."

I remembered. For the last month, all Dowell could talk about was his trip to Savannah.

"That explains it," I said. "I'm just a little worried about her, and then to find out she called . . . "

"I understand." He examined his nails. "She didn't say anything, though."

"But it was her? You recognized her voice?"

"I'm pretty good about recognizing voices." He sounded smug.

I didn't dispute his statement, though I was far from sure.

"Thanks, Dowell. If she calls back, try to find out where she is. And give her my home number and tell her to call me there if she wants."

"Sure, Callie. Jeez, you wouldn't believe all the reporters we've had checking in since you found that skull. Lily said not to talk to them, and to be careful, 'cause some of them would be undercover and might not tell me they're a reporter."

"Excuse me, but could you recommend a good restaurant? I just checked in and I don't know the area."

Dowell turned to the well-dressed man standing at the desk. "You're in luck, Mr. Holloway, this is our restaurant manager and she can tell you all about what they serve in the Seahorse Café."

I launched into my polished spiel about the restaurant while I thought about Margie. Why did she call?

"Thank you, I think I'll give it a try," the man said. "You know, you look familiar." He looked at me appraisingly.

"Hope to see you this evening," I said, and left before he realized *why* I looked familiar.

The door to Lily's office was still closed, but it was very quiet in there—too quiet.

I went back to my menus, but again, I couldn't keep

my mind on them. At this rate, the winter menus would be done sometime next summer.

My pictures were lying beside my bag, and I picked them up and started flipping through them. The first pack was from a friend's wedding in September, out on the gazebo in front of the hotel. It had been a perfect day and the wedding was beautiful. I looked at the radiant bride and tried not to think about my own wedding day, at the magistrate's office. It hadn't seemed important at the time, but now I wished I at least had the memories of a wonderful ceremony. Memories were all I had now.

The next pack was of Jake as a puppy: Jake lying on the bed asleep; Jake playing with Ice; Jake carrying around his fluorescent volleyball. I opened the next envelope.

They were pictures for renter's insurance. I had taken pictures of the interior of the house right before I evacuated for a hurricane this summer. Yes, it took me over three months to get them developed. The last picture on that roll was a beautiful sunrise, and I looked at it, thinking about having it blown up and framed.

I opened the last pack and pulled out the glossy pictures. Margie's tanned face smiled up at me.

I flipped to the next picture. It was Margie in her uniform leaving the hotel. The next picture was Margie, indistinct and shadowed, getting into her car. Here was Margie on the beach in her bikini; Margie in front of her house, working on the herbs in the flower box; Margie in her bedroom, lying on her bed.

There were twenty-four pictures of Margie.

I sat back and stared at the pictures. A tickle of memory was coming back to me, but I couldn't quite grasp it.

I didn't take those pictures of Margie. Who did?

Nine
A Bartender's Nightmare

I leaned back in my chair and pressed my hand against the side of my head. What was I trying to remember?

Suddenly it came to me.

It was this summer, in August. I was cruising through the restaurant, picking up plates, filling water glasses, making sure everybody was all right.

I remembered looking out over the ocean. It was nearing dusk, and the reflection of the crimson sunset in the west was shading the ocean a pale, glimmering rose. As if on cue, a pod of dolphins slid through the silky water, moving south.

I turned to an older couple sitting beside the window.

"Do you see the dolphins?" I asked, and pointed. They exclaimed in delight, and soon everyone in the entire restaurant was craning their necks to see.

The bar had been busy as Jarred Kent, the karaoke guy, started his show. I tried not to wince as a young woman in a super-short miniskirt gyrated to "I Love Rock 'N Roll." Jarred was bouncing around the bar in his usual energetic manner, and I had to laugh as he made a dramatic slide across the hostess stand, knocking off the phone and a stack of menus en route.

I brought up a case of Bud and Coors Light from the

walk-in fridge downstairs, and then started clearing tables for Matt.

That's when I found the roll of film lying under the bar table. I picked it up and looked around the bar, but it could have been lying there for hours. Whoever had left it was long gone.

"Callie, can you get me some more strawberry daiquiri mix?" Matt called, looking pained. He had a troop of children standing at the bar asking for six virgin strawberry daiquiris. A bartender's nightmare. I slipped the film into my coat pocket and planned to drop it in the lost and found at the front desk.

I never did. I promptly forgot about it until a month later, when I found the roll of film in my suit pocket. I put it with the rest of my film to be developed without remembering where it came from.

I stared at the photos I held. Who had been taking pictures of Margie? It was obvious that she was unaware of the cameraman as he stood outside her bedroom window. It was a perfect example of stalking.

One of the pictures caught my eye. Margie was laughing, her head turned towards the person beside her. All that was visible of the other person was long dark hair, a hint of a bikini strap around a slender neck, and an earring—an odd green and red metal frog, large and dangly. I wondered if the woman with the earrings might have seen the man who was taking pictures of Margie.

I felt like pulling my hair out. I tapped my foot on

the floor and played with my little gold spectacles. I don't need glasses, but I had gotten in the habit of wearing them over the last year and a half as a kind of disguise.

I tapped my foot some more and picked up the phone. I looked up a number in my Rolodex and then dialed.

"Dale Grain, please," I said.

It was several minutes before Dale Grain came on, time which I spent shuffling through the photos and tapping my foot.

"This is Dale Grain." His voice was husky and he sounded out of breath.

"Dale, this is Callie McKinley, over at the Holiday House."

"Oh, no."

I tried not to take offense at his tone. See, Dale thinks he has a good reason not to like me because of what happened last summer. But it wasn't my fault that the police found a Class Five hurricane heading straight towards the Outer Banks more interesting than a dead body in the freezer.

"I've already heard about the skull. If you say you've found a hand in the blender, I think I might shoot myself."

"You don't really think Lee killed that girl, do you?" It wasn't what I meant to say, but Dale Grain did that to me for some reason.

"Now you're going to tell me how to do my job?"

"No," I said meekly. "But I do have a small problem."

"I knew it. You always have a small problem when there is something major going on. Wasn't it enough you found that skull? What is it?"

"I didn't find the skull," I began, and then modified my tone. Beggars can't be indignant. "Lee found the skull in the dune. I just caught him running it through the dish machine. Anyway, ah, one of my waits has disappeared."

I heard a rustling sound, as if Dale was getting out a pad of paper.

"Go ahead."

"Her name is Margie Sanders and she's worked here for over two years. She's very reliable. Well, the other day, Saturday, I found a note that she was going away—"

"She left you a note?"

"Well yeah, but then when I talked to her roommate, she said that Margie packed up in the middle of the night—"

"She packed up her things?"

"Yes. Anyway, I found these pictures—"

"How old is she, Callie?" Dale's voice sounded tired.

"Twenty-three. Anyway, someone took these pictures of her, and when I went to pick up my film . . . "

He listened to the rest of my story in silence. He was making me nervous, and I talked faster and faster, trying to jam in all the information in less than a minute.

I finished, and there was silence on the line. For a

long moment I thought Dale put me on hold and that I would have to repeat the story again. When he spoke I breathed a sigh of relief.

"Callie, I appreciate the fact that you're worried, but there's not much I can do. Get me some numbers—her parents, her friends—and I'll make some calls. But all I can do is request that she call in to let us know she's all right and ask if she needs our help. The girl's over eighteen and she left notes for both you and her roommate. You know she's okay, because she tried to call you today. I know her leaving doesn't make sense, but that's just how things are sometimes. The Outer Banks are filled with people who are running from something, and some of them don't stay too long. They pack up in the middle of the night and leave, just like your waitress."

"You don't understand. This isn't like her at all. She's never even missed a shift before."

"But she lied on her application, right?"

"It looks that way," I said with reluctance.

"Then you didn't know the girl, not really. Get me the numbers and I'll call, but I can't go chasing down a missing waitress just because you're mad she quit on you."

"That's not fair." I was aware that my voice was sulky and I tried to stop it. "I'm worried about her."

"I've got a detective from Virginia standing at my door, so I've gotta go. Give me a call back with the names and phone numbers." He hung up.

I sat and held the phone a minute and then dialed the front desk to ask if Doug was working.

"He just got through delivering suitcases for a bus tour. He's standing right here," Dowell said.

"Can you ask him to come see me, please?"

A few minutes later, Doug stood at my door looking nervous.

"Come in please, Doug. And close the door."

Dragging his feet, he came in and sat in Chef's chair.

"What's going on, Doug?" I asked. "I think you know something about Margie you're not telling me. I'm worried about her."

Doug looked down at Chef's desk and fidgeted with a pencil. He wouldn't look at me.

"Doug?"

"I followed her Friday night," he blurted out. "I know I shouldn't have, but I liked her so much, and I thought she liked me, and then she just told me she didn't want to see me anymore. No reason. Said she had to think about some things. She had been acting so strange lately, and when I saw her coming out of the hotel I was in my car getting ready to pull out. I waited a few minutes and then I followed her. She went to Kelly's, and she always told me she never went there. She went inside, and after a while, I went in too. I figured if I ran into her I could say that I wanted to see the band, because it was a pretty good one that night. I didn't see her at first, and then I saw her talking to some guy, but it was so crowded I really couldn't see who it was. I got nervous, because I still didn't want her to see me, and then I went to the bathroom. When I came back out she was gone. I hung out for a while and I guess I drank too much, because next thing I knew, it was last call and she still wasn't back. So I took a cab home. All of that last bit is pretty sketchy, I don't remember a lot of what happened." He stopped and started playing with the pencil again.

"And?" I said, because I sensed there was more.

"I called her," he said in a low voice. "I was drunk, and kinda pissed off. I mean, if she was seeing someone else, I wish she woulda told me. I thought I loved . . . it's only polite, you know?"

I said nothing. Just two days ago, Doug had told me that he and Margie weren't "exclusive" and that he didn't care if she was seeing someone else. It was clear that was a lie.

Doug saw the look on my face. "I liked her so much. And she liked me, I swear she did. I just didn't get it."

"So what did she say?"

"She was crying," he said, and the pencil broke in his fingers. He looked down at it. "She said she couldn't take it anymore, but that she couldn't go back to her parents."

"Why not?"

"I don't know. She wasn't making much sense. I asked her who she was with that night. I told her I knew she loved me and asked her why she was doing this to me." Doug's voice broke, and he picked up half of the broken pencil and stared at it.

"What did she say?" I asked.

"She just cried and said she did love me, but that she was messed up and I was better off without her. Then she said she wished she had never met him in the first place, that she couldn't believe what he did."

"What did he do?"

"I don't know!" Doug almost shouted. "I don't know who she was talking about. I guess it was the guy she was with that night. She was crying and talking about him and her father. I really didn't understand a lot of it, and I was drunk, you gotta understand."

I sat back for a minute. "Why didn't you tell me any of this before?"

"Jeez, don't you understand how embarrassing this is for me? I wouldn't have told you now, except I'm worried about her. I don't know what to do."

I thought a minute, and shoved the photos of Margie over to him. "Did you take these, Doug?"

He thumbed through the pictures with trembling fingers. "No, I didn't take these."

"Did you send flowers to Margie in the last couple of weeks? Tell me the truth, Doug."

"No," he said. "It must have been that guy, whoever he was. God, I wish I had seen who he was, the bastard. He said something to her, and she was *crying*. Margie never cries."

"It's okay, Doug," I said, but something about those last words shook me to the core. What happened to Margie that night?

"You said she was talking about her parents. Have you ever met them? Do you know where they live?"

Doug shook his head. "Margie never talked about her parents much. One time I asked if she had told them about us, and she said of course, but I could tell she was lying."

I sighed. "All right, Doug. Will you give me the names of her friends, and their numbers if you know them?"

He nodded and scribbled down some names and numbers on a piece of paper.

"I'm sure Margie is fine, but I would like to find her. If you can think of anything else that might help . . ."

"I can't just wait for her to come back," Doug said. "I want to talk to her." He got to his feet, knocking a container of pens and pencils off Chef's desk. He didn't even notice. "I want to talk to her!" His voice rose and tears came to his eyes.

"Calm down," I said. "She'll come back when she's ready. Did you see anybody else at Kelly's that night? Anybody you recognized?"

"Of course," Doug said, wiping at his eyes. "I knew a lot of people there."

I forgot that the Outer Banks was a very small place in the fall. Something was bothering me, though. Someone else had mentioned being at Kelly's on Friday night. Who was it?

Doug's walkie-talkie crackled. "I gotta go," he said, and was out the door before I could say anything else.

Margie was seeing someone, or at least she was talking to someone who made her uncomfortable. *I thought he was nice at first, but now he just won't leave me alone.* Then there were the flowers in her room. Who was this mystery man? Was it the man Doug had seen talking to her Friday night? If it was, what did he say or do to make her leave? How did Doug fit into this? Was he telling me the truth this time?

The pictures worried me. Someone had taken pictures of Margie as early as this summer. Did that have anything to do with what was going on now?

I looked down at the menus, and then with a sigh I pulled out Margie's application. Doug said that she mentioned her father the night she left. Did she go home? I needed her parents' phone number to give to Dale; I wanted to ask them a few questions myself. Maybe *some* information on Margie's application was accurate.

I tried again to call the second person on her reference sheet. "Michael Denehey, doctor."

This time a woman answered. She sounded breathless and young. "Yes?"

"May I speak to Michael Denehey?"

"Who?"

"Michael Denehey."

"I'm afraid you have the wrong number. This is

the uh—Hiller residence." She giggled a little as she said it.

"Newlywed?" I guessed.

"Yes. Three weeks ago. How did you know?"

"I remember when I was first married and how strange it felt to have a new name," I said.

"It is strange, isn't it?" She giggled again. "I expect I'll get used to it."

"I'm sorry for bothering you, but an employee of mine listed this number as a reference, and I'm a little surprised that she gave me the wrong information."

"Maybe you dialed it wrong," Mrs. Brian Hiller said, and read out her number.

"Nope, that's it," I said. "Is this 678 Plains Trail, Becks Hill, New Hampshire?"

"Oh my goodness, no. You've called Michigan."

I thanked the young woman and congratulated her on her marriage.

I read the application front and back. When Margie filled it out, she had given the Ocean Inn in Nags Head as her local address. Apparently she had just arrived for the summer and hadn't found a house yet. Most college students who lived here for the summer came with a group of friends and already had a house.

Under "Education" she had listed Northmount High School in Becks Hill—no address or phone number—and Cedar Valley College in New Hampshire.

Under "Previous Experience," she had listed a Smiley's Bar and Grill in Becks Hill.

I called the number for Smiley's, and was not at all surprised to learn that it belonged to an auto mechanic in Michigan.

I called information. The operator could not find a place called Becks Hill, New Hampshire.

Much Ado About Something

As far as I could tell, Margie had picked a town out of her hat and made up names and numbers on her application. She wasn't even careful about it. Though she used the same area code for all the phone numbers, it wasn't for a town called Becks Hill, it was the area code for somewhere in Michigan.

I was disappointed. Suddenly Dale Grain was making more sense and I was feeling taken. Granted, I was not the one who hired Margie, and it wasn't my fault that none of her references were checked—which wasn't unusual on the Outer Banks. Despite the fibbing on her application, she had been a good, reliable employee.

Until now.

I flipped through her file, looking at the employee-of-the-month awards, the special commendations, the IRS forms.

Wait a minute.

I flipped back to the IRS form. Margie had to be using her real social security number. Wouldn't the IRS have noticed a bogus number by now?

I did some quick thinking and picked up the phone. I decided not to call Dale Grain but called Kyle at Sharkey's instead.

"This is Kyle."

"Hi Kyle, this is Callie. Doesn't one of your many brothers own a used car dealership?"

Kyle agreed cautiously and listened while I told him about Margie's forged application.

"So would your brother do you a favor?"

"What do you need?"

"I was wondering if he could run a credit check on Margie, just using her name and social security number."

"I don't know. Kennedy would know, I guess." His voice was reluctant, and I remembered hearing somewhere that there was bad blood between Kyle and Kennedy. "What will it accomplish, though?" Kyle continued. "She may not have any credit, and if she does, so what?"

"I'm not sure," I admitted. "Her address before she moved here would be nice, since she lied about it on her resume. I just can't think of any other way to get information fast. I'm not real good at this, you know. It's not like I can call up Dale Grain and demand he run a background check on my missing wait."

"Already tried, huh?"

"Yes!" I laughed. "Well, he certainly put me in my place, that's for sure."

Kyle agreed to give his brother a try and took down Margie's name and social security number. He didn't sound thrilled, but at least he wasn't being his normal obstructive self.

We hung up after a few more good-natured insults. I called Dale and left a message with the names and phone numbers of Margie's friends.

Then I put my thoughts of Margie behind me and concentrated on the new menu.

It was early in the evening, and though we weren't busy yet, we would be soon judging from the dripping, dark night. No one would want to go out in that for dinner.

I stared out over the restaurant. The Sea Horse Café was on the fifth floor of the Holiday House Hotel, and we had a great view over the ocean when it wasn't foggy and raining. Inside, the restaurant was polished wood floors, white tablecloths, and rose napkins peeking out from the glasses like blooming flowers. The lounge was situated on a platform at the back, dominated by a long, U-shaped bar and gleaming tables.

This summer a hurricane—plus a small incident with a gun—had blown out one of the wide plate-glass windows, and in the aftermath of the storm the restaurant was given a face-lift. I was pleased with the results.

"Callie, how you doing?" Charlie was at the bar in a flowered Hawaiian shirt and that too-perfect tan. I winced, at both his loud shirt and his robust voice, which rolled to every corner of the restaurant.

"Doing good, Charlie," I lied. "Any luck on the house?"

"Getting close, but no cigar!" He laughed, a full, deep chortle. "Looked at this one today that was just gorgeous. Ocean views forever, four master bedrooms all with Jacuzzis, a pool, and hot tub."

"Sounds nice," I said. "Sounds expensive."

"Well, when you've got it you might as well spend it."

I watched as more people came to the door. So far, Kate had it under control.

"How's your Jeep?"

"It's touch and go every time I start it."

"I guess I could take a look at it. What are you doing tomorrow?"

"I work at twelve. You really don't have to—"

"What are friends for? Anyway, between laps around the bar, Matt here was just telling me that Margie is gone. What's up with that?"

"Apparently she had some personal business to attend to. I'm a little concerned about her. She disappeared Friday night without telling anyone."

"Friday?" Charlie frowned.

Suddenly, it clicked. I remembered what had been bothering me when Doug told me he saw Margie at Kelly's Friday night. "Did you see her Friday night?" I asked. "Didn't you say you were at Kelly's?"

"Funny you should ask, because I did see her at Kelly's. Didn't think much about it until now, but she looked upset. I saw Doug wandering around looking like someone ran over his dog. Too bad they were fighting. Life's too short for that kind of crap."

"Why did you think they were fighting?"

"I saw them," Charlie said, downing his drink and signaling Matt for another one. "When I was leaving, Margie was getting in her car and Doug was yelling at her. I stayed around to see if she would need help, but she just got in the car and left. I don't like to see a man yelling at a woman like that. It's not right."

I frowned. Doug yelled at Margie? He said he didn't talk to her at Kelly's.

"Did you talk to her at all? I don't mean to grill you, it's just that I'm worried." I injected sincerity into my voice, though I was far from sure Charlie was telling me the truth. Unfortunately, it never sounded like Charlie was telling the truth, even when he was. It was a byproduct of his salesmen days.

"I said hello, asked her how she was doing, that sort of thing. She didn't say much. Like I said, I think she was upset."

"Did you and Margie ever, you know, date?" The question just popped into my head and out of my mouth before I had time to think it through. What if Margie had been dating Charlie and felt the need to run from him for some reason? He was at Kelly's, and *someone* had been sending her flowers.

"Good Lord, no!" Charlie looked startled and inhaled a swallow of bourbon, which set him to coughing. "Linda would kill me. I've got two kids, for God's sake! And she's a little young for me, don't you think?"

I smiled. "It was just a thought."

"I think she's a great girl and I enjoyed talking to her, but we never dated," Charlie continued, sensing my doubt. Was he protesting too much?

I looked back at the front door and saw Kate give me a meaningful look as the line lengthened. "Well, thanks, Charlie. I've got to go."

"Call me tomorrow and give me directions to your house. We'll fix that Jeep right up, I gua-ron-tee it!" The sound of his laughter followed me as I hurried away.

For the rest of the night I seated customers and soothed ruffled feathers when people complained about the lousy view. The clouds and rain were doing a good imitation of pea soup outside the window. The man I had talked to at the front desk, Mr. Holloway, was sitting by himself at a table eating chicken and shrimp Alfredo over linguini. He thought he recognized me; I hoped he hadn't figured out why.

"Are you enjoying your dinner, Mr. Holloway?"

"Very much so." His thick brown hair was slicked back from his forehead, and he gazed at me myopically. I noticed he was reading an article about the skull in one of the local papers. He was taking down notes in a small black notebook. *He's probably a reporter*, I decided. "Mark Holloway," he said, and held out his hand.

"Callie McKinley," I said, and we shook hands, but I was already looking for a way to escape. For me, talking to reporters ranks right up there with pulling out my eyelashes or being audited by the IRS.

"You're the restaurant manager, right? How long have you been here?"

"Since this summer."

"Hmmm." He seemed to lose interest.

"Well, I'm glad you're enjoying your meal," I said. "Enjoy the rest of your evening." I made my escape, my heart pounding. Reporters had ruined my life, and I would be happy if I never talked to another one again.

In the kitchen, Jerry and one of the new line cooks were sliding prime rib, fried shrimp, and Tuna Oscar into the window.

"Girl, it's some kind of hot in here," Rob, the new waiter said, waving a hand in front of his face as he piled food onto a tray.

"How are you getting along?" I asked him. Kate said that he was the consummate professional, if a bit high-strung. It was hard not to like him.

"This place is like a fresh breeze to my soul. I better get this food where it's going or that little old lady is going to hunt me down. I already saw her headed this way on her walker." He sailed out of the kitchen.

"You sure can pick them," Chef said, shaking his head, but he was grinning.

"Look who's talking."

The clang of metal hitting the floor spun me around into the wide-eyed gaze of Juana, the bus girl who was rolling silverware. She stooped and grabbed up the fork without missing a beat.

"Three seconds!" Luigi, one of the waits said as he came into the kitchen.

The three-second rule was the rule that allowed you to pick anything up off the floor as long as it had only been there for three seconds. I don't know who made it up, but it was in the restaurant business's Magna Carta.

"Put it in the bus tub to be cleaned, Juana," I said.

"'A lord to a lord, a man to a man; stuffed with all honorable virtues.'" Lee was behind the dish line, sliding racks of glasses through the maw of the machine.

"*Much Ado about Nothing*," I said, and Lee shrugged. Someday I would have to ask him where he picked up all his quotes.

"I told you you shouldn'tve called the police," he said, staring at me with his small, slightly crossed eyes. "They've been giving me a hard time, like maybe I killed the chick. Gave me a polygraph and everything."

"I'm sorry, but they'll figure out you're innocent."

"I told 'em that the sand was all dug up and Bingo just went crazy. He's got a great nose, you know. He's always digging up mice and moles. When he came back from chasing that guy, he dug up the skull in just a few minutes."

"What do you mean, when Bingo came back from chasing that guy? Who was he chasing? You didn't mention that before."

"I did!" Lee was as indignant as if I had accused

him of lying on his mother's grave. "The police said I made it up too, but it's true! Bingo took off sudden-like after some guy walking on the beach. Started barking and just ran like all get out. I called and whistled, and when he came back he dug up the skull where the sand was all turned up."

I stared at him in surprise. Was it possible that Lee had startled someone digging up the skull? "What did the police say?"

"At first they acted like it was no big deal, and then they asked all kinds of questions. I told them it was just someone going to the beach, no big deal. I didn't see him close up anyhow." Lee went back to his steaming machine.

"Hiya Callie, how you been? Want a Coke?" Buddy, the other dishwasher asked in his slurred voice. Buddy had been with us since this summer, and if he was a little slow, he was one of the hardest working kitchen people we had. He was carrying a cocktail tray balanced with eight Styrofoam cups.

"No thanks, Buddy," I said, and he put one down beside me anyway.

"Listen!"

I stuck my head around the edge of the dish line in time to see Chef turn up the volume on the radio.

"The skull found outside the Holiday House Hotel in Nags Head, North Carolina was positively identified as that of Angel Knowling, a woman murdered in Newport News, Virginia five years ago."

Eleven

It Hits The fan

"The victim's husband, Keith Knowling, is still being sought for questioning in that crime. Nags Head detectives are cooperating with detectives from Virginia to discover when the skull was buried in the dune." The announcer's voice brightened as he launched into the latest football scores.

I glanced over my shoulder, somehow expecting to see Lily standing there with murder in her eyes. Sighing, I went to the kitchen phone and called her home number. She answered sweetly, as though expecting a lover's voice instead of mine.

"They've confirmed the identity of the skull," I told her.

She was silent.

"It's the dead woman from Virginia. It's a murder investigation."

"Christ." I heard the rustle of fabric, was it the silky *shhhhhhrus* of silk? Lily's love life was the subject of much speculation at the hotel, mainly because she was so secretive about it. She went out a lot, but she was never seen with any particular man, or woman.

"This really sucks," she said.

"I know."

"Couldn't you have just ignored the skull in the dishwasher? Let Lee put the thing on his TV?"

"Lily."

"Okay, okay." She sighed, and I braced myself for the explosion. "You did the right thing," she said instead. "You had to report it. But why the heck did that man have to bury his wife's head here?"

"That's a good question," I said. "Maybe they came here on their honeymoon or something."

"So he buries her head here? How sick can you get?"

"Sick enough to cut off her head."

"Good point. As if we haven't had enough reporters as it is. "

Over the phone I heard the sound of the doorbell.

"Oh great," Lily muttered. "I've gotta go. I'll be there in a little bit."

"One more thing," I said.

"What?" she snapped loud enough for Chef, who was standing beside me, to raise his eyebrows.

"Never mind." I was going to tell her about the fibs on Margie's application, but it didn't seem as important anymore.

Lily hung up.

"Well?" Chef said. Buddy was standing behind him, imitating his hand-on-hip posture. He saw me looking, grinned, and then picked up his broom and continued to sweep under the counters.

"She's not happy. Imagine that. She'll be here soon."

"Callie," wailed one of the waits. "I need bread and

butter at *all* of my tables and there's a line at the door. Help."

"I'm on it," I said, and I didn't have time to think about skulls or the police for two more hours.

I walked into Sharkey's and smiled at the familiar faces that turned my way. A Tanqueray and tonic was waiting for me by the time I got to the stool next to Susan.

"How are you?" Susan asked, her plump, powdery face creasing into a smile.

"So-so," I said. My Jeep had waa-waaed for several minutes before it started, and I was afraid it wouldn't start again. I thought about telling Susan that, but I knew it wasn't what she wanted to hear.

I could see she was aquiver with questions. She knew the latest news about the skull, but she was giving me room to bring the subject up myself. I didn't exactly want to talk about it, but if I didn't Susan's feelings would be hurt. Life sucks sometimes.

"It's not great," I offered.

"If the sky fell in, the ocean turned to blood, and we got a 'F' on our health inspection, things would still be better," Chef drawled as he came up behind me. "No one ever said that life with Callie McKinley was going to be easy."

"I heard a tsunami was going to hit the Outer Banks at 11:36," Elizabeth inserted helpfully. Tonight she wore a blond Pamela Anderson wig and a tight red miniskirt. If my legs looked that good at eighty-six I would be happy for the rest of my life.

"At 11:36? Not 11:35, or 11:37, but at exactly 11:36 a tsunami is going to hit the Outer Banks?" Chef asked, with what sounded like real interest.

"She's been watching the Discovery Channel again," Susan said, and blew a cloud of smoke in Elizabeth's direction.

"I'll have my usual, and make it a triple," Chef said to Melissa, who filled three glasses with soda water and set them in front of him.

"Why not stay out of bars?" I asked. "It can't be easy to watch everyone else drink and not have one yourself."

"What am I going to do at home? Watch *Melrose Place*? No thank you. I'm off the white freightliner, not dead. My soap opera takes place right here every night."

"Did ya'll hear I passed my real estate exam?" Melissa asked. "I want to sell those big oceanfront cottages. Did you know some of them are going for two million dollars? I could make a killing on just one sell. Can you imagine?"

Susan was listening to all this and tapping her fingers on the bar in rising impatience. "Can we please talk about what's going on with the skull?" she said. "I heard the news on the radio. What's going on?"

I tried not to wince. I had had enough of the police

asking questions to last me the rest of my life. It took all that was in me not to run out the door when Dowell called from the front desk to report that a detective wanted to question some of the staff.

I took a long draw from my drink and fumbled in my purse. Where were they?

I checked my coat, and then stood up to see if I put them in my trouser pockets.

"Callie has obviously lost her marbles," Chef said. "Here, you can have mine." He reached in his pocket and flipped a marble in my direction.

I looked at it in amazement and wondered how long Chef had carried it for this very purpose. "Cigarettes," I said. "I'm looking for cigarettes."

Finally I found a crumpled pack at the bottom of my purse.

Susan was looking at me with eyebrows raised. "Are you done now? They asked questions?"

"Yes, a detective from Newport News came down, and they've enlisted policemen from the surrounding towns to help with the questioning. They're going through everybody who's staying at the hotel, plus the employees. I guess they think Keith Knowling may have been trying to dig up the skull. They're also going through the old registration logs to see if Angel Knowling ever stayed there. Lily's been with them all night. The reporters are descending like nosy locusts."

Susan coughed, long and hard, and I patted her on

the back. She lit up another cigarette. "Are the guests upset yet?"

"A couple of them canceled their reservations. Most of the people staying in the hotel are fascinated by the whole thing."

"I can't believe it's that poor girl," Susan said. "The 'Murdered Mermaid.' It seems like only yesterday that they found her headless body up in Virginia. Caused quite a commotion."

"I was in California at the time, and I really don't remember hearing anything about it."

"I tell you, a lot of people didn't think that Keith Knowling could have killed his wife. All the neighbors said what a nice man he was."

"But the neighbors didn't see what went on behind closed doors," I said.

"True. What did they know? Let me tell you, what goes on behind closed doors in some marriages is the stuff of horror movies. I know." Susan stared at the beer bottles above the bar and took a long swig of her drink. "There *was* that call Angel made to 9-1-1 because Keith got violent with her. No one knew about that until after she was killed.

"It was a media circus for a while," she continued. "I'll bet it'll get bad again. The magazines love this type of stuff. Missing heads, missing husbands." She looked at me through her thick glasses. "But I guess you know what they like, don't you?"

I grimaced. The media had liked my little story all

right—enough to splash my face on front pages across the country for several weeks.

"The reporters are going to be a pain. Lily said there were five of them staying in the hotel under their real names, and Lord knows how many are here under assumed names."

I excused myself and went towards the women's restroom. Someone was in there, of course. I stood in the narrow hall outside the door and flattened myself against the wall as employees came by with full trash cans and buckets of ice. I amused myself by reading the sign that hung beside the door.

"This is not Burger King. You get it my way, not your way, or you don't get the damn thing."

I loved it.

"I heard it hit the fan over at the hotel," Kyle said from behind me, and I jumped.

"No kidding," I said, and turned to look at him. Tonight he was wearing a pair of dark-framed reading glasses, and as I stared he flushed a little and slid them off his nose and into his pocket.

"What's Project Nutmeg?" I asked abruptly.

Kyle looked startled. Damn. I wasn't good at flirting with men anymore. How had I lost that?

"Oh, you're talking about the secret report the Atomic Energy Commission ordered back in 1948 to find a place to carry out stateside atomic bomb tests."

I waited.

"The southern Outer Banks was among the sites

considered." Kyle shook his head. "If they had carried through with it, Hatteras and Ocracoke would be as hot as Bikini Island right now. It makes me sick just to think about it."

"Makes you feel sorry for the people in Nevada," I said.

"Your turn. Who is the Bonner Bridge named after?"

I *knew* it; I could almost see the page of the David Stick book in my mind. But I couldn't remember.

"Back to your books," he said cheerfully.

Now it was my turn to flush. "Well, I've been a little busy," I said. "I'll be sure to bone up for the test on Friday."

Kyle leaned against the wall next to me, folding one long, jeans-clad leg over the other. "So have you found your waitress yet?"

I shook my head, but then something compelled me to tell him about talking to Margie's roommate. He was a sympathetic listener when he kept his mouth shut.

"Have you talked to your brother about that credit check?"

"I was wondering when you would get around to that." Kyle leaned back and stretched, and I couldn't help looking at the muscles rippling along his stomach under his shirt. He smiled from under his Sharkey's baseball hat, his blue eyes flashing with humor as he watched me.

"I tried calling a couple of times today. I finally

got him at home tonight, and he said he would try to get to it tomorrow. He says I owe him big time. It's not exactly legal, you know." His voice held an unidentifiable emotion. Kyle's family had been on the Outer Banks as long as the Midgetts or the Etheridges. He had brothers and sisters and cousins and who knows what else running around everywhere, but he almost never talked about them. I wondered why.

"I appreciate your help, Kyle," I said, "and thanks for not asking about the skull. I don't even want to think about that right now."

"I expect to hear some intelligent comments on Outer Banks history the next time I—"

"Daddy!" a little voice squealed, and something about three feet tall with blond pigtails came flying down the hall and attached itself to Kyle's knee.

Twelve
Pit Vipers And Karaoke

"Molly," Kyle said, and I was surprised to see a look of pure joy cross his face. Kyle had a daughter? The restroom was free but I didn't budge. I wasn't going to miss this for the world.

He lifted the small girl into his arms and she leaned back, studying his face. "Mommy said you forgot about me," she accused, her tiny bowed lips trembling. She was a beautiful child, platinum blond hair tied with pink bows on either side of her head, big blue eyes that left no doubt in my mind that she was Kyle's child, and tiny blue-jean overalls with pink sequined butterflies.

"I would never forget you, honey," Kyle said in a husky voice, and all of a sudden I felt bad about eavesdropping on such a private moment. I went into the restroom.

Unfortunately, I could hear everything through the thin wooden door.

"Do you still love me, Daddy?" Molly asked. "Mommy said you didn't have time to call me or write me anymore."

"I didn't have your number or address, or I would have, honey."

"There you are," a sweet, airy voice said. "I was wondering where you got to, Molly. Get down from there. You're crumpling your Daddy's shirt. Hello, Kyle. You've gained weight." The voice cooled.

"Hello Stacy," Kyle said. Was that anger in his voice? "No, sweetie, you don't have to get down. I don't care if you crumple my shirt. When did you get back in town, Stacy?"

"About a week ago," Stacy said, the airy note back in her voice. "I see you haven't done much with the place since I left."

"You got back a week ago? And you're just now coming by?" There was a careful quality in his voice, as if he were weighing each word before he said it.

"Don't you dare talk to me in that tone of voice, Kyle Tyler! I've taken enough abuse from you; don't you dare speak to me like that!"

I was hesitant to come out of the bathroom, not wanting to interrupt, but now I decided that an interruption would probably be a good thing.

"Let me just tell you—" Stacy was saying as I walked out. Molly's lip was quivering again and she said, "*Mommy . . .*"

"Hi Callie, look honey, it's Callie," Kyle said. "Molly, this is a friend of mine, Ms. Callie. Say hello, Molly."

"Hello!" Molly said.

"Hello Molly, it's nice to meet you."

The little girl beamed.

I looked inquiringly at the woman standing beside

Kyle. She was tall and slender, with a beautiful figure and long strawberry-blond hair. With a sugary smile she extended a manicured hand. "I'm Stacy, since Kyle seems to have lost his manners." Her tone said "silly men," and there was an indulgent twist to her lips. If I hadn't heard her berating Kyle moments before I would have thought they were on very good terms.

"Stacy, Callie. Callie, Stacy," Kyle said.

I shook hands with Stacy, feeling short and dowdy next to her perfection.

"How nice to meet you, Callie," she said with a sweetness that made me want to claw the saccharine smile off her face.

"You too, Stacy," I said. "Oops, I think Susan is waving at me. If you will excuse me?" I brushed by the three of them, ignoring Stacy's hair as it whipped across my face. She decided to toss her head just as I passed too close to her in the narrow hall.

Susan, who had indeed been watching the little tableau avidly, patted the seat next to her as I made my way back to the bar.

"That Stacy is such a pretty girl," Elizabeth said. "As rabid as a pit viper, but there you are. Some people just don't know how to be nice."

"Whew," I said, and drained my gin and tonic.

"Here, want some tap water with bubbles?" Chef asked, handing me one of his glasses.

"No thanks." I lit a cigarette.

"Stacy can be a little much," Susan said. "She met

Kyle about six years ago when she worked here as a waitress. They got married, she got her real estate license, and suddenly she thinks she's a big shot. From sweet little girl to bitch in ninety seconds flat. She and Kyle lasted about two years, just long enough to have Molly."

"Isn't she a precious child?" Elizabeth asked, batting her long eyelashes. "Simply precious."

"They're divorced? Kyle never mentioned it."

"Kyle's funny about Stacy. She really worked him over good. She stayed around for a couple of years after the divorce, did real well with real estate, and then she started moving. Virginia, South Carolina, Florida. And every time she moves, she forgets to tell Kyle where she's going, and every time he tracks her down so he can see Molly. He drove fourteen hours to Tampa, Florida last year so he could be at her birthday party for two hours, but then Stacy made him leave, said they were going out of town. She moved again a month after that and Kyle hasn't known where they were—until she showed up tonight."

"Why didn't Kyle mention it?" I asked, bewildered and a little hurt. Kyle and I weren't exactly friends, but we were definitely acquaintances.

"I told you, Stacy worked him over good. He doesn't like talking about her. He's talked to several lawyers about trying to sue for full custody of Molly, but he's afraid Stacy will disappear for good if he does it."

I sat in stunned silence, trying to absorb the fact

that Kyle had an ex-wife and a five-year-old daughter. Kyle, who knew my most guarded secret, never even mentioned her.

"Don't feel bad, honey," Susan said, patting my hand. "He doesn't talk about them much. It hurts him too bad."

"So what's she doing back?"

"She's looking for a job, I know that. She's lost her real estate license in North Carolina, so she's having to scramble to find something. You think Kyle will give her her old job back?" She winked at me.

I looked over towards the hall, but the three had disappeared into the back office. I shrugged, trying to mask my inexplicable hurt, and turned back to the bar. "Melissa, I'll have another drink."

I turned to find Susan regarding me through a cloud of smoke, her smug expression similar to the caterpillar in *Alice in Wonderland*.

"What?"

Susan just smiled.

Jarred Kent was finished setting up his karaoke equipment and made his way to the end of the bar carrying songbooks.

"I'd hate to see what would happen to this end of the bar if you weren't here to hold it up," he told us. He put a songbook down in front of me.

"Just because you don't drink, it doesn't mean you can make fun of the rest of us," Susan said, but she smiled.

"You want a shot?" Chef asked. "Come on, drink one for me."

"Who's singing tonight?" Jarred asked, bouncing a little on the balls of his feet.

"Callie is, I hope," Susan said, and nudged me.

"I hope so, too. Where's Charlie? He lost a bet last time I was here and he's supposed to sing some Frank Sinatra," Jarred said.

"That Charlie," Susan said in an irritable voice. We waited for her to say more, but apparently that was the extent of what she had to say about Charlie.

"He tries," Jarred said, and dashed away to say hello to someone he knew.

"Fill out a slip or I'll fill one out for you," Susan said, pointing at the songbook. "You haven't sung in a while."

I laughed and wrote my name, the name of the song, and the song number on one of Jarred's forms. It still felt strange to sing whenever I felt like it. It was hard for me to believe that I had waited so long to do it again. Somehow in my head, singing had gotten inexplicably tied up with what happened in California, and it was a long time before I felt comfortable singing.

We laughed at the drunk man trying to sing "Man! I feel Like a Woman!" by Shania Twain, and then Jarred Kent called me up to the microphone.

Callie, Callie, Callie!

I looked around at the locals who were smiling and banging on the bar as they urged me to get up and sing. I felt light and happy, as I always did when I sang. How had I given this up for so long?

The first strains of John Prine's "Angel from Montgomery" wafted through the speakers, and I smiled my thanks at the crowd's enthusiasm and closed my eyes.

As I sang, I thought about singing in the church choir when I was still in elementary school. I thought of the band, the Purple Electrics, my two friends and I created in high school. In college, I had been asked to sing the "Star-Spangled Banner" at football games, and sororities asked me to sing at parties.

When I moved to California, a friend of mine at a local club heard me sing karaoke and asked me to fill in one night when his singer didn't show up. From there on out, I sang at several local bars—never for money, just for the pure love of it.

As I finished the haunting strains of the song, I thought about the terrible months when the reporters were showing up at the bar where I sang, critiquing every line, taking pictures, making ugly something that I enjoyed. The night a reporter interrupted a song to ask me if I thought Henry Gray, the famous movie actor, would help me with my singing career was the night I swore off singing.

For over a year and a half I hadn't sung in public. I had been on the Outer Banks for two months when Lenny Marks asked me to sing with him. That was when I really knew how much the Outer Banks had affected me. I was able to sing, and I was able to tell my close friends who I really was.

I went home before Sharkey's got too rowdy. It's amazing how a couple shots of liquid courage can convince your average Joe Blow that he's Frank Sinatra. I couldn't sleep that night, tossing and turning and finally flipping on the light and trying to read. As usual, as soon as my eyelids started fluttering, I would turn off the light. Then my eyes would snap open and I would be wide awake. Finally, around five in the morning, I fell asleep with the light on.

I dreamed about a warm December night in California, when an addict's need for money and drugs led him to point a gun at me and a six-year-old boy. I dreamed about a man with rage in his eyes stabbing his wife over and over again.

I woke up before he cut off her head.

Thirteen

Death Stares And Credit Checks

Mist wreathed the sun like an opaque silk scarf as I took my coffee to the beach. A blanket of white lay over the smooth ocean, and tendrils of fog played with the tops of the waves as they rolled towards the shore. I yawned. My sleep had been anything but restful.

Jake galloped through the shallows carrying an orange volleyball I had brought home to him on a whim. He loved it and took it everywhere with him.

Back at the house, I saw that I didn't have to be at work for another two hours. I looked out at my Jeep sitting in the driveway and resisted the urge to take a gun to it. Not that I had a gun, but the urge was there. I needed to take it to the shop, but Charlie *had* offered to look at it. If it was just something simple, I could avoid paying the outrageous amount beach mechanics demanded for their services.

Sighing, I picked up the phone. I didn't have to like Charlie, but he really tried to be nice.

Charlie had just returned from eating breakfast, and I wondered again what type of unlimited funds he must have to stay at the hotel for weeks and eat out every meal. Must be nice. He was happy to hear from me and promised to be over in a half an hour. True to his word, he showed up half an hour later, just as I finished getting ready for work.

"Nice place," Charlie said, gazing around my living room with approval. "Do you rent or own?" His voice echoed off the cathedral ceiling, and Ice stared down at him from the loft.

I looked around the tidy living area, open and spacious with a loft above.

"I rent. I have a roommate, but she's not here most of the time." Which was a good thing as far as I was concerned. Kim was not a monster, but she was self-centered, loud in the mornings, and unwilling to do her share of the house chores. Ever since she met a new man, she had also been absent, which was just dandy with me.

"Good boy," Charlie said, holding his hand out to Jake.

Jake sniffed for several moments, and then wagged his tail and allowed Charlie to rub behind his ears.

"I miss my dog. Julep's a big Golden Retriever."

"He sounds gorgeous. I'm sure your wife is taking good care of him."

"Hopefully." His voice was odd, and I glanced at him in surprise.

"Oh, Linda and I are having trouble. I guess that's why I've been content to stay here at the beach so long."

"I'm sorry. I'm sure it'll work itself out."

"Let's see what we've got," he said, and followed

me out to the driveway where his red convertible was parked behind my Jeep.

"Nice Jeep," he commented, patting the hood. "It has four-wheel drive? Must be nice out on the sand. I hear the blues are running. I'd love to get out there in something like this."

He seemed to be waiting for an invitation, and I just smiled without saying anything. I found that I liked Charlie more when we were alone, but he still made me uncomfortable for some reason. Was it because he seemed so very aware of me as a woman? He had a habit of leaning in too close when he talked, taking any opportunity to touch my hand, or my arm, or my leg. What was wrong with me? Why was I so uncomfortable when a man expressed his admiration for me in subtle ways? I realized that I had been like this since I left Dave, maintaining my own space, distancing myself from any potential relationships, terrified that I would be hurt again.

Charlie poked and prodded for twenty minutes, muttering under his breath and wiping his greasy hands on a rag. I stayed out of his way except when he asked me to start the engine while he fiddled under the hood. The fog swirled wetly around us and I held out a hand, thinking somehow I could catch the wispy stuff.

"This fog's something else," he commented.

"They say it's unusual."

"It's the starter, all right," he said after a while. "Hate to tell you that. It'll cost you a pretty penny, I'm afraid."

"Great," I groaned. "Just what I didn't want to hear."

I offered Charlie some coffee or a drink, but he said he had to go. I watched him pull the flashy red convertible onto the road, accidentally switching on his windshield wipers before finding the lights and roaring off.

It was twelve when I got to work, right on time. I put my stuff down in the empty food and beverage office and walked down the hall to see if Lily was in. Furtive glances were thrown my way and voices lowered as I passed.

I was sick and tired of being blamed for finding the stupid skull. I couldn't very well ignore the fact that I found a skull in the dish machine, could I? Lee found it first, after all. No one was berating *him* for not leaving it in the dune.

I poked my head into Lily's office and found her on the phone, newspapers spread haphazardly across her desk.

"Are you an idiot, or do you really think that's an intelligent question? And yes, please quote me on that!" She slammed the receiver down and glared at me. On the scale of Lily's death stares from one to ten, it was a twelve and a half.

"Hi Lily," I said with obnoxious cheerfulness. I leaned over the desk and started reading the headlines. "Ah, I guess that explains why you're in such a good mood."

The phone rang and Lily snatched it up, gathering the papers into a ball against her chest.

"What?" she barked, and shoved the newspapers at me. "A spiritualist? No, I don't care if you've got a message from Jesus Christ himself, I'm not going to give you a free room. Good-bye!"

She slammed the phone down so hard that the whole desk shook. "These reporters are *seriously* getting on my nerves. It's bad enough that they're writing this trash about us, but they're sneaking around poking into everything. I'm halfway thinking of throwing every last one of them out of the hotel."

"Probably not a good idea," I commented.

She sighed. "I guess not. Read those for me," she ordered, pointing at the papers. "I'm sick of looking at them. Tell me if there's anything about the hotel that I should take offense at. I'll call up the offending papers and rip them a new orifice."

"Okay," I said.

In my office, I sat down at the computer and hit the switch to turn on the monitor. Not only did I need to work on the new menu, now I needed to work on a check-list to get the kitchen back in shape for a new inspection.

The phone rang as the screen flickered to life.

"Callie?"

"Yes."

"My brother got an address and some credit information on your wait," Kyle said.

"Really? Great."

"It's kind of funny, because she stopped using the account about two and a half years ago, but the cards are still active. And the address I've got is in Kentucky, a town near Lexington, my brother thought. Didn't you say she was from New Hampshire?"

"I thought she was," I said, a little dismayed. Margie out and out lied to me. I knew I had asked where she was from and she told me New Hampshire. It was one thing for her to lie on her resume, but the fact that she had lied to me face to face hurt. I wouldn't have pegged her accent for Kentucky either.

"Anyway, she listed fifteen years under 'how long at current address.' She's only what, twenty-two or three? I think it's probably her parent's address. What do you think?"

"Yeah," I said.

Kyle gave me the address in Kentucky and I thanked him and hung up. I thought a minute, and then turned to my computer and logged onto the Internet. After just a few minutes I found a website with a reverse phone directory. I put in the address Kyle had given me, and presto, I had the telephone number for an Andrew Sanders.

Was it Margie's dad? I crossed my fingers and dialed.

"Hello?"

"Mrs. Sanders?"

"Yes?"

"I know this will sound like a silly question, but do you have a daughter named Margie Sanders?"

There was a long silence, long enough for me to say, "Hello?" Had we been disconnected?

"May I ask who you are?" she said finally, in a quiet, listless voice.

I decided on the simplest answer. "I'm a friend. I haven't talked to Margie in a while, and I was just going to see how she's doing."

"I'm sorry," Ms. Sanders said. "I'm sorry." Silence again, but this time I heard the tiny hiccup of a repressed sob. "I thought all her friends knew. Margie was killed in a train wreck over two and a half years ago."

Fourteen

Peacocks, frogs, And fish

I was numb as I thanked Mrs. Sanders and told her I was sorry for her loss. She was too upset for me to ask the questions I wanted, and anyway, I didn't think of them until I hung up the phone.

Margie's mom thought she was dead.

I'm a little slow sometimes. This wasn't sinking in as fast as it should.

Margie had let her mom think she was dead for two and half years. Or did I make some sort of colossal mistake? The social security number led me to her mother, who thought she had been dead for the exact length of time Margie had been on the Outer Banks. Did she fake her death, or was there another explanation I was missing?

If Margie *had* deliberately let her mother believe she was dead, that didn't make her sound very nice. Mrs. Sanders had been very upset about her daughter's death. Why would Margie do that?

As hard as it was to admit, I was beginning to realize that I hadn't really known Margie. And though she never talked about her past, at least I felt like I knew the real Margie, the way she was on the inside.

Now I wasn't even sure if I knew that.

As if you're any better.

"Shut up," I said.

Stephen was passing outside the office and he leaned through the doorway. His face was coated with a light sheen of sweat and a cigarette dangled from his lips.

"I didn't even say anything," he protested.

"Hi, Stephen. I think I'm losing it."

"Well, if you're telling the voices in your head to shut up, I'll tell you, that's not a good sign."

"Oh, shut up!" I said, and threw my pen at him. He ducked and I could hear him laughing down the hall.

I wondered if Stephen knew who I was. My face had recently been plastered across the front of *Time* magazine, so I wouldn't be surprised if the entire beach knew who I was. Thankfully, a lot of the people who lived on the Outer Banks came here to escape civilization and weren't real keen on keeping up with what happened in the "real world."

But what about the people who found out who I was? Would they think they had never known me, that I had been duplicitous for changing my name and not telling anyone who I was?

But I wanted to get away from all that.

"Exactly," I said. This time no one was listening.

After that deadly December night in California, I had felt an overpowering need to escape from the media who were hounding my every step. I lasted through the trial, but after I lost my job, my husband,

and my desire to sing, I packed up and left, first for the Florida Keys and then the Outer Banks. I picked "Callie" as my new name, an old nickname my grandfather Sam called me when I was small. I had told no one who I really was.

It took a while for the Outer Banks to work its magic on me, and for me to be comfortable enough to tell my secret to my friends. Even now, only Lenny Marks, Susan, and Kyle knew the truth about me for certain. I suspected that Lily and Chef knew as well. For all I knew, quite a few people had guessed the truth about me, but they seemed to respect my desire for privacy.

During that year that I was in hiding down in the Florida Keys I had little contact with my family and no contact with my husband. I chopped them right out of my life. I was so wrapped up in my own survival, I had no time for anybody else.

So what did all that have to do with Margie?

Simple. It meant that she and I might not be that different. She may have a very good reason for doing what she did. Who was I to judge?

Resolving all of that still brought me no closer to finding out where she was now. And somehow I thought her past had something to do with why she ran in the first place.

Meanwhile, I had a restaurant to run, and we were doing a bug-out tonight. After the bar was closed, pretty much everything movable in the kitchen would be put on racks, wrapped with plastic, and rolled out into the restaurant. Everything in the restaurant and bar would be piled on tables and covered with tablecloths so that maintenance could come in and spray for bugs.

Tomorrow, we got to put everything back.

It was a pain, but it was necessary. Bugs are inevitable: roaches arrive at the restaurant in boxes; fruit flies love orange juice; ants love the grenadine out on the deck bar; several types of bugs piggyback a ride on the fresh produce. All we can do is spray for bugs, keep the kitchen and restaurant as clean as possible, and pray.

I really think that in most places a restaurant kitchen is cleaner than most home kitchens. Most people don't have a strict cleaning regimen which they follow every day. Do home kitchens have thermometers in the refrigerator to ensure that the food is kept at the proper temperature? Do dishwashers spray a minimum of 160-degree water over dirty plates? And most importantly, does someone come in every couple of months to make sure all these health codes are followed?

The phone rang and I snatched it up, muttering. "What?" It was my mother.

"Hello, dear," she said.

"Hi Mom."

"I was wondering if you remembered whose birthday it is tomorrow."

I looked at the calendar, wincing. "It's not like he'll even remember."

"Laurie," my mother said in a gentle voice. "That's what we're here for, to remember for him."

It was a very un-mom thing to say. Not in general, but for my mom to say it. She's a very self-contained person, not given to fits of emotion or passion.

"He's getting worse," I said.

"A little. We've had some problems with him at the nursing home. I'm sure we'll get it straightened out."

I hadn't seen my grandfather Sam in three months. I looked at my appointment book and saw without surprise that I had scheduled myself off. Maybe I had remembered his birthday subconsciously.

"I'll be there," I said. "Dinner?"

"That's fine. Your aunt and I were thinking about Bennigan's in Norfolk by the mall at five. You're welcome to spend the night if you like."

"Thanks. I might. I'll see you at five."

I hung up and sat looking at the rough drafts of the menus spread in front of me. With all that was going on, it was almost impossible to get anything done.

The phone rang.

"What?!"

"Your fish tank's here," Chef said over the phone.

"Great," I said, and meant it. At last I had something to take my mind off Margie.

I took the elevator up to the restaurant and spent a happy hour conferring with Sadie, the pet store representative who brought the fish tank. I had her set it up on a wood cabinet near the front door; the cabinet had previously held an ornate ceramic clock and an aluminum foil flamingo fashioned by Buddy the dishwasher.

Before long, Sadie had the fifty-gallon tank filled with water and bright blue and yellow fish. She worked to arrange the rocky castle and seaweed in attractive positions as the fish darted away from the flashing rings on her fingers.

"How's that?" she asked, her arm in the water up to her bony shoulder. I noticed she had a small butterfly tattoo.

I peered critically at the tank, but the placement looked fine. "Beautiful."

Sadie's face spread into a gap-toothed smile. "These guys are real active. The kids always love 'em."

She brought her arm out of the water and dried it with a rag. Her short hair was spiked around her narrow face, and iridescent earrings hung from her earlobes. I watched the green and blue peacocks sway from her ears for a moment. What was so familiar about them?

Sadie saw me looking and reached up to finger her ears. "You like them?" She smiled kindly, looking over my conservative suit and simple gold jewelry.

"Yes, I do," I said, and the memory clicked. It was the picture of the anonymous woman and Margie. The woman was wearing glittering red and green frog earrings, similar to the ones Sadie wore.

"Where did you get them?"

Sadie was packing up her supplies and she glanced

at me over her shoulders. "We sell them at the pet store. The owner makes them: peacocks, cats, ducks, dogs . . . "

"Frogs?"

"I'm sure. The animal people like 'em, that's for certain."

I leaned forward and examined Sadie's earrings. They were made from delicate, filigreed slips of metal, some silver, some green, and some blue. The eyes were made with tiny red beads.

"They're exquisite," I said.

"They're my favorite pair."

She finished packing up her stuff and promised to be back in a couple of days to check on the tank. I smiled at the colorful fish darting around their new home; they were sure to be a guest-pleaser. They would catch the eye as the guest was walking by the restaurant and with luck bring him in to investigate. They would keep kids occupied when they had to wait for a table.

I went back into the kitchen and found Chef and Leah talking about the health inspection notice.

"Honey, these counters are so clean, I'd feed my new grandbaby off them. What's she mean, giving us a 'B'?" Leah asked, her voice rising with anger.

"It was just bad luck." Chef was being very patient, in his "professional" mode. That could change at any time of course, and Buddy would be cleaning egg yolk off the wall.

"Bad luck? That lady might as well have come into my *home* and told me my dishes weren't clean! Where does she get the nerve?" The health inspector had socked Leah where it hurt the most; she was dearly proud of her sparkling, shining kitchen.

Downstairs, I tried working on the new menus again, but my eyes kept straying to the stack of newspapers Lily had given me. After a while, I sighed, pushed the menus aside, and picked up the newspaper on top.

Lily had been busy. It usually takes a couple of days for us to get the major newspapers delivered out here. Somehow Lily had managed it sooner. Not only that, she managed to get every grocery store magazine available, including *Inquisitor*, *We Want to Know!*, and *Liar! Liar!*.

The major Hampton Roads, Virginia papers like the *Daily Press* and the *Virginian-Pilot* were the most accurate. They kept the sleaze to a minimum, and spent a lot of time on the five-year-old murder. I read with interest.

Angel H. Knowling was twenty-three when her nude body was found behind her house. It was a quiet neighborhood, and the neighbors were shocked. The papers dredged up interviews from five years ago, and the neighbors had all said what a happy couple the Knowlings seemed to be.

Keith Knowling was a biology teacher at a nearby high school. The grainy pictures showed a beefy white face and bruised eyes obscured by glasses. In the picture, Keith looked about as harmless as a wet kitten, and it was hard to believe he could be capable of killing someone. He married Angel when he was twenty-five and they moved into a small house. Keith inherited a little money when his grandfather died, and he bought himself and his new bride a beautiful, secluded home on a creek. Keith seemed flawless: he rode his bike for cancer relief; he was a "Big Brother;" and he had directed the school's production of *Macbeth* the year before.

Angel married Keith when she was eighteen, the day after she graduated from high school. They had a big white wedding, and everybody said how happy Angel had been. "All she ever wanted was to find a good husband to take care of her," one of her aunts said, and I wondered how well the woman had known her niece. Angel's picture showed a pure white oval face, big eyes, puffy lips, and a mass of curly dark hair. She looked a little sexy to be an angel, but her smile was sweet, even if her eyes were opaque in the picture.

Angel didn't have a job; she took care of her husband. Her neighbors rarely saw her except when she was gardening, which she loved to do. One of her neighbors confided that the quiet Mrs. Knowling liked to swim in the muddy creek behind her house. Several of the neighbors had seen her over the years.

The night she died, she was swimming nude in the creek, her clothes folded with care on the dock. Keith Knowling stabbed her twenty-five times, and, in the privacy of the dark, fenced-in backyard, cut off her head.

His prints were everywhere. He had disappeared by the next day when a man in a passing boat saw a pale form lying under a weeping willow in the Knowling's backyard. A subsequent check of police records revealed a domestic disturbance call from Angel in the month leading up to her death. A lawyer came forward to say Angel had consulted him about a divorce. The theory was that Keith killed his wife because he found out she wanted to leave him.

I put the paper down, feeling sick. What happened in those last months to turn what looked like the perfect marriage into hell on earth for Angel Knowling?

I moved on to the *Inquisitor* and was not surprised to see a picture of the Holiday House Hotel at the top of a story about Angel Knowling's skull. This reporter decided that Angel's ghost must walk the halls of the hotel searching for her head. A "reliable source" disclosed that a headless ghost dressed in white had haunted the hotel for years. It made a great story.

The next magazine took a far different tack. This reporter claimed Keith Knowling had lived in Montana for the last five years, with a wife and new daughter, and was working as a roofer. The man had disappeared over the weekend, just as the rumors about Angel's head began to circulate. The fuzzy picture that ran with the story bore little resemblance to Keith Knowling.

The fourth paper picked up the ghost theme again, but this time with an interesting twist. This reporter was a busy little bee. He dug up the story about the mermaid sightings on the Outer Banks and connected her to Angel. It was Angel, he theorized, swimming in the ocean searching for her head.

I slammed the papers down and then clipped a note to the *Inquisitor*—the one with the picture of the Holiday House—saying: "Are you going to use a knife or your bare hands to rip the new orifice?" and put it aside.

To make matters worse, all the papers picked up on the fact that the five-year anniversary of Angel's death was on Sunday, only four days away.

Something was bothering me, and I flipped through the papers again, studying the tiny newsprint. It was a horrid little story, but what in particular was bothering me about it?

Sighing, I shoved the papers away. I had other things to worry about. I had bug-out tonight, the new menu was due out in a week, and I promised I would help with the strenuous cleaning regimen prescribed by Chef and Leah to get the kitchen back in shape. On top of that, Margie's disappearance had left a huge hole in my schedule, even with my new hire.

Margie. What was I going to do about her? I couldn't seem to leave it alone. I couldn't shake the image of her sitting on the floor in the storeroom staring at the wall.

Something clicked in my mind. I grabbed one of the newspapers and flipped to the photo of Angel Knowling.

Jesus. It seemed unbelievable.

There was an unmistakable resemblance between the dead woman and Margie Sanders.

Fifteen

Twinkle, Twinkle, Little Star

It was four o'clock in the morning by the time I got home after bug-out. I slept for two hours and then went back in and helped put away the stuff for the morning shift. After that, I went home and crashed until almost noon.

It was my day off, and I was due in Virginia by five. I messed around the house, desultorily washing clothes and cleaning, and trying not to trip over Jake and Ice. Jake had lost a little of his puppyish exuberance, though he still liked to pound Ice on the head with his over-sized paws. Ice liked the "piggyback" game, where he jumped from the couch or the table onto Jake's back, riding him like a bucking bronco until Jake managed to dislodge him.

I was trying not to think, and I was doing a fairly good job of it. Still, the thoughts of Angel Knowling and Margie Sanders kept creeping back into my consciousness. As soon as I saw the resemblance between Angel and Margie, I called Dale Grain. He listened to my disjointed conjectures, but did not seem to understand my urgency.

"Your waitress left on her own," he pointed out. "I talked to her roommate and she confirmed that the girl packed up and left a note. I called the rest of the numbers you gave me. None of her friends knew where she'd gone; they also said Margie hadn't told them that somebody was stalking her. I left messages for her to call me, but it's clear she left on her own."

"I know, I know," I grumbled, "but the resemblance between the two is striking. Don't you think there might be a connection? What about the fact that Margie Sander's mother thinks she's dead? What about that?"

"Obviously there has been some sort of mix up with the social security numbers. By the way, you do realize that it's illegal to run a credit check on someone without their knowledge?"

"Yes, yes," I said with rising impatience. "But how else was I supposed to find out who her parents are? Don't you think there must be some kind of connection between Margie's disappearance and her resemblance to Angel Knowling?"

"It's a coincidence," Dale said. "What do you think, that Margie Sanders is actually the long-dead Angel Knowling? Because I can tell you, it's not so. Angel Knowling is dead. It's conclusive. There is no connection, Callie. You're taking a passing resemblance and building a theory out of sand. It won't hold up. If you hear from Margie let me know. I'd like to talk to her." He hung up.

I was getting tired of Dale Grain hanging up on me. Was he right, though? Many young women shared common features. An oval face and dark, curly hair weren't that unusual, and the picture of Angel Knowling *was* grainy and dated. I couldn't be sure.

At almost three o'clock, I told the animals good-bye and pointed my Jeep towards Virginia. I had made an appointment to have it looked at next week, and was praying it would get me to Virginia and back.

During the tourist season, the locals always complain about the traffic on the Bypass and Beach Road. I've heard that the way you know "they're back," meaning the summer visitors, is when you see the first U-turn on the Bypass.

In the summer, they cruise along in the left lane of the fifty-mile-an-hour Bypass at a whopping twenty miles an hour, and are apt to change lanes in either direction with no notice. And, of course, there are the Pointers. The Pointers are a very nice family from somewhere up north who are so busy pointing out the various Outer Banks sights (from the ocean, to the dunes, to the new "Dirty Dick's Crab House" sign) that they neglect to watch where they are going.

Traffic is traffic is traffic, however, and I was not happy about being stuck in the Hampton Road's variety.

I traveled in the middle lane over Interstate 64—which seems to be in a perpetual state of repair—keeping a careful eye on the other drivers around me. My fellow travelers were, respectively: tying a shoe, switching out a CD changer (the one in the back seat), and trying to clean the outside of the windshield from the inside. It was hard to avoid the little old man in the big Cadillac who thought that the right two lanes were his exclusively.

I found my mother, my aunt, and my grandfather Sam inside the restaurant. They had already ordered. My aunt doesn't play games with food. You don't sneak food off of her plate for fear of a fork stabbing, and if you're late for dinner, you get your food if and when you can.

"We weren't sure how long you would be, so we ordered," my mom said apologetically. Aunt Alice smiled, not in the least fazed.

"How was your drive, Laurie?" Mom asked. Laurie was my birth name, a name I gave up when I went into hiding.

"Fine."

My mom looked like me. She didn't act like me, but she looked like me—or I guess I looked like her. She was dressed in pale blue today, a slimming combination accented by an amethyst necklace and a purple scarf around a smart ponytail.

My aunt looked like no one in the family. Where the rest of us were dark-haired and quiet, slim, and on the short side of medium height (except for my brother Henley who was taller than a pine tree), Aunt Alice was rolling curves, jolly, irrepressible, and not even five feet tall. She was incapable of letting others speak for any great length of time.

"Traffic was pretty bad, though," I said.

"Oh, isn't it just terrible? I was telling Kitty here—" Aunt Alice rambled on, while my mom, "Kitty," short for Katherine, rolled her eyes.

"Oh, it's you," my grandfather said, chewing on his slipping dentures and reaching for me with a gnarled hand.

I took his warm, hard hand and looked at the oh-so-familiar face. His burgundy and gold baseball cap emblazoned with "Redskins" was askew on his head, and the plaid shirt and blue pants hung on his skinny frame.

"Hi Sam," I said.

"I was just telling the big-un," Sam angled an elbow at my mom who was taller than Aunt Alice by four inches, "that you should come over some more. We got peas, and corn, fresh right out in the garden—" Sam waved vaguely out the window and then trailed off as he looked with confusion at the other diners around us.

"You ready to go?" he asked my mother, sliding his chair back with a screech and trying to stand.

"Sit down, Sam," my aunt ordered, and pulled him down to his chair. She was still visibly pleased with the "big-un" comment.

"We haven't eaten yet," my mom explained to Sam in a soft voice. "It's your birthday, and Laurie's here. Don't you want to stay and talk to Laurie?"

"Who's Laurie?" Sam asked, and smiled at me.

While I was in California fighting my own battles,

my grandfather's mind slowly slipped away. At first no one noticed. *Sam forgot to pay his electric bill again. Sam got lost on the way to visit, do you think he should still be driving?*

After a while it had become all too clear that Sam was suffering from Alzheimer's disease. For almost two years, my mom and aunt tried to take care of him at home. But he had become too much for them to handle and they had to put him in a nursing home.

To their surprise he loved it.

He seemed happy, he just wasn't the Sam who had helped raise me from a baby. He wasn't the Sam who taught me how to sing, who taught me so much about life and called me "Callie" for the cat named Kalamazoo in my favorite Hoyt Axton song.

Sam tried to leave several more times as we ate. My mom and aunt were full of questions about Angel Knowling's skull, and I filled them in.

"I had a friend who worked with Keith Knowling," my aunt said. She worked in the Norfolk school system and always had the latest gossip.

"She was so shocked when this all happened five years ago. I think she met Angel at a school function. She said Angel was sweet, but that she seemed kind of restless. My friend said that you felt like Angel wasn't listening to you when you talked to her; she would nod and smile, but you got the feeling she didn't hear a word you said. Keith, on the other hand, he was a talker. He loved to talk. My friend said it was hard to shut him up. She always thought he was a good man, said she was impressed with the extra time he took with the kids at school, though he spent so much time at work she wondered how he ever had time for his poor wife."

My mom patted her mouth with a napkin. "Around the time Angel Knowling was killed, a lady contacted a journalist friend of mine." Inexplicably my mother blushed. "She wanted to give him the 'real' story of Angel Knowling. When my . . . friend looked into her, he discovered she had been Angel's piano teacher for ten years. He called her back, but she decided she didn't want to talk after all."

I was still wondering why my mother was blushing, but I was intrigued by her story.

"Did your, uh . . . friend . . . ," and darned if she didn't blush harder! Did my mother have a boyfriend? " . . . try to contact her after all this recent fuss?"

"Yes. She still didn't want to talk to reporters about Angel."

"Angel, angel, twinkle star," Sam said in a falsetto voice. "How I wonder where you are." He chomped into his cheeseburger and chewed with his mouth open.

"So have you heard from your deadbeat husband?" my aunt demanded, and my mother shot her a quelling look. My return to the McKinley family fold was a delicate subject. It was only in the last couple of months that I had started to feel comfortable visiting my family again.

"No, I haven't," I said, in what I hoped was a "no more questions, please" tone of voice. But my aunt has never been one for subtlety.

"How about Henley? Have you talked to your brother?"

"I haven't spoken to him either," I said equably, my gut clenching. "He'd probably go straight to the news-papers."

"Alice," my mother said sharply, "shut up."

So many family secrets. We were a very small family, and sometimes we just knew too much about one another.

"Anyway, Cynthia called from London yesterday," my mom said with forced cheer. "She's doing well."

"Great," I said with feeling, though I had only talked to my sister Cynthia once since she moved to London.

And that about exhausted the family talk. We moved on to less sensitive subjects, and even Aunt Alice didn't seem inclined to rock the boat very much.

"It's getting dark," Sam kept saying, gesturing at the windows where falling dusk was shrouding the parking lot. "Gotta get home now, you hear?"

He grabbed my mother's hand and tried to pull her to her feet.

"No Dad," she said. "You haven't had your birthday cake yet."

"Come on now, it's time to go," he said, but he sat down, mumbling under his breath.

The staff brought my grandfather a huge, freshly-made chocolate chip cookie covered in chocolate syrup and whipped cream. They surrounded us and sang "Happy Birthday" as he grinned his big, happy grin and clapped along in delight. My grandfather always loved to sing; he still did, even if he couldn't remember the words.

I don't think anyone saw my tears.

Sixteen
Mom Comes Through

It was after eight by the time we finished dinner, and Mom talked me into going home with her and spending the night. I called my roommate, who was home for once, and asked her to watch Jake and Ice while I was gone. She agreed with ill grace. Mom was pleased, though she didn't say so.

It was strange going back to the house where I had grown up. It had been years since I had been home, and the house was now arranged to suit Mom's needs. The bedroom I shared with my sister until I was fifteen was now an office. My brother's bedroom, which Mom told me was where my grandfather had lived for two years, was now a sterile guest bedroom.

My mother raised us alone with the help of my grandfather. Except for occasional men friends, I had never known my mother to be serious about a man. Now, in her house, I saw the unmistakable signs of a man who visited her frequently: a razor in her bathroom; a fishing magazine on the table; men's size twelve dress shoes in the closet. I didn't say anything. She would tell me when she was ready.

I found myself confiding in Mom about my job

and the difficulties I had faced since half of the food and beverage staff left this summer.

"Sounds a bit hectic, hmmm?" Mom said. She was the master of the understatement, unlike my aunt and my brother Henley who always spoke the first thing that came to their minds.

I also told her about Margie and the resemblance I thought I had discovered between she and Angel.

"How could there be a connection?" Mom asked. "The police have identified Angel's body and her—er, head. Your waitress couldn't be Angel."

"I know," I wailed. "Don't you think I know?" Suddenly I felt thirteen years old: *Callie you need to clean your room. I know Momma, I will. Soon. I know I need to do my homework. I know, I know, I know.* That was the refrain of my unruly teens, when I was so sure I was right about anything and everything. How did Mom put up with me?

"So, what possible connection could there be?" It was the same oh-so-reasonable voice I remembered from childhood, but now it was comforting, not irritating.

"I don't know," I said. "I guess none."

"It is strange that your waitress Margie seems to have no history." She was playing devil's advocate, trying to be fair, trying to see the situation from all sides. "I guess it is possible that she's Angel's sister or something, though I still don't understand what it would have to do with her disappearance."

"I don't either," I admitted. "It just seems like too

much of a coincidence that Angel's skull is discovered the week before the fifth anniversary of her death, and then my waitress—who happens to look a lot like Angel—disappears the same week."

"She left of her own accord, from what you've said."

"I know."

We were going around in circles, and eventually we started talking about other things.

That night I couldn't sleep, and I lay awake staring at the familiar walls where I used to feel so safe and secure. I wished for just one night that I could feel the way I did as a child, when Mom and Grandpa would take care of everything and summer vacation was always just around the corner.

The next morning, Mom had left for work by the time I woke up. On the kitchen counter next to her hefty supply of assorted hot tea bags was a note:

Laurie-

Even as a child, you always wanted to know how and why and when. As an adult, I know you have learned the hard way that there are some things you will never know. I called my friend, and this is the name and number of the woman who contacted him about Angel Knowling five years ago. Maybe talking to her will ease your mind.

Love,
Mom

A name and number were at the bottom of the note.

I sat for a minute and stared at the green lawn and towering pine trees in the backyard. Right outside the window was a lopsided birdhouse Henley had made for Mom when he was in the sixth grade. My old jungle gym was still there, and I saw with surprise that it had a fresh coat of paint. Was Mom secretly longing for grandchildren?

My thoughts spiraled to Margie and Angel. It was only a passing resemblance, wasn't it? And, really, what business was it of mine?

Mom was right, though. I have never been able to accept what people told me on faith. My Sunday school teachers had despaired of my constant questions. What if there was a connection between Margie and Angel? I couldn't shake the feeling that Margie was in more trouble than maybe even she realized.

With sudden resolve, I picked up the phone and dialed the number. I noticed it was a Hampton exchange.

"May I speak to Betty Lewis?"

"Yes, this is she." The voice was aged to almost mildness.

"I was wondering if I could come by and talk to you about Angel Knowling," I said without preamble.

"I'm sorry, I'm not talking to reporters. Thank you for calling."

"I'm not a reporter," I said before she could hang up. "I . . . it's hard to explain. I want to understand what happened to Angel."

"You're not a reporter?" Her voice was skeptical.

"I've had two phone calls just today from reporters, and you expect me to believe that you're not one of them?"

"No, ma'am. I'm not. I'm someone who understands what it's like to have the media dissect every facet of your life and still miss the real person," I said, surprised as the words came out. "I think Angel deserves better."

"How do I know you're not a reporter?" she asked, and I knew she was wavering.

"My name is Laurie McKinley," I said.

There was silence for a few moments and I opened my mouth to say more, but then she sighed. "If you're really who you say you are, then okay. I know what you look like, so don't think I won't know if you're lying when I see you."

"I'm not lying."

"Well, I'd like to talk to someone about it. My son is tired of hearing about the whole thing, and I don't have anyone else who'll listen. I know why Keith killed her, you know."

"You do?"

"Oh yes. You come and talk to me and maybe I'll tell you why he did it."

Seventeen

Talk About Complicated

It was nearing ten o'clock when I pulled into the parking space in front of Betty Lewis's neat, vinyl-sided town home standing in a row of clones in the rambling apartment complex.

I knocked on the door and heard a horrible yapping start up. Mrs. Lewis flung open the door holding a black and tan Yorkshire terrier. The dog was squirming and snarling at me, a small blue ribbon holding the hair back from his face.

She had cleaned house since I spoke to her. I could smell Pine-Sol, and could see where she had tried to clean around various knickknacks, leaving wide rings of dust around their bases. An entire wall at the far end of the room was devoted to picture frames. Washed dishes gleamed in the sink, visible through a wide doorway.

Mrs. Lewis was in white slacks, sensible white shoes, and a pale blue top. Her gray hair was caught up in a bun at the top of her head giving her a faintly girlish look. Her jowls drooped alarmingly around her mouth and her lucid blue eyes were friendly and alert. She seemed in good health, though I smelled an unidentifiable odor that I had always associated with my aunt, who had diabetes.

"I see you weren't lying," she said as she showed me to a couch covered with a pretty afghan. I sat down.

She sat down in a chair across from me, patting the dog and crooning to him. I noticed that she had a tic that ran from the side of her face down to her neck. I tried not to watch as the muscle tightened spasmodically, pulling down the edge of her mouth.

"My poor Angel, always thinking that a man was going to solve her problems." Her large, age-spotted hands clenched the growling dog on her lap.

"So how did you meet Angel?" I tried not to watch as her neck jerked like a fish on a hook.

"I lived in Deep Creek many years ago, and Angel used to take piano lessons from me. I didn't need to teach, you understand; my husband made a fortune before he died. I liked doing it."

I hoped she didn't notice my quick glance around her neat, modest home. If her husband had made a fortune, it was not obvious in her humble surroundings.

"I taught piano for forty years, but the arthritis has finally won out." She held out her big, bony fingers glittering with cheap-looking silver rings, and massaged the swollen knuckles.

"My Angel was always such a pretty-looking thing, but so shy! She took lessons from me for over ten years, and she was quite good. She was the star performer in my Valentine's Day recital two years in a row. Such an angel! You know, her name really fit her." She smiled at the memory, and I realized she must be very lonely. My heart went out to her.

The dog had subsided to a tense crouch on Mrs. Lewis's knee, staring at me malevolently and rumbling an occasional warning. She gave him a sharp pat on the back. "Now, now, Oliver, don't growl at the nice lady." The dog continued to growl. His look said he knew a nice lady when he saw her.

"So what happened?"

"Well, Angel always talked to me. You see, the poor little thing didn't have anybody else. She was so full of dreams! We used to talk for hours about boys in her class she was interested in, movie stars, and singers she'd like to marry. She had her wedding and the names of her children planned out before she was twelve. Angel always said she wouldn't marry anyone unless he was at least as good as her daddy, though I never saw the man give her the time of day. Even after she stopped taking lessons from me, she came by after school and we would sit and talk." The old woman's eyes grew dreamy.

"Then she met him." Her gaze hardened. "That horrible man she married. Keith. She fell head over heels for him. I always thought if—well, you can't change the way things happen. She loved him, and even though her parents wanted her to go to college, she got her way and married him the day after she graduated. All she ever wanted was her own home and a man to love. Seems old-fashioned in this day

Wendy Howell Mills

and age, but that was Angel. So she married Keith, and my, oh my, she was in love with that man. Had stars in her eyes, she did."

She paused, and again she retreated into her memories, but this time her mouth was pursed in anger. I looked around at the room, the stained blue carpet, the doilies on the coffee table, and the ornate lamps. A battered Steinway piano crowded against the back wall.

Mrs. Lewis continued. "She was so happy at first. She stopped coming by; you know how young love is. They would go on trips together . . ."

"To the Outer Banks?" I asked.

She shrugged. "I don't know. They went to Myrtle Beach on their honeymoon, but I'm not sure where else they went. Everything seemed perfect. After a while though, she started coming by again." She gazed at the piano and the pictures. "She was lonely. Keith spent a lot of time at work and riding his bike. I think he wanted to be in a marathon, so he was always taking long rides. She was stuck at home all by herself. She was bored and disillusioned. She started talking about going back to school, and I encouraged her. She thought she might like to be a nurse, and I know she would have made a good one.

"Then," she said, and put a hand to her neck where the tic was jumping wildly. "Then Angel met my Lucas." Mrs. Lewis closed her eyes, and Oliver the dog started to wiggle. "Lucas has been away in Hollywood, you know. He used to tell me that when people thought of the biggest stars in Hollywood, they'd think of Lucas C. Lewis first. He had a hard time out there, though he was in a couple of commercials. What a place California must be! Do you have any children? No? Well, if you did, you'd give your dying breath just to see them happy.

"Lucas came for a visit one day when Angel was here. It was the first time he'd seen her all grown up. Before, she was just a dreamy-eyed little girl he loved to tease. Something clicked that day and they fell in love. He was so sweet, and he was just right for poor Angel. They saw each other in secret whenever they could.

"One time, when Keith came back from a teacher's conference, he must have hit her. Angel never complained, but I saw the bruises. Then she stopped coming to see me."

"So you think Keith killed Angel because of her affair with your son?" I asked.

"Keith didn't know who Angel was seeing, he just suspected that she was seeing someone. How scared she must have been! Angel and Lucas decided to run away together and get married. Of course, she was going to divorce Keith, but Angel and Lucas had such plans! They were going to have three children. Grandchildren . . . " Mrs. Lewis closed her eyes and smiled. "They were such a perfect couple, young and innocent, both of them interested in the same things.

If only they had met first—but you can't be curing spoiled milk. Keith must have found out about their plans, and he killed Angel to stop her from going. I'll never forget Lucas's face when he found out. He was so upset."

"Why didn't you go to the police?"

"We were going to, but we decided it would ruin Angel's good name. She was dead and there was no sense dragging all the skeletons out of her closet. Normal people just wouldn't understand the kind of love they had. Lucas wanted to tell at first, but I talked him out of it. I didn't want my boy tied up in that business."

She was stroking Oliver and her neck tightened, pulling her mouth down into a leer. I felt sorry for her, stuck here alone with her nasty dog, living her life vicariously through her memories of the two lovers.

I rummaged in my bag and pulled out one of the pictures of Margie. "Have you ever seen this girl?"

She squinted at the picture, and I got up and went over to her chair to hand it to her. She stared at it for a long time.

"She looks like Angel, doesn't she?" she asked in a soft voice. "But I've never seen her before. Who is she?"

I sidestepped the question. "Angel didn't have any sisters, did she?"

"Oh no. Only the one brother, and he was so much older. I think that was why she was so lonely. It was hard for her to make friends too, because she was so shy. Why, I think I might have been the only true friend she ever had."

I put the picture away, disappointed. It had been a wasted trip after all. Whatever resemblance Margie had to Angel, it was just a coincidence.

I headed west on the interstate, and on a sudden impulse I took the exit towards Old Dominion University.

Even though I had attended college in northern Virginia, I spent a lot of time in high school at the large ODU library.

I turned off Hampton Boulevard onto the campus, and with difficulty found a parking place. It was strange walking among the groups of chattering college students. I was only six years out of college myself, but I felt immeasurably older than these brightly-dressed children.

I entered the library, and it was like walking into a bright, warm embrace. The library reminded me of happier days, when my biggest worry was whether Eddie Fisher was going to invite me to prom. My stomach muscles began to unclench as I walked into the glassed-in reference section, which had been moved since last I was here, and saw computer terminals with cursors blinking in welcome.

I sat down and dug into my bag for a pen. I had

come to ODU on a whim, because I felt like I wasn't getting any closer to finding Margie Sanders. I couldn't shake the feeling that I had to find out *who* she was before I could find out *where* she was. The visit to Betty Lewis had been a bust, but the trip to Virginia didn't have to be wasted.

I wanted information about the train wreck that supposedly killed Margie Sanders, but I wasn't sure how to go about it. I coasted through the library's homepage and clicked on the Dow Jones Interactive icon, which gave me access to tons of newspapers.

I typed in "Margie Sanders," but the computer didn't find any reference.

I escaped from that screen, and kept hitting escape until I came to a screen that I overlooked the first time. The database I was searching was only for the last two years. I chose to search for the last five years, and again typed in "Margie Sanders."

Still no luck.

I tried "train wreck and Kentucky." Nothing.

I tried "train wreck and New Hampshire." Nothing.

I tried to think of which states a train from New Hampshire to Kentucky would have to go through and came up blank.

I tried "train wreck and Pennsylvania" just for the heck of it, and got nothing.

I tried "train accident," the year the accident would have happened according to Margie's mom, and "Margie Sanders," and still came up with nothing.

Okay, time to regroup. I was working under the assumption that any train wreck that had actually killed someone would have to be national news. I was assuming that the train wreck would have happened between New Hampshire—where she said she grew up and went to college—and Kentucky, where her parents lived.

But "train wreck" was not getting me anywhere. I was getting way too many hits to wade through. I needed to narrow it down.

I sighed and sat back in my chair. I'll never know where the urge came from, but I typed in my own name, "Laurie McKinley."

The screen blinked out an entire page of summaries.

I scrolled through them, remembering many of the first stories when I was heralded as a hero for saving the young son of movie star Henry Gray. Here was the interview I gave in the hospital room, still stunned by what had happened. Next was the interview with Henry Gray, taking time from a major movie production in Spain to come back to be with his injured son. He spoke warmly of me, and I remembered the first time he came to see me in the hospital.

Then, because there was nothing else newsworthy going on, the articles took on a darker tenor. Reporters began to speculate that Henry Gray and I were involved, that I had been stalking his wife and that was why I had been in the 7-11. The probing into my background began: an old boyfriend was interviewed;

friends I never heard of began telling how I had always been a little obsessed with things.

Worst of all was the interview my brother Henley gave. He swore later that his words had been twisted around, but the article was damaging nonetheless. I still hadn't forgiven him. I asked all of my family not to talk to the press, but Henley decided "for my own good" to clear the air.

It all died off after a few months, and I got well enough to go back to work. But I had been replaced, and no matter how much everybody made me feel welcome, I could see the questions in their eyes. Then the trial started, and the nightmare began all over again. Had I known the killer? People came out of the woodwork to say that I'd always had strange friends. As I was the primary witness against the two killers, I was dragged through the mud, and the media hopped and skipped along with every new juicy tidbit.

When I found out from an insensitive reporter that my husband was having an affair, I swore off reading or watching any of the coverage. As soon as the trial was over, I left.

My finger was on the scroll-down button, and the stories were sliding past with increasing rapidity. I abruptly hit the power button on the monitor. The screen shrank to a gleaming white line and then disappeared with a pop.

I sat back and closed my eyes, focusing on breathing. My heart was hammering and my skin felt clammy.

Gradually though, the panic receded and I opened my eyes.

I turned the monitor back on and typed "Amtrack" and the year the train wreck was supposed to have taken place.

Bingo. There it was.

It had been in Louisiana. I never would have tried that. The train had derailed at a traffic crossing and killed two people on board and one in a car. I scrolled through the article summaries, but there were no names for the victims. I started downloading specific articles and stretched, little pops echoing down my spine. This was going to take a while.

A half an hour later, I knew more than I had when I started. The train in Louisiana had been en route from New York to New Orleans, and a malfunction in a railroad crossing sign caused the tragic accident. The wreck inspired a spirited public debate over the safety of railroad crossings all over the country. I had to wade through several articles in that vein before I got to an article that focused on the human-interest side of the story.

The old man in the car was killed instantly, and a young woman and a little girl were killed inside one of the mangled train cars.

The young woman's name was Margie Sanders. She was from Kentucky.

Even though I was expecting it, it was still a shock to see it in print. Margie Sanders, a junior at Boston

University, had caught a train from Boston to New York and then got on the train that would kill her in Louisiana. There was a grainy picture of the procession of cars to her burial site.

I hit "page down" and saw a picture of Margie Sanders, taken the month before she died.

I stared in shock.

"Who the hell is that?"

Eighteen
I Own The Weeds

All of a sudden I realized just how tired I was. Staring at the picture, the headache that had been worrying at the edge of my brain grabbed the back of my head and bit, hard.

It was simple, really. The Margie Sanders who was my head waitress was not the same girl as the Margie Sanders who died in the train wreck.

It made sense, of course. How could the girl be waiting tables if she was dead? I guess I was thinking that there had been a mistake and Margie Sanders wasn't dead; she had run to the Outer Banks for her own reasons.

However, according to the newspaper, the casket had been open at the viewing. The girl was dead. And the blond girl smiling in her blue velvet graduation gown was not the Margie Sanders I knew.

I wondered if I had followed the wrong trail. But how many Margie Sanders could have died in a train wreck in the same year? When I checked the social security number that Margie was using, it led to the woman in Kentucky whose daughter died in a train wreck two and a half years ago.

My headache got worse.

I was back to square one. I had no idea who Margie was, and as far as I could tell, she was using the social security number of a dead girl. Wonderful.

I downloaded several more articles and printed them out without reading them. I just didn't have enough energy to read any more today, and I had over an hour's drive to get home.

I exited onto the new turnpike and opened the windows to try and enjoy the crisp, fall afternoon. As I drove, my thoughts fluttered around in the past and settled on a memory that I had hoped to forget.

I was coming out of the courtroom where I had just given my testimony. I was shaking. The defense had been rough with their questions, and Dave had his arm around me as he hustled me past the yelling reporters and their bright, bright lights.

"Laurie, how did it go? Do you think the jury will find him guilty?"

"Laurie, have you talked to Henry Gray? What about Andy Gray?"

"Laurie, did you know Henry Gray was on Today this morning and he wished you luck?"

"Laurie, did you know Dave is having an affair?"

I felt Dave's arm stiffen around me, and my lawyer pushed his way through to the front and gave a small speech about civilization and the fruits of justice while Dave and I made our way to the car.

He didn't say anything as I got into the car, and neither did I. I think I was too numb to feel any emotions.

"Is it true?" I asked.

I could feel Dave looking at me, his eyes dark and worried. "Laurie, I wanted to tell you. It really means nothing, believe me, but you've been so distant lately . . . Laurie, I love you," he said, and we pulled away from the courthouse.

I nodded. Couldn't he see I felt empty, that nothing mattered? I felt as if someone had gone inside of me and ripped out every part that could feel. I didn't want to talk about it. I didn't want to think about it.

"Will you say something?" he said, and I could hear the anguish in his voice. I looked over at him, and was almost surprised to see tears well up in his eyes. Dave never cried. He looked handsome in his dark suit with his golden blond hair retreating a bit from his wide forehead. His light blue eyes were searching my face, but I don't know what he saw. I know I saw my husband, the man I had loved for five years, the man who I wanted to have children with, the man who had betrayed me.

"What do you want me to say?" I said, the words echoing inside me as they dropped into the silence.

It hadn't escaped my notice that Dave didn't try to deny what the reporter said. He easily could have. The reporters had already accused me of having an affair with Henry Gray, for God's sake. Dave could have said it was all untrue. I knew then that he had been waiting to tell me for some time. I saw it now, even if I hadn't before.

"It's over with her," Dave said, putting a finger under his collar and looking out the window. "I love you more than anything, but you're shutting me out. I'm sorry about the baby, but I'm hurting too. Talk to me, Laurie!"

And I said nothing.

When I got to work the menus were waiting for me, and I actually got quite a bit done before I had to go to Thursday afternoon staff meetings.

I decided that it would be best for me to forget Margie Sanders, or whoever she was. She must have a good reason to do what she did, and if she wanted to hide, who was I to say she couldn't?

It wasn't that I stopped worrying, I didn't. I guess I realized that Margie could take care of herself. She had been doing it for the last several years, hadn't she? There was no indication that she was in trouble, just that she was scared and felt the need to leave.

And I was the last person to say anything about someone being scared and needing to leave.

The detectives were busy asking the staff questions and looking through old registration records. It was a mammoth job, and they hadn't come up with any proof that Keith and Angel ever stayed at the hotel. There *wouldn't* be any proof unless Keith had paid with a credit card. They had expanded their search to nearby hotels and restaurants.

Maybe it was just a fluke that Keith Knowling buried the skull in the dune behind the Holiday House. I couldn't help but wonder why he did it, though. I felt a connection to Angel, a protective instinct for the girl-woman who couldn't defend herself. I would defend her, as I hadn't been able to defend myself.

Angel and I could not have been two more different people. But I sensed there was more to the girl than anybody knew. I guess that was how I felt about myself. Even now, I carried secrets in my heart that I had never told anybody. Doesn't everyone? I felt more safe and comfortable now than I had since I left California, but I still couldn't bring myself to talk about the past.

Was that how Angel felt, as if she had a great burden of secrets and dreams that she carried with her everywhere? Was she afraid that if she ever started talking they would all pour from her like a load of gravel, sliding and bouncing out until she lost all control?

A detective showed me a picture of Keith Knowling, but I didn't recognize him. No one did, as far as I heard. The man was about as nondescript as they came: medium height, mousy brown hair, medium brown eyes. Who would remember him?

They were trying to find people who had worked at the hotel long enough to remember if Keith and Angel stayed there before her death. The murder took place five years ago almost to the day, so they would have visited the hotel at least five years ago. Lily and Ray, the front desk manager, were the only ones who had been at the hotel for more than five years, and neither of them recognized the pictures.

The one person who had been working at the Holiday House longer than Lily and Ray retired two months ago. Old Jonathan had worked at the hotel since it was built. He was retired from the postal service when he started working at the front desk of the Holiday House, and by the time he retired for the second time fifteen years later, he was ready for some peace and relaxation. Knowing Jonathan, he wasn't relaxing. I hated to do it, but I sicced the police on him.

After the endless staff meetings, Lily caught me in the hall and shoved a newspaper at me. "Check out page three," she ordered, and went into her office.

I flipped to page three and saw the article.

Outer Banks Mermaid?

One week after the skull of Angel Knowling, known as the "Murdered Mermaid," was found outside of the Holiday House Hotel, everybody is talking about the Outer Banks Mermaid.

"She's been around for years," said Happy Jenkins, a crabber out of Colington. "I've seen her twice."

So who is this woman who has been swimming in the waters off the Outer Banks?

No one knows.

People from Hatteras to Kitty Hawk have reported seeing a long-haired woman swimming in the ocean, mostly around dusk and dawn. Some have reported that she is naked; others swear that they have seen a tail.

Some people say it's just mass hysteria.

"Someone sees a dolphin or a bird or something, and next thing you know, it's a beautiful woman with long green hair and a fish tail. Give me a break!," said Hugh Williams, a broker at Starfish Realty.

Others say she's the ghost of Angel Knowling. However, there have been reports of mermaid sightings going back as far as fifteen years, long before Keith Knowling allegedly killed his wife.

Those who claim they have seen the mermaid are convinced she's real.

"Just because you've never seen a mermaid, there's no reason to think that those of us who have are crazy!," said Elizabeth Tarrington. "Maybe you've never been abducted by an alien either, but don't you tell me it's not possible!"

"She's real," Happy Jenkins said. "I'm not crazy."

I smiled and closed the paper. I'd seen her too, and I didn't think I was crazy. Then again, what crazy person thinks they are?

I went back to my office and finished the schedule. When I was done, it was time for the restaurant to open so I went upstairs.

Most of the staff was gathered around the new fish tank, arguing over names for the fish.

"Let's call him Weed," Luigi said in his not-quite foreign accent, slouching against the side of the cabinet. "The blue fish gets in the weeds more than any of us."

Everybody laughed as the neon blue fish flashed through the floating seaweed. Since "in the weeds" meant being very busy in restaurant lingo, the name made a certain kind of sense.

"Well, I think it's absolutely adorable," said Rob. His tie was a bit flamboyant, and his flaming red hair was a little startling, but from all accounts he was doing well.

"At this one restaurant I worked at they had this saying hanging in the kitchen: 'Five minutes, I own the weeds. Ten minutes, I'm in the weeds. Fifteen minutes, I'm weeded.'"

"I'd say Weed gets out of the weeds a lot better than the rest of us," Kate joked, swinging her long brown hair out of the way as she bent to peer at the fish. "I want to name one of them Mellow Yellow." There was a queer silence.

Mellow Margie was Margie's nickname. I didn't like the feeling that we were honoring the dead by naming a fish after her, but I wasn't going to say anything.

An older couple came in waving an "early bird" coupon, and the two servers hid groans of disgust.

"I can order anything on the menu, right?" the woman was asking as Kate led her to a table. "I can order anything, and you'll give my husband a free entree? What about a free salad, or a free glass of wine? Is that included?"

Luigi groaned out loud and gestured magnanimously to the other server.

"You can have them."

I went into the kitchen and found Leah's hind end protruding from under a sink. I could hear the fierce sounds of scrubbing and a muffled oath as she hit her head.

"Hey, you!" she said, seeing my feet.

"How you doing, Leah?"

"You just going to stand around? Get to work, girl!"

I glanced down at my green linen dress and sighed. I picked a scrubee up out of the bleach water and started cleaning.

It wasn't long before Buddy wandered by and saw me.

"Callie, you're going to get dirty," he chided, his thick glasses making his eyes look small. His faded blue T-shirt struggled to contain his stomach. "You go on, I'll do this."

"Thank you Buddy," I said, glancing down at Leah's butt waving back and forth as she scrubbed. I stepped away, hoping she wouldn't notice I had absconded. As I left, Buddy started into a freewheeling cartoon dialogue. I couldn't understand most of it, though I heard "What's up, doc?" a couple of times.

"When is Margie coming back?" Buddy said, and I glanced back at him in surprise. It was easy to under-estimate what he could understand. If you'd asked me, I would've said that he hadn't even noticed she was gone.

"I'm not sure, Buddy," I said. "She didn't tell anyone where she was going."

He shook his head as he scrubbed at the white tile above the sink. "I don't think Margie was very happy."

"Really?"

"She smiled, oh, she smiled all the time. But she looked like she felt pretty sad inside. I told her to cheer up and then she smiled again." Buddy grinned, a sunny, uncomplicated smile.

I couldn't help but feel guilty. Had we all ignored Margie's pain? Had Buddy been the only one to see it?

"Did she go away with that man?"

"What man?"

"I saw him when I was taking the trash out, behind the dumpster. He was watching Margie."

"What night was this? Do you remember, Buddy?"

He shrugged. "No, just one night. But I wish Margie had said good-bye to me, because she never came back."

Buddy saw someone watching Margie on the night she disappeared?

"Did Margie talk to this man?"

He looked down. "She got in her car and he got in his. They left."

"What did he look like?"

He started to fiddle with the zipper on his sweatshirt, pulling it up and down, up and down.

"Buddy?"

"Luigi!" Chef yelled. "In the window!"

"Did you know him, Buddy?"

Buddy kept his eyes on the zipper. "I don't know," he said.

"Are you sure, Buddy? What did he look like?"

"Callie!"

"Just a man," Buddy said and zipped his sweatshirt all the way up. "I couldn't see him."

"Callie, we're going under here! Glub, glub, help me, help me!" Chef cried.

As I hurried over, Chef slid two chicken sandwiches through the window.

"Can't you train the waits to up-sell?" he asked in a snotty voice.

"Sometimes all people want is a chicken sandwich," I said. "You can offer them the lavender chicken, you can offer them the filet mignon, but all they want is a blasted chicken sandwich. You can't always blame it on the wait."

"Yes, I can," Chef said, and turned back to his flat top.

I turned away as Luigi rushed in to grab his chicken sandwiches.

Who did Buddy see the night Margie disappeared? Doug said that he was in his car when she left the hotel, not hiding behind the dumpster. Had he lied? According to Doug, he also hadn't talked to Margie at Kelly's, though Charlie had seen them arguing. Then again, if it wasn't Doug, who was it?

I went out into the restaurant, but there were only a few tables occupied.

"That man's kinda weird," Kate said. "Him." I looked where she was indicating. It was Mark Holloway. He had five newspapers piled up in front of him as he ate.

"He's been coming in breakfast and dinner, and he's always reading the papers. He's real nice, but he doesn't say much. Luigi said he asked him the name of the dishwasher who found the skull in the dune. Weird, huh?"

"I'm pretty sure he's an undercover reporter," I said. "Tell everybody to be careful what they say around him." I intended to suit action to words by staying as far away from him as possible. Reporters made me itchy.

I told Kate to call me if they got busy and headed down the front elevator to my office.

"Ms. McKinley, a girl just called for you and I sent it up to the restaurant. I thought you were upstairs." It was Stella, a front desk trainee.

"Did you recognize her voice?" I asked. "Was it Margie?"

Stella cocked her head at me, her dazed green eyes looking more confused than ever. She had been here two weeks, so I know she must have met Margie, but it was too much to expect her to recognize the girl's voice.

Ray, the front desk manager, lifted his eyebrows at me in frustration.

I picked up the in-house phone and dialed the restaurant. Luigi answered with a curt, "Seahorse Café."

"My, that sounds welcoming," I said. "Did a girl just call up there for me?"

"The phone rang, but no one said anything," Luigi said. "Can I go home? We're dead up here."

"Ask Kate," I said, and hung up.

"Was it her?" Ray asked.

"I wish I knew."

I went into the back and checked my employee mailbox. I slid my fingers into the dark cubbyhole and felt a piece of paper pushed far into the back.

It was a plain white envelope addressed to me. I tore open the seal and pulled out the piece of paper inside. It was a copy of a press release, addressed to two of the Outer Banks newspapers.

The headline read: **Laurie McKinley Hiding on the Outer Banks.**

Nineteen

Plastic Eggs And Platonic Kisses

It was Christmas, almost two years ago and two thousand miles away in Palo Alto, California, and despite the warm weather, there were Santa Clauses and candy canes hanging from light posts. Christmas music was on every station and I flipped though them all, eager for something other than "Jingle Bells" and "White Christmas."

I looked down at the run in my stocking. I had dropped a pencil out of my purse last night as I struggled to get a grocery bag out of the Jeep. I was in a rush because I had a pregnancy test in the bag, so I left the pencil on the seat and hurried inside.

This evening, as I was sliding into the Jeep, I had snagged my favorite silk stockings on the pencil. It was Dave's fault, of course. Everything was Dave's fault. If he hadn't backed out of this Christmas party at the last minute we would be in his cushy Buick instead of my Jeep.

Dave hated my office parties, but I didn't particularly enjoy his either and I still went. He *knew* my boss was going to announce my promotion tonight. It would have been nice if he were there to share in my moment of glory, even if I was ambivalent about the new responsibility. Just when I decided to make some changes in my life . . .

Dave had been distant the last couple of months. Something was going on, I knew, but we both worked so much we hadn't had a chance to talk about it. Maybe we could go on a cruise this spring. I'd always wanted to go on a cruise, and the time away would do us both good.

I saw a 7-11 coming up, and I slammed on the brakes and turned into the parking lot. The mood I was in, it would be Dave's fault if I got in a wreck. I still couldn't help smiling when I thought of him last night, asleep on the couch wearing only a pair of cotton sleeping pants. I had been in love with him for six years, and even though he was often selfish—sometimes cruel—he was a good husband, and I couldn't imagine being married to anyone else.

Inside, I went straight to the aisle with toothpaste, aspirin, and deodorant, and found the pantyhose eggs. The smell of chili-cheese burritos was in the air, and a little boy in blue jeans and a T-shirt was standing in front of the pet food section.

"Do you think I can take Spots when I go visit Daddy?" the little boy asked his mother, a slim woman in stylish suede pants and dark sunglasses.

"If he doesn't mind," the woman said. "God knows I wouldn't. Hurry up, Andy. We need to be going."

"We need two bags of Puppy Chow," the little boy insisted. "Spots is growing fast."

I smiled, turned back to the pantyhose, and began fumbling with the little eggs, looking for my size. What genius thought one day: "Hey, we can put pantyhose in plastic eggs!" You wonder about a person whose mind works that way.

A microwave dinged and I decided to go with two pairs, just in case.

"I want some donuts," little Andy said.

"I've got to get some milk. I'll be right there."

And that's how both Andy Gray and I ended up at the front of the store just as Bobby Little, in a raggedy leather jacket with no shirt and "666" tattooed on his dirty bald head, pulled a gun on the cashier.

"Money," he said. Nineteen-year-old Jinx Doherty pulled out a small machine gun and nervously swung it back and forth in front of him.

I froze when I saw the gun, and now I inched back into the aisle, trying to get out of the line of fire.

"Don't move!" Jinx yelled at me, his blond dreadlocks swinging as he turned the gun in my direction. "It's not cool, man," he whispered to Bobby. "Let's get out of here."

But Bobby was so jacked up that his hands were shaking and he couldn't stand still. He screamed at the clerk, demanding money and threatening to shoot her.

Little Andy Gray was standing across from me, tears streaming down his face as he watched the men with guns not five feet away from him. I wondered where his mother was, and how helpless she must be feeling.

"Bobby man, a cop just pulled up. Bobby, it's all going to shit!" Jinx cried, and I saw the red and blue lights washing over the interior of the store. Jinx moved behind a column, his young face terrified.

Thank God, it was almost over!

"Mommy," Andy whimpered.

"What? What did you say, you little faggot?" Bobby's face contorted with rage as he screamed the words.

"Bobby, man," Jinx said.

"I heard what you said." He raised both hands to steady the gun and pointed it at Andy Gray's head.

I reacted on instinct, stepping forward and pushing the little boy down behind me. I'm not sure what I intended to do; fall on the floor with him? Jump to safety on the other side of the counter? I don't know now, and I don't think I knew then. I've thought about it many times, relived it in my dreams more times than I can count. I wish I'd had a better plan of action, but in the end I stood and watched as Bobby Little pulled the trigger.

I couldn't move, and that feeling will haunt me until the day I die.

"Don't shoot the chick, man," screamed Jinx.

The bullet sailed towards me as I stood there frozen. Then the glass door of a refrigerator holding cans and bottles of sodas exploded behind me.

"All righty," said Bobby Little to me, and the light of insanity flickered in his eyes.

Still, I couldn't move, even when he hit me in the

face with a heavy, ring-studded fist. My cheekbone broken, I fell to the floor and landed on top of Andy.

Then he squeezed the trigger two more times.

Bobby laughed in crazed delight, and I was helpless as he jiggled the gun and took aim again.

At that moment, when I knew I was going to die and there wasn't a thing I could do about it, several police officers slammed into the store and shot Bobby. He fell on the floor, and I watched as blood bubbled out of his mouth and his lips moved soundlessly.

I closed my eyes.

I opened my eyes.

I was back at the hotel, still standing in front of the employee mailboxes. I held the press release in my hand, the press release that would reveal the location of my sanctuary to the world.

Andy Gray happened to be the son of Henry Gray, the mega-star of countless karate movies. At the time, I had no idea that the little boy in the store was his son, or that the woman in sunglasses was his wife.

I was in the hospital for months, in and out of surgery to remove the bullet from my side. My cheekbone was broken and the graze across my arm got infected.

Even worse was that by the day after the shooting, my face was splashed on newspapers from coast to coast. Whatever my intention was when I stepped forward to push Andy Gray to the floor, I was labeled a hero. I've never done anything like that before in my life, and it's still hard for me to read those articles without blushing because I feel like a fraud. I'm not sure if I'd do it again if I had any idea of how much pain there would be or how close I would come to death. Or maybe I would. I don't know. It was something that I did without thinking, and I've lived with the consequences.

The first consequence was a gift I received in the face of tragedy. Andy Gray has become as dear to me as a little brother, and I will never forget him. I have the undying gratitude of Henry Gray, which I could probably live quite well without, but it's nice nonetheless.

The second consequence was, and is, the hardest to bear: the loss of my privacy.

For six months, first after the shooting and then during the trial, my life was under constant scrutiny. It was not something I sought out, and it was not something I enjoyed. Every facet of my life was laid bare to public dissection.

The worst moments came when the rumors started that Henry Gray and I were having an affair. A photographer caught him kissing my cheek. It was a platonic, thank-you kiss, but there it was in print and the gossip magazines ran with it. It was particularly juicy because Henry and his wife were going through a vicious divorce.

I lost my job, I lost my husband, and I lost my family

for a while after my brother Henley gave that interview to the press. I think I even lost my sanity. It took a year in Key West recuperating at a hotel my best friend owned to bring my life back into perspective.

And now someone was threatening all that I had worked so hard to build here in the Outer Banks. I changed my name and I altered my appearance by losing twenty pounds, cutting my hair short, and acquiring glasses. But I'd changed inside, too. In a lot of ways I look on that old Laurie McKinley as a naïve younger sister. Callie McKinley is harder, more jaded.

Some people know who I am, most don't. Now it would start all over again.

Oh, I didn't expect the strident media attention of two years ago. But the speculative looks, the murmured conversations cut off mid-sentence as I approached, the inevitable questions would start up again—and I didn't think I could bear it.

Twenty
All The Little Creatures

"You look like hell," Kyle greeted me as I came into Sharkey's.

"Thanks," I said.

It was ten o'clock at night, and the bar was just beginning to fill. Steve Laten played a few chords on his guitar, and then launched into a song about Libyan fighter jets set to the tune of "Stairway to Heaven." That Steve, always a hoot.

"I've had a bad day," I said, sliding into the empty seat beside Kyle. "Is that so strange? People have bad days all the time. Must you comment on the fact? What if I just found out I had terminal cancer, or my dog just died? Wouldn't you feel like a real jerk for saying that?"

"Just as bitter," Chef said, from the other side of Kyle. He looked much too chipper to me and I scowled in his direction. He turned back to the tourist sitting next to him. From the disjointed conversation I overheard, it sounded like he was telling her that he was here on vacation from Milwaukee, and that his wife had left him while they were on their honeymoon. I scowled again when I caught him pointing me out as the estranged wife.

Kyle considered me. "Okay, Callie, how are you

doing today? You look like you've had a bad day. I hope you feel much better soon." His voice was syrupy with sarcasm.

"Thank you, Kyle," I said, matching his tone. Melissa slid my usual gin and tonic in front of me, and I took a long swallow. Kyle watched me.

"Do you ever drink?" I asked him. "What, are you a recovering alcoholic or something?' I was being nasty, but I felt like taking my troubles out on somebody.

"No," he said. "I had an alcoholic mother."

We started at each other combatively.

"Okay, okay," I said. "I'm being a bitch. I'm just upset about something. I know your life can't be perfect either right now, with your ex-wife showing up. I'm sorry."

"What's up?" He stared at me, his head cocked.

I looked away.

"What happened?" he asked in a softer voice.

I hesitated, and then I told him about finding the press release in my mailbox.

"I spent the entire afternoon with Lily, and she pulled every string she had to keep the story out of the papers. They received the press release this afternoon. We won't know until Sunday whether they're going to print it or not. I'll be eternally grateful to Lily for trying." My voice was light and disinterested, though inside I was a mass of jelly. What would I do if it came out? Leave? I didn't want to leave! But I truly didn't think I'd be able to stay if it came out.

"Lily can be a good friend," Kyle said, and I saw that my façade had not fooled him.

"Yes, she can."

Lily had really come through for me. She was brash and tough-talking, but when the chips were down, she had asked no questions when I came to her with the press release in hand. As the general manager of a large hotel she had a certain amount of clout, and she used every bit of it to help me keep the story out of the papers.

"To make matters worse, it turns out that Lee the dishwasher was actually living in Virginia at the time Angel was killed, so the detectives are back to looking at him as a suspect. Lily had to find him a lawyer while all this was going on. To his credit, Chef is the one who actually found the lawyer, the same one he used this summer."

"My God," Kyle said. "How horrible. So who would do something like that to you?"

I shook my head, but appreciated that he understood without my telling him what the threat of publicity meant to me. It occurred to me that I sometimes underestimated the value of my friends.

"But who did it?" Kyle said again.

I stared at him and frowned. I had taken the question as rhetorical. "I don't know," I said. "We talked to Dowell, and he said he found the letter on the counter addressed to me, so he put it in my box. It was just some busybody who found out who

I was and thought it was his or her civic duty to notify the press. That's my guess."

Kyle sipped his soda and tapped the straw against his bottom lip. He looked so much like a little boy I felt the sudden urge to hug him. Since I usually wanted to strangle him, the urge caught me by surprise.

"What's going on with your missing wait?"

The abrupt change of subject confused me. "Oh, God, I don't know. I haven't had a chance to think about her today with all this stuff about the press release." I filled him in on what I found out about Margie at ODU: she was using a dead girl's social security number; the train crash in Louisiana; the picture of Margie Sanders in the paper, which was definitely not the Margie Sanders I had known for the last five months. As an afterthought, I told him about the resemblance between Margie (or whoever she really was) and Angel, and the fruitless trip to talk to Betty Lewis.

"Dale Grain has about got me convinced that I'm off base with all of this. After all, what could my waitress have to do with a murder that happened five years ago?"

Kyle chewed on the straw as people laughed and talked around us.

"I think you better be careful," he said after a moment. "I'm not surprised you didn't think of this, because I know you've been so worried about that press release. But what if someone is using it to distract you? You've spent the entire day worried about it. What if the story is published? You'll be upset, answering questions, completely distracted."

"Yes," I said, still puzzled. The only excuse I had was that I was emotionally drained by the prospect of a news story about me. Otherwise, I would have seen it right away.

"Callie," he said, "what if someone did it on purpose? Someone generated that press release to keep you busy so you wouldn't have time to look into Margie's disappearance or Angel Knowling's death, I don't know which. You told me you've been asking questions and doing research. You found out a lot about Margie, for example, that she probably doesn't want anyone to know."

"You think Margie sent the press release to get me off her trail?" I asked incredulously.

"Margie or someone else with the same motive."

I thought about it. It made a certain amount of sense, but then again, it could also just be a coincidence. But the coincidences were piling up and I didn't know what to think.

"All I'm saying is that it's possible that someone is trying to distract you from asking so many questions. If the press release doesn't work, there's a chance they might try some other way. Just watch your back."

I looked down at my drink and realized that it was gone and that I had almost finished the ice as well. "I hear you, but right now I don't want to think about it anymore. If that makes me an ostrich, so be it. I don't want to think about Margie, Angel Knowling, or the press release anymore tonight." I was at the end of my endurance.

Kyle studied me for a moment and then gave me a pat on the shoulder. "Okay, no more serious talk. Did you hear that Echo Masters got caught walking down the Beach Road buck naked yesterday?" From there our conversation moved mercifully on to safer, mundane subjects, and I began to relax. I wanted to ask about his daughter and ex-wife, but he was so intent on distracting me with funny little bits of gossip, I hated to ruin it by bringing up a serious subject.

Steve was taking a break, and in the sudden lull in the noise level, we heard a man's voice from the end of the bar.

"I was comin' in through Oregon Inlet, and there she was just swimming along about a half a mile off shore."

I turned to look at who was speaking. The man looked familiar, and when I turned back to Kyle I saw he was listening too.

"It's Larry, he owns the *Ocean Dream*, a charter fishing boat," he whispered.

I turned back to the charter boat captain who was continuing his story, seemingly unaware that the entire bar was listening to him.

"I said to Bob, 'Is that a fe-male swimming along, or am I dreaming?' and Bob, he said, 'You ain't dreamin'. Well, then the chief money-man—he's brought in a puny little sailfish and won't shut up about it—he said, 'By God, it's a mermaid.' Which of course is what I'm thinking, but before I could say anything, the man climbs up on the rail and says, 'I'm going to catch me a mermaid,' and jumps in. After a case of Bud, I guess he thought he was Superman or something. We had a line of boats behind us coming through the inlet, and everybody had to go around while we circled back and rescued the stupid idiot." Larry leaned back and took a long swallow of the drink. I revised my thoughts. Charter Boat Larry was very aware of his audience.

"By the time we got him all straightened out, she'd disappeared. I don't know what the lady was doing out there, but I saw her with my own eyes. Didn't see any fins or nothin' like that, but she had long hair and she was beautiful."

The bar was silent as he finished up his story, and then everybody started talking at once. I turned back to Kyle.

"Did you see the article about her? Elizabeth is hoping Oprah will see it and want to have her on the show," he said.

"I saw the mermaid," I said. "I wonder who she is?"

Kyle shook his head. "Only on the Outer Banks."

The next morning when I went into work, Lily was lying in wait.

"Callie girl, get in here," she boomed as I passed

her open door. I was trying to do a walk-by to see if I could tell what kind of mood she was in before I went to talk to her.

"What's up?" I asked, stepping into her office. Today she was subdued in a dark purple dress and matching coat, but her wild copper curls were flying free around her head. Her eyes were narrowed in thought or hate, I couldn't tell which. If I had succeeded on my walk-by, I would have decided she was not in an amiable mood to chat.

"Why're you so happy?" she snapped. Any warm, fuzzy feelings we had amassed the day before when she helped me squash the press release were gone.

I shrugged, which I knew she hated. I was in a good mood for some reason. I had been in a good mood when I woke up from a sound night's sleep and walked out onto my deck into a beautiful Outer Banks morning.

She snorted in disgust. "What's going on with your missing wait? Dale told me you had some crazy idea that she might be Angel Knowling raised from the dead. What the heck are you doing? Aren't things bad enough already?"

I winced, but looking at it like that, it did seem ridiculous. "There is a resemblance between the two," I protested, but my heart wasn't in it.

"That's crazy!"

"I also wanted to tell you was that there's something strange going on with Margie's identity. She's not really Margie Sanders. I have no idea who she is."

Lily took a deep breath and exhaled. "What*ever* do you mean?"

So I explained to her about Margie's bogus application and the social security number that belonged to a dead girl.

"Oh wonderful," Lily said when I was done. "This is getting better and better. She'll show up eventually, you wait and see. I heard the police got a tip that Keith Knowling is in Wyoming or someplace like that. Lee's back, but I don't think they're convinced he's innocent. What a mess."

I spent the rest of the morning helping set up the banquet room for a family reunion, wishing that Lily would find a replacement for Janet, our old banquet manager. I arranged flowers and puffed up tablecloths in attractive clouds, and tried not to think about Margie Sanders, or whoever she was. I seemed to be spending a lot of time thinking about either Margie or Angel, and I wondered about that. What was it about these two young women that so fascinated me? Did they remind me of myself?

Around twelve, I decided to go to Mulligan's for lunch. As usual, the restaurant was crowded with business people taking a half an hour for a quick, good meal.

After finishing my crab cake sandwich, I headed to Kmart to pick up some fall decorations for the banquet buffet. On my way back to the hotel, huge gray clouds were advancing towards the beach and the wind was rising as I passed French Fry Alley, a collection of fast food restaurants in Kill Devil Hills.

A green sports car with out-of-state plates suddenly decided to change lanes into mine and then screeched the tires and honked the horn as he realized I was there.

I calmed my breathing, and then did a double take as I saw a colorful sign that said "All the Little Creatures" in curlicue writing. It was the pet store that took care of the hotel's fish tanks.

Without thinking, I swung into the parking lot and found the pet store snuggled next to a flip-flop and bathing suit shop.

The door was wide open, and the earthy smell of cedar shavings and saltwater was enticing. I inhaled deeply as I stepped inside.

The room was clean and brightly lit with plants hanging everywhere. There were trees in the corners shading aquariums full of vivid, darting fish, and plants hung from the ceiling, their frondy tentacles brushing the top of the rabbit and gerbil cages. A small fountain and pool housed more plants and a three-foot-long iguana. Three or four kittens lay heaped in a ball in a corner of a cage, and two small black lab puppies scrambled on the floor in a makeshift fence.

"Can I help you?" I turned to see a statuesque woman standing behind the counter, her long fingers sorting through neon-colored dog collars.

To one side of the counter was a rack filled with rows of glittering metal earrings, and I recognized them as the same type I had seen in Margie's picture.

I turned back to the woman, who was regarding me with large, friendly eyes. She was tall, with skin the color and texture of honey and long, dark hair flowing over her shoulders. She was about my age, I guessed, and she smiled at me.

"Do you know who makes these earrings?" I asked, reaching out to finger the delicate metalwork.

"Yes," the woman said. "I do." She extended her hand. "I'm Dee Burkes. Are you interested in buying?"

"Oh!" For some reason I hadn't expected that. I reached into my purse and fumbled for the picture of Margie and the unknown woman with the earring. I handed it to her and she peered at it expectantly. I saw recognition pass over her face, which was replaced with a frown. Dee looked back up at me without saying anything.

"This is going to sound weird," I said, hoping she wouldn't think I was a kook, "but did you make that earring?" I leaned forward and pointed to it, almost hidden in shadow.

Dee studied the picture, turning it this way and that, and then just holding it still, a small furrow creasing her forehead.

"Yes," she said, and looked back up at me. "What's more, I think I'm the one wearing it in the picture."

Twenty-one

Unpainted Aristocracy

"Oh?" I said, keeping my surprise to a minimum. I planned to ask her if she remembered who bought the earrings. This was much easier. "You knew Margie?"

Dee stared at me a moment, as if wondering whether or not to lie, and then nodded. She put the picture down and braced her hands on the edge of the wooden counter.

"And you would be?"

"I'm Callie McKinley. I'm the restaurant manager at the Holiday House Hotel."

Now it was her turn to try and hide her surprise.

"Margie's boss!" she said, almost to herself.

"I'm a little worried about her—you do know she's missing, don't you?"

"Everybody knows," she said, staring down at the picture.

"When was the last time you saw her?"

Dee looked up at me, and I would have loved to know what was going on behind her dark eyes. "Probably a month ago," she said. "But I think I know when this picture was taken. It was August, and I had just made those earrings. I liked them so much that I decided not to sell them. I met Margie on the beach outside the Holiday House, and we laid out and talked for most of the day. It was her day off, as I recall."

"Did you see anybody taking pictures?"

Dee laughed and flashed the whitest teeth I had ever seen. "Honey, it's the beach. It seems like every tourist and his momma is taking pictures. They take pictures of the ocean, of the dunes, of the lighthouses, any pretty girls they come across. You know what? I've even seen them pull off the road and take pictures of my sign. What's so special about my sign? But there you go."

She was right. I now saw that it would be very easy to take pictures of someone without them noticing. Another tourist taking pictures would not arouse suspicion in anybody's mind.

"Yes," I said. "How well did you know Margie?"

"We were friends," she said, but I got the feeling she was being evasive.

"How long have you known her?"

"A couple of years."

"You've known her since she first moved here?"

Dee nodded but didn't say anything. She wasn't being obstructive, but she wasn't exactly being helpful either.

"Okay," I said, making a decision. "I'll tell it to you straight. I'm worried about Margie. I don't know if you know or not, but she wasn't telling the truth about where she came from, her name, or anything. I found out she's been using the social security number of a dead girl about the same age as her. Now, I know Margie, and I'm sure that she has her reasons for what she's done. But I think she may be in trouble, and anything you can tell me will be helpful."

Dee turned a yellow collar over in her fingers, the metal ring tinkling as it hit the counter. She didn't look surprised.

"I knew Margie before she perfected the act," she said. "She's been hurt real bad, and I'm feeling very protective of her, if you know what I mean. I'm not sure what to tell you. I get the feeling you're trying to help, so I'm going to tell you some of what I know. I knew Margie wasn't her real name. I was staying in the room next door at the Ocean Inn when she first moved down here. She was always looking over her shoulder, and she was skinny as a rail. I knew she was hiding from something, but hell, most the people down here are hiding from something. I helped her find a job. I used to work at the Holiday House, and I knew Darryl Menden, the restaurant manager. He hired her, and when I moved to my new apartment, I let her move in with me for a while until she found a place on her own.

"Those first few months . . . she was in bad shape. I sunk into a pretty good depression when my husband left me, but Margie—Margie was beyond that. I don't know what had happened to her, but I have never seen somebody so sad and yet still able to function. It was a couple of months later when she moved out, and by that time she was getting good at what she was doing."

"What do you mean?"

"She was getting good at the hiding game. She remembered to look around when someone called her Margie, she stopped crying at night, and she stopped making the little slips."

"What slips?"

"Oh, you know, like one day she'd say she was from Connecticut, and the next day she'd say she was from New Hampshire. One day when I had a lump on my wrist, she examined it and gave me a long, complicated medical name for what it was. When I asked her about it, she just turned away and said she read it somewhere. She did that a couple of times, before she perfected the sweet, innocent girl act. It was like she was trying to *become* someone else. She became very smooth after a while, and I even forgot about it sometimes. I was mainly happy that she seemed to have pulled herself out of her depression. I didn't care how she had done it. We kept in contact, but after those first months, she was never as open with me. She was friendly, and funny and sweet, but she would only open up to you a certain amount. Then I saw the paintings . . . " She hesitated.

"'Paintings?"

"A couple of months ago I was in one of the galleries on Gallery Row, and I saw two paintings. They reminded me of some of the stuff Margie was doing when she was staying with me, but they were unsigned. When I asked the owner about them, he told me they were Margie's. How come she never told anyone about them? She must have been so proud, but she didn't tell a soul about them as far as I could tell. It just goes to show how secretive she is, even now."

Dee stared at me after she finished and I could tell there was something more. I waited.

"Okay," she said. "Your aura is all right—all cool blues and greens. I think you really are trying to help."

As I tried to figure out what to say to that, she continued. "Margie called me last night. She sounded scared, but she said she needed to talk to somebody. She said she had to decide what to do. She was rambling, and I couldn't understand half of what she was saying. Stuff about being old enough to face her dad, but wanting to do it on her own terms, only she wasn't sure she could do it."

Dee broke off.

"Facing her dad?" I was bemused.

"She hung up a little bit after that," Dee said. "I asked her where she was, but she wouldn't tell me. She said that she was safe for now; she just had some thinking to do."

The front door opened, and an angular blond woman came in asking about the puppies. When it looked like she was going to be a while, I mouthed "thank you" to Dee and she waved a hand in acknowledgment. Her face looked resigned, as if she hadn't quite made up her mind if she had done the right thing or not.

I thought of what Dee revealed as I traveled back to the hotel. What happened to Margie? Something had traumatized her it was clear, but what could make a person pick up, change her name, and leave? Until I knew that, I wasn't going to find her.

I sighed and turned my attention to something tangible, the passing scenery. I never failed to enjoy cruising the Beach Road at a sedate thirty-five miles an hour, enjoying occasional glimpses of the ocean and the unique designs of the cottages. I passed Nags Head Pier, crowded by a row of colorful houses, and thought with nostalgia of the old Footsball Palace the new houses had replaced.

The Footsball Palace had been old, tired, and dirty, but with the lights of the video games flashing, the shouts of triumphant winners, and the laughter of young kids, it had been transformed in my memory to one of those glittering places in my childhood where everything had been okay.

After Sharkey's, I passed the row of rambling, weather-beaten cottages known as the "Unpainted Aristocracy" or the "Nags Head Ladies." A national historic district, some of these houses were over one hundred years old and were built to withstand the capricious Outer Banks weather

As I arrived at the hotel I waved at Stephen, who was chaining his ten-speed to a fence, and went straight to my desk. I was working on dinner plans for a women's group due in next week. I was also laminating room service menus, which had to be distributed to all 175 hotel rooms by November first.

After a while, I called the front desk and asked if Doug was working. I had been meaning to ask him about the argument he had with Margie the night she disappeared. Had Doug been too drunk to remember? Had he lied for some reason?

"Honey, the boy hasn't shown up to work for two days. I always liked him too, but I can't accept this type of behavior, you know?" Ray was harried, and sounded disappointed. I could hear phones ringing in the background.

"Could you give me his phone number real quick?"

There was a moment of silence, and then Ray gave me the number. "It's no use calling, he hasn't been returning my calls for the last two days," he said, and hung up.

No harm in trying. I dialed the number and listened to the brief message ("This is the party house. Speak.") and then to several beeps that came after. I asked Doug to call me and hung up the phone.

Why hadn't Doug shown up to work for the last two days? Did it have anything to do with Margie's disappearance?

"Ugh," I said out loud as Chef came into the office.

"I can leave," he said, and dropped a clipboard on my desk.

"No, it's not you. I'm just still thinking about Margie." I picked up the clipboard. It was the cleaning list I had typed up, and a string of initials ran down the side of the sheet.

"What's wrong with it?" Chef asked, sitting at his desk and running some figures through a calculator.

I looked at the list. It was about halfway completed, and "LH," "BM," "LL," and "Chef" appeared frequently—initials for Leah, Buddy, Lee, and Chef.

"I don't know," I said. "What's wrong with it?"

"I don't see 'CM' anywhere on it."

"I know, I know. I'm sorry. I've been overwhelmed lately, but I'll try to help out."

"That's nice," he said, and picked up his phone.

"Have you seen Jerry? I need to ask him about tonight's special."

"I'm sure you'll find our restaurant chef where he usually is: wherever I'm not. Right now, that would be up in the kitchen. I'll be going up soon; I'll chase him down here for you."

As he started putting in his food order I turned back to my laminating. Jerry couldn't stand Chef, and the situation was only getting worse. One of them was going to have to go, and soon.

Twenty-two

As The Hotel Turns

It was Friday night and the hotel was full. We were having a Tupperware convention downstairs, and I spent my night running back and forth between the restaurant and the banquet ballroom.

The kitchen was hot and crowded as Jerry and a line cook manned the restaurant orders, and Chef and Leah slaved over chicken wings, lasagna, and hotel pans stacked with green beans for the banquet.

"The chicken wings are going like crazy," I yelled to Chef as I came through.

"Ugh," he said in disgust. His coat was immaculate, but sweat was running down the side of his face into his mustache. An incessant beeping, like a dump truck backing up, underscored the radio and the kitchen noise, but no one seemed to notice it.

I went over to the restaurant side of the kitchen and found the window full of food. Jerry was pounding his fist on his side of the line. "Is anybody going to pick up this food or do I have to stand and watch my sauces break all night long?"

Without speaking, I picked up the ticket lying on top of a fried oyster dinner. The ticket told me that the server was Luigi, that the food was going to table forty-three (hopefully), and that I needed to pull the oyster dinner, a chicken and mushroom risotto, and a surf and turf combo. I piled the plates onto a tray and carried them out to the dining room, passing Luigi on the way.

"I've got your food for forty-three," I called to him, and he nodded without speaking.

The waits were weeded and Kate was manning the hostess stand and the waiting list. I delivered the food and started bussing another table. There's an art to stacking a tray so it's balanced as well as filled to capacity, and I always got a perverse pleasure out of doing it right. I carried the tray back to the kitchen and started unloading it.

"Don't put them in there like that."

I stuck my head under the shelf holding the glass racks and saw Buddy and Lee in the narrow confines of the dish room. Billows of steam swirled around them as they fed piles of banquet plates into the machine.

"Lee," Buddy said again. "Chef said not to do it like that."

Whatever Buddy was objecting to, Lee seemed to ignore it. A moment later he started with "Two households, both alike in dignity," and continued reciting *Romeo and Juliet* verbatim. He changed his voice as he got to the different parts and swung his arms theatrically. Not to be outdone, Buddy began reciting one of his favorite cartoons.

"You're both insane." Neither heard me—then I

was glad they didn't. By all accounts, Lee was still under suspicion for Angel's murder. He would *have* to be insane to do that. I shivered a little. I reminded myself that the police had yet to discover any link between Lee and Angel.

I finished bussing the tray and hurried back downstairs, squeezing past a wait who was carrying three large, slopping containers of salad dressing.

I circled the ballroom, but everything was under control. All the guests had gone through the buffet, and the waits had already distributed coffee and tea to those who wanted it.

I went back upstairs to the restaurant and prayed for the night to end.

"You forgot to set up table forty and forty-one," I said, and the two servers swiveled on their heels to peer at the back of the restaurant.

"Ooops," said Luigi, his crumpled shirt hanging on his skinny frame.

I sighed in frustration as I surveyed the restaurant. Kate had gone home early with a headache and I was checking the waits' closing work.

"And you need to sweep. I see crumbs everywhere." I continued to list several other things they had forgotten to do.

I watched them as they grumbled and moaned about having to continue cleaning when they were ready to go home. I missed Margie. When she was working, everything got done.

"I'll be happier than a mouse in cheese when we find someone to replace Janet," I told Chef as I sat down.

Lenny had been playing for over an hour, and the dark lounge was filled with smoke and people.

"I don't know anyone in their right mind who would want to work here with all this stuff going on," Chef muttered. He had his eyes on a pretty young woman sitting on the other side of the horseshoe-shaped bar, and she was staring back at him in fascination.

"You do have a way with women," I said.

"Huh." He got up and made his way around the bar. The young woman pointed invitingly to the chair next to her.

"That man is amazing!" Charlie laughed. He was wearing another Hawaiian shirt, this one pink and yellow. From his flushed face, I guessed that he was probably drunk. "I don't know how he does it."

"I'm not sure why women fall for it," I said, a little moodily. My thoughts were dark tonight.

"Bad night, huh?" Charlie picked up his drink and moved over to the seat next to me.

"Yeah, well, it wasn't the best."

"I think I found a house. I put a bid in. I'm waiting to see what they counteroffer. Thank God. Loretta's threatening to come down and find a house herself, and that would mean four of us in the hotel. Believe me, it wouldn't be pretty." He laughed.

"Especially since you two are having trouble." I

frowned. Something he said struck me wrong, but I wasn't sure what.

A man entered the bar, and I saw that it was Mark Holloway, the not-so-undercover reporter. He sat next to Charlie and ordered a Bloody Mary.

"I see they let you off every once in a while," he said to me, and I smiled, wishing I could politely leave. He took a swig of his drink and introduced himself to Charlie.

Charlie stared at Mark for a minute, and then shook his hand. "You look like a guy I went to college with," he said, smiling.

"People always say I look like someone," Mark said. "Is it always this foggy here?"

"This is my first fall, but everybody's saying it's pretty weird," I said. I wondered how long it would be before he started asking about the skull.

Not long.

"What's going on with the skull your dishwasher found? I keep hearing about that madman who buried his wife's head in the dune," Mark said.

"Sick, isn't it?" I said.

"Very," Charlie agreed.

"They any closer to finding that bastard?"

I was surprised at the intensity in Mark's tone. "I don't think so."

"They keep saying he's over in Nebraska or somewhere," Charlie said.

"Your dishwasher didn't see anything when he found the skull?"

"No, he didn't see anything."

Lenny's set was over, and with relief I saw he was coming my way.

"How's Callie?" He sat beside me. His gray hair was in a braid that hung down the back of his black T-shirt, and he wore an elaborate leather and silver belt around his narrow waist. I always forgot how tiny Lenny was until he put down his guitar. His voice was as deep as James Earl Jones's, and everybody said Willie Nelson sounded just like him.

"I'm good. How's Jennifer?"

Lenny laughed. "Old Jennifer is hanging in there." His guitar was polished to a golden shine, and he treated her like gold. He had several, but Jennifer was his favorite. "So how about getting up and singing after my break?"

I hesitated. "I feel funny singing here."

"You shouldn't feel funny about singing anywhere," he said, tapping his cigarette against the ashtray.

I smiled.

"You got the light in your eyes. I think you're just like me and the guitar."

"I'll tell you," I said, "that year and a half when I stopped singing was the hardest time in my life."

Lenny nodded like he understood, and I think he probably did. He never mentioned my background, but he was one of the first people on the Outer Banks to recognize me. I saw that now, though he waited several months before pushing me towards the microphone. I was grateful to him, though I had never thanked him. He knew, just like he knew everything else.

"You're welcome," Lenny said, and finished his drink.

After a while, Lenny went back to work. I was just thinking about leaving when Stephen wandered over, depositing his tool belt on the bar.

"Hi Callie," he said with a grin. He was drinking a long-neck Bud, and he took a swig of it as he watched me out of the corner of his eye.

"Hi," I said. "How are you?"

"I'm doing just great, especially now," he said, drawling his syllables out in the slow, languorous, Southern way. "You look very appealing in that dress."

"Thanks," I said. "Are you like this with everyone or should I be flattered?"

"Like what? I like you. If I have something to say to a woman and she has something to say to me, I figure why not strike up a conversation? Who knows?" Stephen grinned again, as if maybe I had a *lot* to say to old Stephen-O. I tapped my fingers on the bar and shook my head when Matt lifted a gray eyebrow at my glass.

"They say you have a real pretty voice. I didn't know you sang."

"I've been singing for a long time," I murmured.

"I never could sing much, except in the shower of course." His glance roamed over me and I repressed the urge to tug my neckline up. "So, how long have you lived on the beach, anyway?"

"About five months." My thoughts were far away.

"I lived here about five years before I moved to Raleigh," Stephen said, taking a puff of his cigarette. "Grew up in Alabama, near Talladega. I've worked in construction ever since I was fourteen, but when the cotton mill shut down the place went to hell in a handbasket and nobody was doing much building. I decided to move up here to make an easy buck or two. I'm getting older, you see, need to slow down a little." He puffed out his chest, expecting me to massage his ego and say, "Of course you aren't getting old, Stephen!" When I didn't say anything he said, "Not that you have to worry about getting older."

I looked at him a moment. "Are you always this full of bull, or is it just with me?"

Stephen looked about as surprised as I felt, and then he laughed. "I knew you had some spirit under there, girl," he crowed. "Honestly, I'm harmless. I talk a lot, but I don't mean no harm. I like you, you know. I like the way you always look so serious, and then you'll smile and it's like a light bulb came on in a dark room. I like the way you talk, low and quiet, and you don't waste any words, you say what you mean. I like the way you look, pretty and feminine, and professional, too. I like *you*, Callie, and I want to know everything about you."

It was the first real conversation I'd had with Stephen, and I felt myself thaw to him. He was handsome, tanned face weathered a bit by the sun and wind, dark eyes under a heavy, brooding brow. And what girl can resist a man who appreciates her finer qualities?

"Thank you, Stephen," I said, and then he ruined it.

"Did I win any brownie points? Do you want to go have a drink down at Sharkey's?"

"No, not tonight, I'm afraid. I've got to go." I stood up.

"Wait—" he protested.

"See you later," I said, and left.

I stopped by the front desk and asked Dowell if Margie called.

"Sorry, Callie," he said. "Nothing."

"Bye Callie," Stephen said, and I turned around to see that he was going out the front door. He winked suggestively. "I'll see you around."

Dowell shook his head as Stephen left. "That guy. I don't know why you girls go for him." His tone was a little envious. "Did you ask Stephen if he knows where Margie went? They were pretty tight there for a while, right after she and Doug broke up."

"They were dating?" Jeez, how had I missed that?

"He was interested, that was for sure. Enough for Doug to get all bent out of shape and tell him to leave Margie alone, even though she and Doug weren't dating anymore."

"'As the Hotel Turns,'" Ray said as he came out of the back. "It's always something around here, isn't it? Who's that new wait you hired? He's cute."

"He is, isn't he?"

"I don't think Margie and Stephen were actually dating," Ray said, returning to my original question. "The other night Margie was leaving and Stephen was down here waiting for a cab. He asked Margie where she was going and if he could come. Just like that. Can you believe his nerve? Margie said, 'Nowhere, for God's sake, leave me the hell alone!'"

"Golly," Dowell said, eyes wide. "Doesn't sound like Margie."

"No," I agreed. "What did Stephen say?"

"He just looked kinda stunned," Ray said. "I was too, to tell you the truth. Margie's always so sweet to everybody. He must have really pissed her off."

"What night was this?"

Ray thought a minute. "Friday night? I think so." The phone rang and he answered it.

"Stephen's a great guy, don't get me wrong," Dowell said. "He's a real good painter. The old guy who usually does the painting had gotten pretty bad. He'd stay here for three, four months, just milking us for free room and board while he did one room every two or three days. Lily finally had to tell him he couldn't come back this year. She told him she loved him to death, but she needed someone who could do the job in a timely manner. He cried. She said some other stuff, but she got up and closed the door, so I couldn't hear. Not long after that she hired Stephen. I heard him in there smooth-talking Lily. She doesn't take that kind of stuff real well, you know, but she sat in there smiling like she believed all the crap he was dishing out." Dowell's voice grew bitter.

"So he's like that with the ladies," I said, disappointed. "I thought so."

"He's a great guy," Dowell said. "But honestly Callie, I'm not sure he'd be that good for you. I mean, he's been dating two or three of the housekeepers that I know about . . . "

"Two or three of them?" I said, feeling a bitter taste in my mouth. Yes, I had been taken in by the smooth-talking Stephen. I felt like a fool.

"Oh God, yes," Dowell said. "And he liked Margie all along. He asked me some questions about her when he first started working here."

"Hmmm," I said. I could feel Dowell staring at me, deciding if he should say anymore, but I didn't feel like encouraging him. I didn't want any rumors starting that I was madly in love with Stephen.

I went back to my office and sat staring at the blank computer screen. I felt so helpless that I didn't know what to do next. Had Stephen been stalking Margie? It sure sounded like it was possible.

"What're you thinking about?" asked a quiet voice, and I almost jumped out of my chair.

I turned to find Kyle leaning against the doorway. "You looked like you were so deep in thought, I didn't want to interrupt you."

"What are you doing here?"

Kyle was dressed in a dark blue Sharkey's T-shirt

and jeans, and his hair was still wet. "That's what I like about you, Callie. You're always direct." He stared at me a moment. "I was thinking about going to Quagmire's and sitting out on the deck. They'll be closing for the year soon. It's a warm night, and the fog is lifting."

"Have fun," I said.

"You're going to make this difficult, aren't you? I came by to see if you wanted to go with me."

"I've never been there," I said, while I tried to think. My palms were sweating and I hoped he didn't notice how shallow my breaths had become. Jesus, was I having a panic attack? I hadn't had one in months. "You're not going to have another ex-wife pop out of the woodwork with maybe triplets this time, are you? You could have told me, you know."

"Just like you told me you're still married?"

"That's different. I don't want to go."

"Come on, it won't kill you," he said irritably.

"All right then, if you're going to badger me," I snapped.

He grinned.

I thought for a moment about flirting, about husbands, about the rest of my life. "Let's go," I said.

Twenty-three
Love Comes Calling

I woke up humming Willie Nelson's old song, "Angel Flying Too Close to the Ground," and my face was hot with embarrassment. It took me a minute to remember my dream. I had been standing on stage singing, and I looked down and realized in horror that I was naked.

"God, that was awful," I said.

"Roarow," Jake said, lifting his head and peering at me through sleep-scratchy eyes. He dislodged Ice who was lying curled up against his side, and Ice got up and flounced to the floor.

"Always a critic," I said, and Jake flopped his head back down. Ice bent his hind leg over his head and started cleaning his pure white belly.

It was still early, and the light seeping though my venetian blinds was milky white. I stared up at the textured ceiling and thought about Kyle.

We had gone to Quagmire's, a sprawling restaurant on the beach in Kill Devil Hills with two stories of decks. Kyle and I sat on the top deck and simply talked. Our subjects ranged from shipwrecks to Adolph Hitler, and then to the mystery of Margie's disappearance, which was worrying me like a sore tooth.

We talked a little about our personal lives. It was almost as if we had called a truce, and I found myself enjoying his company. The Outer Banks were born and bred in him, and I had never encountered such a fierce love for a *place* in my life.

"In 1750, the North Carolina Colonial Council described the people of the Outer Banks as being 'very wild and ungovernable.' I don't think much has changed. We're just quieter about it," Kyle said, gazing out towards the dark ocean.

"Those of us who were born here are just plain stubborn and independent to begin with, and those people who choose to move here are different, too. They are the people who don't mind living on the edge of the vast Atlantic, in danger every summer of being washed away. They don't mind the lack of modern conveniences and that the nearest real city is almost a hundred miles away. They don't mind that they may have to wait tables or sell houses to live here. It makes for an interesting group of people.

"The sad thing, the very saddest, is that we're ruining what we love about this place with overdevelopment. How many ten-bedroom cottages do we actually need? These houses sit empty for nine months out of the year and we have whole neighborhoods of ghost houses, just waiting for the summer. Meanwhile, every year it's harder for the people who live here to afford housing. Pretty soon we'll be as developed as any of the other resort cities and we'll have lost something precious." He paused and looked abashed. "I just went off on a tangent, didn't I?"

He asked me about my past, and I could tell he was giving me an opening to talk about the shooting, but I sidestepped the question and talked about college and California.

After a while, he talked about his daughter a little. He told me how Molly had looked when she was born, how the first word she said was "sand," and how she couldn't take a bath without Hugs, her stuffed bear, sitting on the side of the tub. He didn't mention his ex-wife, and I didn't ask.

At last call, we said our good-byes and Kyle caught my hand.

"I've enjoyed talking to you," he said formally, as if we didn't see each other almost every day.

"Me too," I said, and for a moment I thought he would kiss me. Instead he said "Good-night," and shut the door to my Jeep.

Thinking back over the night, I realized that there had been something impersonal about our conversation. We talked for hours, but neither of us stayed on personal subjects for more than a few minutes.

"We're just a couple of scaredy-cats," I told Ice, who was freshly groomed and regarding me with lazy golden eyes.

At the foot of the bed, Jake lifted his sleek brown head and inspected me with one eye—the blue one. His brown eye was closed against the muted light slipping through the venetian blinds. He groaned in disgust and flopped his head back down on his paws.

"Oh no you don't," I said, nudging him with my toe. "You kept me awake all night chewing on that stupid squeaky toy. You're not sleeping now."

Jake groaned again and rolled over on his back, paws in the air.

I looked around at the new bedroom suite that I had bought a month ago to replace the boxes and cartons I had been living out of for over a year. The homemade quilt from my grandmother highlighted the golden sheen of the pine.

I realized that I was subconsciously thinking about how hard it would be to pack up all the stuff I had accumulated over the past months. In the back of my mind I was already planning to leave if the article about me came out.

"Maybe things will turn out all right," I said, but this time neither the cat nor the dog was listening.

When I went downstairs, the animals hot on my heels, I wasn't surprised to see the thick fog that swirled in front of the sliding glass doors. The cat and dog sat and watched the tendrils of mist wash across the window while I made coffee.

It was eerie walking to the beach. The air was chilly against my skin, but I hadn't been able to find my coat, so I settled for wrapping my hands around my elbows. Visibility was cut down to just a few feet, and even the ocean was muffled as we climbed to the top of the dunes. I sat down at the top of the stairs and watched Jake disappear into the fog. Ice sat beside me and looked around with a distracted air. He wasn't about to leave my side.

I heard faint splashing and knew Jake had found the ocean. After a few minutes he was back to shake sand and water in our faces.

"Bad dog," I said, wiping sand from my face, and Ice glared at Jake. Jake licked my face in apology and trotted back into the fog.

"I don't think I've ever seen fog like this," I told Ice, but he was too busy grooming the sand off his fur to pay me much attention.

When we got back to the house I went up to my desk in the loft. I wondered where my roommate was. Judging from the messy kitchen, she had come and gone this morning, and I was just thankful she wasn't there.

It had been like that with Dave at the end, when just being in the same room with him rubbed my nerves raw. We never fought. We never talked about it, though he had tried over and over. But I was through; I had had enough, and I couldn't take any more. I sometimes wondered if I had a nervous breakdown of some sort, because everything seemed unreal when I looked back on those months. Right now it was hard for me to even remember how I had felt.

I wondered why I was thinking of Dave. I had been doing that a lot lately, and it was usually after I had seen Kyle. Was I feeling guilty? Dave and I were still married after all, even if the marriage had been over for a long, long time.

I sat down at my desk and watched the fog swirl against the window for a few minutes. Ice followed me upstairs and jumped onto the desk to keep a close eye on my wastebasket. He considered it his solemn duty to attack and kill any paper aimed at the basket.

I pulled out the manila file containing the unread articles about Margie Sanders. I spread them across my desk and read about the girl whose name Margie had borrowed.

The real Margie Sanders had been a student at the prestigious Boston University. She had been in her junior year with a bright future in medicine ahead of her. She was bright, pretty, and popular; she was in a social sorority, as well as several academic fraternities.

It was a fuzzy, indistinct picture in a Boston newspaper that provided the answer I was looking for. It was a picture of two girls, arms akimbo as they stood in front of a dorm building.

I stared at the picture for a long time, the realizations sinking in one by one.

One was the girl I knew as Margie. The other was the real Margie Sanders.

I read the story underneath the picture. The girl I knew as Margie was really Sandra Meadows from Hammets Hill, Massachusetts. She was the real Margie Sanders' best friend, and she was on the train when it wrecked. The two girls were on their way to New Orleans after completing their harrowing final exams. Sandra Meadows was pre-med at Boston University, and she planned to go into OB-GYN.

It was only a couple of sentences in a long article about the train accident, but it gave me the information I needed. Not that it answered any questions. What happened three months after the real Margie's death to make Sandra run away and assume her dead friend's identity?

Did Sandra's past have anything to do with what was going on now?

I picked up the phone. It was a matter of minutes before I had two different listings for "Meadows" in Hammets Hill. I was just glad her name wasn't Smith or Jones.

On the first try I hit pay dirt—such as it was.

I asked for Sandra Meadows, and a cautious woman's voice told me that she wasn't available.

"Are you her mother?" I asked.

"Yes," she said, and there was a slight, breathy stutter to her voice. "Who is this, please?"

"Just a friend," I said. "I was wondering if you could tell me how to reach your daughter."

"She's out of the country," the woman said, "studying abroad." The words sounded worn and rehearsed.

"Are you sure?"

She hesitated. "Do you know something about her? Because if you do—"

"Have you talked to her in the last week?" I asked.

"The last week? I haven't talked to her for almost two and a half years! Do you know something about her? Please tell me where you're calling from!"

It almost broke my heart, but I put the phone down without saying anything. I had no intention of betraying the girl's secret, but it was necessary to find out if her parents knew where she was. Any hope I had that Margie ran home to her parents was squashed.

The phone rang and I picked it up and cradled it against my shoulder and ear.

"Laurie?" a familiar voice said.

I was silent, willing my breath to come evenly, my heart to stop thudding.

"Callie, is that you?"

"Yes, it's me." I closed my eyes. So many memories.

"I needed to talk to you," he said. "How are you doing?"

"I thought we agreed you would only call me in an emergency. Why are you calling, Dave?"

"Laurie, God, I miss you. I've been thinking about you a lot and . . . I just wanted to hear your voice." His voice was warm and strong, so familiar.

"Well, here I am," I said flippantly. "What do you want to talk about?"

"I want to see you. I know you're somewhere in North Carolina. I want to come visit you, and maybe . . . maybe work things out."

"I don't think it's a good idea," I said. "Not right now."

"Laurie, you know it's never going to be a good time. You've got to make time for this. We're married for God's sake!"

"We haven't been married for over a year."

"It was just a mistake, Laurie, just a mistake. Are you really never going to forgive me?"

I was quiet for a moment, gathering my thoughts. "You did more than cheat on me. You let me down when I needed you most. I needed you desperately during those months, but you were so jealous of all the attention I was getting that you turned your back on me. Where were you when the newspapers were accusing me of stalking Henry Gray's wife? Where were you on the days the pain was so bad I couldn't get out of bed? You said you were at work, but we know better now, don't we?" I realized I was almost yelling, and it shocked me into a sudden silence.

"Laurie, all I can do is say I'm sorry," Dave said.

"I know. I know that, and I've already forgiven you in my heart. But I've learned to live without you, and I don't think I have any desire to ever live with you again. I know I could never trust you, and I don't think I could live with that between us."

"Jesus, Laurie," he said, and his words cut into me.

"Good-bye Dave," I said, and hung up the phone.

After that, I started cleaning house and tried to ignore the tears leaking down my cheeks. I threw myself into vacuuming, scrubbing bathrooms, and dusting. Outside, the sky brightened as the sun climbed to its zenith.

It was my day off and I was fighting the urge to go into work. There was still a lot to be done on the menus, but I was tired—both mentally and physically—and I needed the time off. It was easy to tell myself that, harder to convince my conscience.

I made myself angel hair pasta with a tomato cream sauce over fresh squash and chicken, and settled down on the couch. There was a wonderful old World War Two movie on and I snuggled into a comforter with Jake stretched out at my feet and Ice curled under my hand.

I'm not sure when I fell asleep, but it was to the sound of gunfire on the TV. I dreamed fitfully.

I was in the convenience store staring at the sodas and ice cream and thinking about making a float—but that wasn't right. I came in here for pantyhose, but I picked up the container of ice cream and walked to the counter. It was the same 7-11 as always, but instead of Andy Gray holding his bag of Puppy Chow, it was Margie, and she turned to me with a sweet smile.

"Hi Callie. How many covers did we do tonight?"

I realized that melted ice cream was dripping onto the floor, and I looked down and saw that the carton was falling apart in my hands.

I heard a shot and looked up in time to see Angel Knowling standing in the doorway, holding a gun and pointing it at Margie. Behind Margie, the bullet crashed into the glass front of a refrigerator, and milk and soda went foaming to the floor.

I realized that Angel wasn't aiming at Margie. She was aiming at a man who was hiding behind Margie, but Angel didn't see her in front of him.

I jumped at Margie to push her out of the way, and something hit my stomach. I felt searing pain as the sound of the gun ricocheted through the small store.

I didn't realize I was screaming until Kyle told me later. I did remember waking up and feeling someone's hands on my shoulders and lashing out with my hands and fists, fighting for my life. I could hear Jake barking frenziedly.

"Callie!"

I continued to struggle, but I opened my eyes and was shocked to see Kyle peering down at me.

"Callie! Wake up!"

I focused on Kyle's face looming over me and blinked.

"What the heck are you doing here?"

Twenty-four
A Nickel for Your Thoughts

I stared up at Kyle in astonishment, my mind still fuzzy from the dream. My hand was clutching my stomach, and I was conscious of Kyle lying over me as he grasped my shoulders and stared into my face. Jake was still barking.

"Are you hurt?"

He sat up and gently removed my hand from my stomach. When I realized what he meant to do, I protested and tried to wiggle away from him, but it was too late. He lifted my shirt far enough to see what I was holding.

I shut my eyes and lay there, tense, as he looked.

"Looks like he got you pretty good," Kyle said, and with light fingers replaced my shirt over the puckered, ugly scar on my right side.

I began to relax and opened my eyes to look up at him. I was shaking, and realized that it was the first time anybody besides a doctor or a nurse had seen the scar.

"What? Were you expecting me to fall out in horror?" Kyle asked, almost in amusement.

I tried to think of how to answer, but Kyle's lips were twitching and the next thing I knew, I started laughing.

"Oh Jesus, you don't understand," I said, trying to choke back the almost-hysterical laughter. "It's not funny at all."

"I know." His baseball hat was askew from where I hit him in the head, and his eyes looked very blue in the dimness of my living room. He leaned forward and kissed me on the lips, a sweet, patient kiss that lingered like the smell of coconut sunscreen on a long, lazy beach day.

Kyle pulled back and looked at me full in the eyes for what seemed like forever. "I think I could fall in love with you," he said, as if just discovering the truth himself. As I stared at him in astonishment, he moved to the end of the couch and I sat up. I ran a hand through my hair and adjusted my shirt. Jake had stopped barking, but he stood at the edge of the coffee table, body tense as he watched me.

"It's okay, boy," I said, and he came over to me and put his head in my lap. I rubbed him behind the ears, and I looked up to see Ice peering down at us from the loft, his ears flat against his skull.

"It's all right, guys," I said, trying to decide what to say to Kyle. How did I feel about him? I hadn't let myself think about love for a long time, wrapping myself in a protective cocoon to ward off inevitable pain and disappointment. Still, there was no denying the honey-pure heat that Kyle's kiss awakened in me, and as I looked at his handsome, honest face, I saw the truth in his statement. I could fall in love with

Kyle Tyler. But did I really want to put myself through that again?

My confusion must have been plain on my face, because Kyle chuckled and changed the subject. "I thought he was going to chew my leg off," he said, holding his hand out for Jake to sniff.

"He must have remembered you from the couple of times I've brought him up to Sharkey's, otherwise he wouldn't have held back," I said, relieved for the reprieve. "You're lucky."

Jake—looking tall and lean and not at all puppyish—glanced at me and then decided that things were back to normal. He wagged his tail and touched his nose to Kyle's fingers.

"No, I don't want to get on this boy's bad side," Kyle said. "I heard about what he did this summer during the hurricane."

Jake circled the living room a couple of times and then lay down alertly by the door. Ice ventured down the stairs and swiped at Jake's nose as he passed.

"So what are you doing here?" Behind him, I could see that the fog had lifted a little, though the day was still overcast and milky.

Kyle pointed to my red jacket on the back of the couch. "You left your coat at Quagmire's last night. The waitress came out with it just as you left."

"Oh." I looked at him, wondering if I could ask how he knew where I lived without sounding rude.

"You said you lived on Windjammer Court, so I just

looked for your Jeep," he said, sensing my question. "It's not a long road."

We paused, and I could hear the faint rumble of the ocean.

"Okay," Kyle said. "What was that all about? I knocked on the door and then I heard you yelling like you were in pain. Were you dreaming about the shooting?"

I looked away from him. My dream seemed unreal and faraway right now, but only a few minutes ago it had seemed so real that my side still ached. What exactly *was* I dreaming about? I remembered I was in the 7-11, I was always in the 7-11, but this time it was different . . .

Kyle was waiting for me to speak.

"Yes," I said. "I was dreaming about the shooting. I dream about it all the time."

"Like this?" Kyle frowned. "You wake up screaming and in pain, *often*?"

"Well, no." I shook my head. "Not anymore. I used to dream about it all the time. Now it's only once or twice a month."

"I'm surprised you can get to sleep, knowing you might wake up to that."

"Well, a lot of times I can't," I said.

I could see the questions in his eyes. He seemed as reluctant to ask them as I was to answer them. He settled for, "Is it always the same dream?"

"Usually," I said. "Not this time, though. This

time was weird." I paused in thought. The dream was slipping away as I tried to remember. "Margie— I mean Sandra—was there, and Angel." I thought for a minute more, and then frowned in frustration. "That's all I remember. The end was the same, though. I got shot." My voice was matter-of-fact.

Kyle looked at me, and I wanted him to ask me the questions. I wanted to tell him what I had told no one else. But he stayed quiet, and I turned my head away, feeling disappointed.

"Have you found anything else about Margie?" he asked, moving away from the personal. Was he as scared as I was of this thing developing between us? He had every reason to be scared of love, I knew. Stacy had worked him over pretty good.

"Jesus, you won't believe this," I said, remembering that I hadn't told him about my discovery of Margie's real name.

"I don't know what to do," I confessed when I finished explaining. "I felt so sorry for her mother. But Margie—Sandra—is a big girl, and she must have a good reason for what she's done. I don't have the right to blow her cover unless it's absolutely necessary."

"I don't know. It doesn't seem right not telling her mother." He paused and looked out the window, and then turned back to me. "Though I guess you've got a lot more experience with this than I do."

"I understand the need to get away. Sometimes that's the sanest thing to do. I also understand that you can't run away forever, and that you have to face the music sooner or later. I can't force Margie to do that. She's got to do it herself."

"Okay, Laurie McKinley," he said.

I flushed. A part of me thought I *could* keep running and never face the music.

"But I do want to find her," I continued. "I just want to make sure she's okay. I want to see if I can find Doug—he hasn't been at work the last couple of days—and see if there's anything else he can tell me."

"All right. Let's go."

He smiled at my quizzical look. "I don't have anything better to do."

A quick phone call to the Holiday House was all I needed to discover Doug's address. A few minutes later, Kyle and I were in his truck on our way to a collection of motley cottages on the sound side of the Bypass, next to the tangled, dark trees of Nags Head Woods.

"How's your Jeep?" Kyle asked as we searched for Doug's road.

I laughed. "Not great. Charlie came and looked at it and he thought it was the starter. I've got an appointment for next week."

Kyle glanced at me sideways.

"What?"

"Nothing."

"Well, why did you look at me like that?"

"I guess Charlie strikes me wrong. That tattoo of his? It looks like a joint tat. My brother Bill got out of prison last year, and he had a tattoo like that, crude and in blue ink. Not the same, of course, but . . . "

"Point taken," I said. "I'll be careful."

Doug's house was close to the highway, a tall cottage with peeling red paint and four cars in the driveway. Kyle pulled his battered pickup truck into the yard and we went up to the door.

"Eh?"

After several minutes of knocking, a lean, smooth-skinned boy in drooping Tweety Bird boxer shorts stood squinting at us. A wave of pot smoke rolled out of the house behind him.

I resisted the urge to yell, "Police! We're coming in!" just to see what he would do.

"We're looking for Doug," I said.

"He's not here," Mr. Tweety Bird said, and started to close the door.

"Hey," Kyle said, stepping forward and stopping the door with his hand. "Do you know where he is?"

Another young man, dreadlocks hanging down over his shoulders, came down the stairs holding a cigarette. "Was' up?" he asked, appraising me from head to toe and ignoring Kyle.

"They're looking for Doug. Told 'em he's not here. I haven't seen him since yesterday. He was real paranoid; I don't know what he was on. He told me to look out the window and tell him if I saw a blue

Taurus. Said there was one following him."

"Weird. I heard him come in sometime last night. I heard him 'cause my room's right next to his," Dreadlocks said as an aside to us. "He wasn't here when I got up, though."

"Was anybody awake? Do you think someone may have talked to him?" I asked. *Doug thought he was being followed?*

"Ah, I don't know," Dreadlocks said and went back up the stairs.

"Red might have been up," Mr. Tweety Bird said. "I think he's mowing the lawn . . . " He wandered down the hall, and his boxer shorts slipped down even farther on his bony hips.

I looked at Kyle and he shrugged, so we stepped inside the open door and hurried up the stairs. I had seen which door Dreadlocks went in, and there was a door on either side of it. One was a bathroom (dripping shower head, mildewing towels piled on the floor, toilet that hadn't been cleaned since before Jerry Garcia died), and the other was Doug's room. It was messy, but not filthy. Battered crate furniture squatted against the walls, a dark blue comforter covered the double bed, and a black sheet hung over the window. A surfboard was propped in a corner, and a bulletin board, covered with pictures and slips of paper, was nailed to the wall.

"Well, it's not pretty, but it looks normal to me," Kyle said.

I wandered over to the bulletin board. The slips of paper were phone numbers with names, and the pictures were mostly of Margie. Dominating the bulletin board was an 8x10 photograph of her. It was a very flattering picture. She was in a white, long-sleeved shirt, gazing off over the shoulder of the photographer with a small smile on her lips. She was sitting on Doug's bed in this very room.

"Hey, Callie, look at this."

I went over to where Kyle knelt before a bookcase. It was filled with comics and journalism textbooks. I remembered Doug saying he had been a journalism major before moving to the beach to pursue surfing as a career.

"What do you have?"

"Look."

Kyle was flipping through a folder filled with news clippings. I was startled to see Angel Knowling's face staring out from one of the pictures.

"They're all about Angel Knowling's death," Kyle said, flipping to the end of the clippings. "All of them. They're all the original articles from five years ago."

"Weird." I stared at Kyle. "Where did you find them?"

"They were lying on top of the bookcase. I'd say he was looking through them recently."

We finished searching Doug's room, and found nothing else of interest. I wrote a note asking him to call me and pinned it to his bulletin board. As we left, we asked the lean, sweating Red about Doug, but he frowned and shook his head. And that was that.

"Hey," Kyle said, capturing my hand as I reached for the door handle. We were parked in front of my house, and the delightful uncertainty that had disappeared when we left had returned. Would he try to kiss me again? I don't know if I was more afraid that he would or wouldn't.

"Yeah?" I turned and found him staring at me.

"I want you to call me if anything comes up. Something is going on here, and until we understand it, anything is possible."

"All right."

He lifted my hand to his lips and kissed it. I got out of the truck in a daze and watched as he backed out of my driveway.

I hope I didn't look as shocked as I felt.

Twenty-five
Hit And Drive

On my way to work that afternoon I stopped by Seamark and picked up a bag of cat food for Ice. The fog was thickening like a good cream sauce when I passed a familiar road. Without thinking, I slammed on the brakes, fishtailing a little on the wet pavement. I pulled into the parking lot of a bait-and-tackle store and headed down the narrow road I had just passed.

I had been down this road many times over the last five months. Old Jonathan had gotten to where he didn't feel comfortable driving at night, and I often gave him a ride home after his three to eleven shift at the front desk. He was still spry and bossy at seventy-two when he retired, and I missed him.

Jonathan's house was an immaculately-kept ground level duplex surrounded by thriving bushes and plants. The old man would never slow down.

"Callie!" he exclaimed as he opened the door. He was thin and a little stooped, but his hair was thick and white and the eyes that gleamed from behind his glasses were bright and alert. He led me into his living room.

"It's good to see you, sit down—no, not there, right there." He sat me down in what was plainly his favorite chair, but I knew better than to protest. Bits and pieces of electronics littered the kitchen counter, but other than that his house was neat as a pin, as always.

"I thought maybe everybody forgot me at the hotel," he said, perching on the edge of his ancient couch. "Ever since they put me out to pasture, nobody comes by to see old Jonathan anymore. Did I ever tell you the story about when the hotel first opened and someone forgot to turn the water on? What a mess!"

"I can't even imagine," I said.

Jonathan saw me eyeing the pieces of VCRs and clock radios on the counter. "Yes, I've been keeping myself busy. It's amazing how many people don't know how to fix the clocks and radios in their houses."

"Jonathan, I thought you were going to *retire*."

Jonathan shook his bushy white head. "No girlie, I don't think I'll ever retire. I'd rather die from doing good, honest work than die of boredom."

I smiled. "You'll never change, will you?"

"I certainly hope not," Jonathan said. "So I've been hearing there's a big hubbub down at the hotel." He gazed at me inquisitively.

"Yes, they found the skull of a woman named Angel Knowling behind the hotel. They're looking for Keith Knowling, her husband. Have you seen his picture in the paper? Do you remember if they stayed at the hotel?"

"Actually, the police already stopped by. As soon as I saw her picture in the newspaper, I knew she looked familiar. It was about five years ago—in September,

I do believe, because it was beautiful fall weather. She was a pretty little thing, not hard to remember. She asked me about the Lost Colony, the Wright Memorial, and the Hatteras Lighthouse. She wanted to go see all the sights. I chatted with her for about a half an hour while I re-caulked their window. It had rained the night before, and that darn window in 328 always leaked in an east wind."

I hid a smile. Even though Jonathan worked the front desk, he had never been able to resist showing up the maintenance department with his fix-it skills.

His eyes twinkled. "She seemed like a nice girl. She said her husband was out getting breakfast, and I had to look at her hand to make sure she was wearing a ring, because she didn't look old enough to married. She was wearing one, all right."

"Jonathan, you know Margie, right?"

"I sure do. That little girl is something. Hard worker and so sweet. She's been at the hotel for over two years now, hasn't she?"

"About that. I was just wondering . . . well, it sounds stupid now. I guess I was wondering if you could think of any possible connection between Margie and Angel Knowling."

Jonathan frowned. "Look kinda similar, now that you mention it. But Margie would have been, what, seventeen or eighteen when this Angel was killed? I don't see how there could be any connection between the two. Besides, they sounded a lot different. The girl

Angel had a strong Southern accent, and Margie, well you know, Margie has that crisp Northern accent. I don't see how there could be any connection. Why do you ask?"

"It's just that they look alike, I guess. I don't know."

I stayed and chatted a few more minutes before saying good-bye and heading back to the hotel.

That afternoon at work, I forced myself to concentrate on the new menus. I had gotten a lot accomplished when Nell, the chief of housekeeping, poked her head in the office door.

"Did you hear?" When all she got was a blank look, she smiled and came all the way into the office. She was dressed in khaki slacks stretched over wide thighs, and a Holiday House shirt strained to cover her monumental breasts.

"I just heard Ray at the front desk talking about it. He got a call from a hospital in Norfolk. Seems Doug, that nice little houseboy? He was run over riding his bike last night. He was unconscious and they couldn't find no next-of-kin, but they found his nametag in his pant's pocket, so they called here. Ray is calling his parents right now."

"Jesus," I said. "I was just at his house. Is it bad?"

Nell headed out of the office. "Don't know yet," she said. "That poor little boy."

She left, seeking fresh ears that hadn't heard the news.

I went to the front desk and talked to Ray, but Nell had already passed on the most relevant information. Ray was almost pulling his hair out with worry. He had just gotten off the phone with Doug's parents and they were on the way.

"If only I had tried harder to get in touch with him," Ray wailed.

"What difference would it have made?" I asked. "You couldn't have stopped the accident."

"If he had been at work last night like he was supposed to be, this wouldn't have happened."

"And that's your fault?"

As I went back into the offices, he called after me. "Charlie Miller has been coming into the bar, right?"

"Blond Charlie? Yes, almost every night. Why?"

"Nothing major, but I've been leaving messages on his phone the last couple of days and he hasn't called me back. He's been paying cash, and he hasn't come down yet this week. If you see him, ask him to stop by."

"Sure."

Lily was in her office on the phone, and I stopped in the doorway.

"His arm? And a concussion? Thank you. His parents should be arriving in the next couple of hours."

Lily hung up the phone and looked at me. "He broke his arm and he's got a concussion. Apparently he was drunk last night, riding his bike near his house. It looks like a car hit him, but they're not sure. He was already laid out in the road when one of his neighbors found him and almost ran over him. They decided to ship him to Norfolk Trauma because of the head injury."

"Poor thing. If it's not one thing, it's another. Oh, something else has been bothering me . . . "

"Well? Spit it out!"

"I hear you're having trouble getting Charlie to pay his bill this week. He bugs me for some reason. Kyle said it looked like he's got a fresh prison tattoo on his arm, and I'm pretty sure he's called his wife by at least two different names. I just wanted to give you a heads-up in case he tries to skip on his bill."

"All right," Lily said. "I never liked him much anyway. I'll keep an eye on him."

I wandered back to my office and filled Chef and Leah in on the news about Doug.

"What's this boy look like?" Leah demanded. "I don't know him."

We explained Doug as best we could, but Leah just frowned. "All I can say, it's too bad it wasn't that bad boy dishwasher, Lee. Would have been a good way to get rid of him."

"Leah!" I said.

"I got intuition about men, you mark my words. That boy always bugged me. And what's that crap he's always spouting? Never can understand a word he's saying."

"It's Shakespeare," I told her. "He's reciting Shakespeare."

"Like I didn't know that!"

"Why in the world do they call it 'hit and run' anyway?" Chef asked. Why not 'hit and drive,' it makes more sense. Speaking of which, what's with that new waiter? I thought his name was Rob, but now he says he wants to be called Don. I called him Rob-Don all last night. You sure know how to pick them."

I exhaled and turned back to the laminating machine. God, I was beginning to hate these menus.

Besides a nasty interlude with a guest who insisted that we didn't know how to make *soup du jour* properly (he ate in a lot of restaurants and the *soup du jour* always had mushrooms in it, he said. It was hard to keep a straight face as I explained that *soup du jour* meant soup of the day) that night in the restaurant was without incident. Downstairs in my office, the phone rang.

I sighed and turned my chair around so I could answer it.

"Ms. McKinley? Callie?" a tremulous voice asked.

"Speaking."

"This is Valerie. You know, Margie's roommate? You told me to call if . . . well, some tourists just brought Margie's dog home. They found her over in Hatteras running around in the middle of the road. I'm afraid something bad has happened to Margie."

Twenty-six

Snapping Turtle

I turned off the computer two hours later and stretched in relief. The menus were done, and not a moment too soon. After Valerie called I turned off the ringers on the phones and locked the office door to ensure that I wouldn't be disturbed.

I promised Valerie that I would come over first thing in the morning, and it was already after eleven. I needed to be getting home.

I headed for the front door, sketching a wave at Dowell behind the front desk.

"Hey, Callie!" Dowell squawked when he saw me.

"What?"

"Where have you been? I tried calling you everywhere. I thought you should know. A couple showed up tonight, late, and showed me a picture of a girl. They wanted to know if I had ever seen her." Dowell took a breath, always the master of the significant pauses.

"Well?"

"Well," Dowell said deliciously, "it was a picture of Margie!"

"Margie?" I stared at him, stunned.

"Yep." He was pleased with my reaction.

"Who were they?"

"Well, I didn't know what to tell them, of course, because you know, I didn't know who they were." Dowell ignored my question and continued his story the way he had intended. "I mean, they didn't look nutty or anything—well dressed, older couple, distinguished if you know what I mean. I kind of hemmed and hawed, and then the woman said she was Margie's mother. She called her something different, Cindy, I think . . . "

"Sandra?"

Dowell frowned. "No. Sandy, that's right. She said she was Sandy's mother, and she was almost crying, so I told her yeah, I knew the girl, though I thought her name was Margie. The man got right in my face and ordered me to tell him where she lived. He was real rude, like he was used to ordering people around. I told them I couldn't, because I didn't know where she was, and that they should probably talk to you because you were her boss. He asked a bunch of questions about you, too." Dowell took a breath.

"What name did they register under?" I said before he could get rolling again.

"Meadows. I remember because I thought it was strange. Isn't Margie's last name Sanders?"

Five minutes later I was in the elevator going up to the fifth floor to the best rooms in the hotel. Margie—Sandra—Margie told me to call her Margie and that was what I would call her—Margie's parents wanted to see me, no matter what time. Mr. Meadows badgered Dowell into calling me at home several times, but Dowell held firm on not giving out my phone number.

I glanced at my watch as I trotted down the hall. It was late and I wasn't sure that I wanted to see Margie's parents, but they were here and I couldn't avoid them. When Dowell called them they asked that I come right up.

How did they find Margie? I had the sneaking suspicion that it had something to do with my phone call, and I was feeling bad about giving her away. I had just called this morning, for God's sake. They must have dropped everything to get here so fast. Now that they were here, I was hoping they could give me some information that might explain where Margie was.

I knocked on the door, and it was opened before I even finished.

The man was wearing a dark, immaculate suit with a snowy white shirt. The immediate impression I had was of a snapping turtle. He stared at me from under thick eyebrows, his head lowered as if he was seriously thinking about biting. The fact that he was round with a pudgy face and a double chin seemed inconsequential to the sheer force this man projected.

"Do you know where she is?"

I shifted my gaze to the pale, weeping woman in light blue standing behind the snapper. She was tall, taller than her husband, but the way she hunched her shoulders suggested that she wasn't comfortable with her height. She had dark hair, straight and bobbed, but it was wispy and she pushed at the strands clinging to her face.

"Be quiet Hannah," snapped the man, without turning around. "Are you Ms. McKinley?"

"Yes," I said, deciding on the spot that I did not like this man. "And you are?"

"I'm Lee Meadows." He held the door open. "Come in." It was an order, plain and simple. Out of sheer cussedness, I thought about turning around and walking away. I had a feeling this man was not used to defiance, but I needed information about his daughter. I bit my lip and walked inside the suite.

Lee Meadows closed the door behind me, walked to the most comfortable chair in the room, and sat down. I took a seat on the couch, and the wife, Hannah, fluttered around and then took a seat on one of the chairs at the table. She was behind her husband, out of his sight.

"Tell me where my daughter is," Lee Meadows demanded. I wondered if he ever said please, and then decided probably not.

"I don't know where she is."

"Ms. McKinley, I'm not playing games. You don't know who you're dealing with. We know you called our house this morning. Tell me where she is and you can go on your way."

He sat in his chair like he was the lord emperor on high. I detested him already. "Mr. Meadows, I don't know who you are, or who you think you are, but it really doesn't matter. I don't know where your daughter is. She disappeared about a week ago. I've been looking for her, but I haven't been able to find her."

Hannah Meadows gave a little moan and I glanced at her. She leaned forward, her hands clasped, her eyes fixed on my face.

"Why should I believe you?" Meadows didn't even turn to look at his wife.

"Why would I lie? Look, Mr. Meadows, do you have a picture of your daughter, so I know for sure we're talking about the same person?"

Mr. Meadows turned and waved a hand at Hannah and she rummaged though the briefcase on the table and brought me a picture. It was a younger Margie, an informal headshot blown up so only her smiling face was visible.

I handed the picture back. "She's been going by a different name," I said. "Why would she do that, do you think?"

"Margie Sanders," Meadows said dismissively. "I know."

Out of the corner of my eye, I saw Hannah shake her head and say something in a soft voice.

"Mrs. Meadows? What did you say?" I asked.

"They were friends," she said after a moment's hesitation. "Little Margie Sanders. She died so tragically."

"That's not important," Meadows said. It was clear

he was angry that his wife had spoken to me directly. "How long ago did Sandra leave? Where was she living? The front desk man said she was waiting tables." His voice dripped scorn as he spoke the words. "Is this true? She was waiting tables part-time while she was in college and I always told her it was beneath her, that if she wanted a job she should get one at a hospital. Where did she go and why did she leave?"

I looked at him for a moment, wondering if he ever looked in the mirror at his own smug, self-satisfied face. "Yes, Mr. Meadows," I said, "tell me, why did she leave? She hasn't been in contact with you in over two years. Why is that?" I stood and headed for the door. "I'll let you know if I find her. Good night."

Meadows said something low and angry, and Hannah let out a little cry of despair as I closed the door.

I was almost shaking with rage. I understood why Margie would feel the need to get away from her father. If her only reason for running away to the Outer Banks was to get out from under that man's control, I understood.

I heard the door open behind me and I refused to look around, certain it was Lee Meadows. When I heard running footsteps and hesitant panting breaths behind me, I turned to see Hannah Meadows at my heels.

"Ms. McKinley, please wait," she said. Her face was flushed with effort, and her eyes sparkled with determination. She looked a lot like Margie.

"I want to talk to you," she said. "Please."

I hesitated a moment, and then nodded. We walked down the hall towards the elevator.

"How did you know where to find your daughter?" I asked.

"We've got caller ID," Hannah said. "When Sandy left, we put it in, in case she called."

I groaned, wondering how I could be so stupid. Caller ID had never even crossed my mind. It was clear I needed to make the step into the new millennium. I left my computer in California, and I didn't even have a cell phone.

"We've had two calls in the last two weeks, both about Sandy. When you called this morning, I could tell you knew something. I couldn't take it anymore. I called Lee at work, because I wasn't sure how to find out where the phone number was from. I don't know how to do that kind of thing." She said it matter-of-factly, as if repeating something her husband had told her time and time again. "He canceled everything for the day and came home. Before I knew what was going on, we were on a plane."

I studied her as we rode down the elevator to the first floor. Her pale blue dress was spotless and unwrinkled, and her hands slender with beautiful oval fingernails. Her only jewelry was a massive diamond on her left ring finger and she carried a shiny leather bag over her shoulder.

She was staring at the elevator door, her hands clasped together in front of her. Her tension was almost palpable, but she did not fidget.

"Let's go to my office," I said as the elevator door opened.

Dowell studied us with frank curiosity when we went past him. Inside my office, I offered Hannah Janet's old chair and sat in my own, swiveling the seat around so I could see her.

"Okay," I said.

She studied me a moment and then opened her bag and dug around inside it. She passed me a piece of paper.

"Read this. It'll help you understand what happened to Sandra."

I took the paper and saw that it was a letter, typed on a computer and signed in Margie's neat hand. Even though she signed "Sandra" instead of "Margie," I recognized her handwriting.

Dad-

All I've ever wanted is for you to love me. I'm sorry that I can't be the person you want me to be. I've tried, I've tried so hard.

The last three months I've gone on as if nothing has changed—but it has! My whole life has changed and I feel like I've just been holding on by my fingernails while everything I've known slips away underneath me. I can't take it anymore.

When Margie died, I realized how little time all of us have. I've been thinking about death a lot, and if I died tomorrow, what would I have accomplished? I never wanted to be a doctor. I thought I did. I had myself convinced that being a doctor was what I wanted more than anything in the entire world. But it's not. I realize that now.

It's the scariest thing I've ever felt in my life. I feel like the world I knew is gone and I'm left with nothing. I don't know who I am or what I want to do. Sometimes I think that if I just died tomorrow everything would be so much easier.

I'm going away for a little while. I'm sorry for doing this to you and Mother. I never wanted to hurt either of you, but I've got to figure some things out for myself. I think I want to paint, but I don't know for sure. Maybe I'll end up being a truck driver, I don't know! I'm more confused than I've ever been in my life.

I'm sorry.

Love,

Sandra

Twenty-seven

Expect The Unexpected

"My God," I said.

"Lee isn't a bad man," she said. "I don't think he quite realizes how overbearing he is. He's a cardiovascular surgeon you know, and he's used to ordering people around. He sometimes forgets he's not in the operating room with nurses and interns jumping at his commands." She lifted dark, wet eyes to me to see if I understood. I nodded, because I saw that she needed me to understand.

"He was so happy when I was pregnant with Sandy. He wanted a boy, of course, but he wasn't too disappointed when we had a girl instead. He was very proud of her accomplishments. Whenever she brought home good report cards and awards from school, he was so happy." She paused and gazed around the office. "He didn't pay much attention to her otherwise, though. I think Sandy realized early on that the only way to get her father's attention was to succeed. So she succeeded. I've never seen a child work so hard to get good grades, to be the best at gymnastics, to be good at everything she tried. She scared me sometimes she was so single-minded in her determination. She used to rub her eyebrows until they were bald, and she got an ulcer when she was twelve. I encouraged her drawing, because I could see she had talent. I even paid for lessons out of my own pocket because Lee refused. I tried to tell her that we would love her no matter what she did, but she didn't listen to me much."

Hannah turned away, and I saw that Margie's casual dismissal still hurt her deeply.

"She always said when she was small that she wanted to go into medicine, and Lee was so proud of her. She got into Boston University, and, as usual, she excelled. Lee was a lot more involved with her as she got into the pre-med courses. They spent a lot of time together. But the pressure! He would go into a rage if she got a 'B' on an exam. He was always calling her, asking her questions about her classes, calling up her teachers and badgering *them*. By the end of her junior year, Sandy stopped coming home and stopped calling us. I think she just couldn't take him anymore. That only incensed Lee, and he would leave long messages on her answering machine asking where she was, asking if she was studying, wanting to know if she really wanted to be a doctor because he didn't know if she had what it took.

"I think she started to crack just a little bit. Sandy and Margie wanted to go down to Louisiana to stay with some of Margie's relatives for a week after exams, and I encouraged Sandy to go. She was looking so exhausted, so—*haunted,* I guess. They left, and then I heard about the train wreck and that poor Margie Sanders was killed. Sandy was sitting right beside her you know, and even though Sandy never said anything, I found out later that she was trapped under the wreckage with Margie as she died. Margie was her best friend. The two were almost inseparable. Sandy wouldn't talk about it, and I can only imagine how horrible that must have been for her.

"That summer, she tried to go on as if everything was normal. But something was very wrong. She quit her job at the restaurant, which Lee was thrilled about, but instead she sat at home all day. She had always been so neat, but it was like she didn't have the energy to even pick up after herself. She still painted, but the pictures were dark and angry and she burnt them all one day towards the middle of the summer and didn't touch a paintbrush again. I tried to talk her into going to see a psychiatrist, but she didn't want to, and Lee thought I was overreacting.

"Right before school started in the fall, she disappeared. She took some clothes, her shoes, and all of her painting supplies, and she left. She even left the brand new Mercedes convertible Lee bought for her. She just disappeared."

Hannah was concentrating on her lap, and I could see the tension in her fingers as she held them still.

"Lee was furious, of course, and he called the police and a private investigator, but I think she had been planning it for a while, because she managed to just vanish. We've gotten several letters from her over the years, always mailed from different places around the country. She always said she was fine and that she loved us."

"I don't know what to say," I said. "I'm so sorry." Margie must have asked friends to mail the letters if they were traveling away from the Outer Banks.

"But to find out she's been using poor Margie Sander's name and identity . . . It's like she's been living Margie's life for her. Keeping her alive the only way she knew how." Hannah put her face in her hands.

"She's going to be okay," I said in a soft voice.

"I would do anything," she said fiercely, "*anything* to have her back." She stared at me, her face tear streaked, as if daring me to deny her.

"Mrs. Meadows, have you ever heard of Angel Knowling?" I was clutching at straws.

"No, I've never heard of her. Is she important to my daughter?"

"I don't know," I said. "I don't know."

I changed tactics.

"Do you know if there's any chance that your husband may have found out where Sandy was, say about a week ago?" Was there any way that Lee Meadows may have been the one to scare off Margie? If she knew he was getting close to finding her, would she have run again?

"No," Hannah said. "My husband may be a lot of things, but he's not a very good liar. I was the one who took the first phone call, which was over a week ago. I told the man that Margie was studying overseas; that was what Lee wanted us to say. He laughed, said he didn't think so, and hung up. Lee was out of town that week, but he was back when you called, and I told him about the first phone call. He was surprised, and set out to find out where they came from. We've never been here, you see. I guess that's why Sandy decided to come here."

Two phone calls? She mentioned that there had been two phone calls, but it hadn't really registered. "Wait a minute. There were two phone calls about Sandy in the last couple of weeks? One from me, and before that, another one?"

"Yes. A man called first. Like I said, he laughed and hung up. I figured it was just a crank phone call and that he was looking for some other girl. But when you called . . . "

"Do you remember what phone number the man called from? Did you write it down?" My heart was beating fast, but I wasn't sure why.

"Yes, of course I did. I wrote them both down." She handed me a slip of paper. "When I saw that the calls were made from the same area code I had to tell Lee. It was the first lead we'd had in so long. That's why we decided to come. He was so angry that I didn't tell him about the first call immediately."

I stared down at the phone numbers. The second one was mine. The first one was the hotel's.

"We called your number first, but Lee hung up when your answering machine came on. He said he didn't want you to warn Sandy we were coming. When he found out the other number was for a hotel, he made reservations immediately. And here we are."

Mrs. Meadows and I talked for over an hour. She was desperate for information, and I told her about Margie's second vanishing act. I also told her about the girl that I knew as Margie—the daughter she hadn't seen for over two years.

On my part, my thoughts were racing with the information she gave me about the first phone call, but I didn't let her see my excitement and worry.

Someone in the hotel called about Margie, that was clear. Who else had found out that Margie was really Sandy Meadows, and why did he call her parents? To confirm his suspicions like I had done? More importantly, was this the man she was running from? Had this man threatened to tell her parents where she was? Why?

The caller could have been an employee or a guest. I ran through the options as Hannah talked.

Was it Doug? If Margie told anybody her real identity, she would have told Doug. He never mentioned it. That wasn't surprising, since I was sure Margie impressed upon him the importance of the secret. Was Doug so worried when she disappeared that he called her parents? That didn't make sense, though. I questioned Hannah about when the first call was made, and it had been the day *before* Margie disappeared. Why would he laugh and say "I don't think so," when Hannah said her daughter was studying overseas?

Maybe Margie had told Doug the truth about her name, and when she broke up with him he tried to blackmail her into coming back with him. The call to her parents? Well, that could have been an "I've called your parents once, I can do it again if you don't come back to me."

It was hard for me to see Doug doing something like that. But if he was desperate enough . . .

Okay, who else? If the phone call came before Margie disappeared, then somehow, someone had discovered the truth about her. The way the caller laughed on the phone suggested that he was up to no good. Someone else had found out the truth about Margie and was blackmailing her to . . . what? Go out with him? Sleep with him? Something more? Who could it be?

I didn't know the identity of Margie's current admirer. It was clear she had one. The flowers in her room and the pictures of her from last summer were proof that *someone* was interested in her. If not Doug, who?

Margie's words on the night she disappeared haunted me: *I thought he was nice at first, but now he just won't leave me alone.* She knew her admirer, that much was clear. Was it Charlie? He was at Kelly's the night she disappeared and I had seen him talking to her before that, but I never suspected that they were having a relationship. But Margie was a secretive person; would I have known? There was something not quite right about Charlie.

What about Stephen? He made no secret of his interest in Margie. She told him to leave her alone the night she disappeared. He was here this summer, when the photos were taken. Did he call her parents over a week ago? How did he find out who she really was?

I sighed, and then smiled when Hannah looked at me inquiringly. "Ah—I was just thinking that I wish your daughter were here so she could hear how much you love her," I improvised.

Tears came to her eyes and she continued talking.

Did it matter who called the Meadows? It was clear that Margie left on her own, that she hadn't been kidnapped. Still, she had been frightened enough of someone to run. She was safe for now—as long as no one knew where she was—but she couldn't come back until whoever it was stopped. If someone had been stalking Margie since this summer, why would he stop now?

Hannah eventually talked herself out and went to bed after making me promise that I would tell her if I learned anything. I ran my hand through my short hair and glanced at the clock, exhausted. So much had happened in the last twenty-four hours. If I could only piece together the parts . . .

I gathered my stuff, locked the office behind me, and walked out to my Jeep, parked in its usual place beside the trash dumpsters. It was a cool night, and I shivered a bit as I got in. I turned the ignition, praying it would start.

A man in a ski mask opened the passenger-side door and slid in beside me.

Twenty-eight

Jeep-Jacked

"Drive," he said in a low voice, poking me in the side with a large, serrated fillet knife. He was wearing a ski mask with a baseball hat over it, a dark Windbreaker, and gloves. Somehow the gloves scared me the most.

I realized what an easy target I must have been. He had stood by the dumpsters and waited for me, and I—who had been so careful in California about my safety—had been lulled by the Outer Banks. The thought of a carjacker had never even crossed my mind. How could I be so stupid?

I stalled as I backed up the Jeep and he casually stretched his arm across my shoulders and put the knife at my throat.

"Don't do that again," he said.

My hands were shaking so badly I could barely steer, but I managed to get the Jeep pointed towards the Beach Road. I looked around, but there was no one to see me. I hoped once were we on the Beach Road someone's headlights would illuminate the masked man sitting next to me. Maybe we would pass a cop. There were enough of them on the road looking for drunk drivers that the chances of one seeing us were good. My hopes rose.

"Left," he whispered, and I turned to look at him. "Don't look, just drive." The pressure on my neck increased. I felt a trickle of blood running down inside my shirt and I shuddered.

"Left," he repeated when I turned onto the Beach Road. I paused in surprise. "Left," he insisted, and I gasped in pain.

I turned left onto the beach access next to the hotel. Now I was really scared. He was taking me to the beach, and there weren't any cops out there.

"Four-wheel drive."

I stopped the Jeep, used the small gear changer in the floorboard to put it into four-wheel-drive low, and rolled forward again. At the end of the parking lot was a ramp leading over the dunes, and when I slowed, he cut me. Blood was running down the front of my shirt now. I gunned the motor and we were up over the ramp and onto the beach.

"Left," he said again, and I winced as the sandy ruts jarred the knife into my neck. Tears were leaking from my eyes. Where was he taking me?

I had driven the Jeep on the beach several times, and I was familiar with the slushy drag on the tires, the slippery feel of the steering wheel as the wheels slid down one rut and into the next. I had to concentrate on driving, because it would be very easy to get stuck, and then what would he do? I was conscious of the sharp edge of the knife against my neck, and I couldn't think. What could I do? The sand was too deep for me to try any wild maneuvers, and even if I did, the knife prevented me from even thinking about trying. I could open the door and jump out . . . but always the knife. Tears were dripping down my cheeks and I was disgusted with myself, but I couldn't seem to stop. What was he going to do with me?

I had sped up, and the next cross rut we hit threw us both forward. The kidnapper clutched at the door handle, and for a moment, the knife left my throat as he regained his balance. Then it was back, pressing harder than ever.

"Sorry," I muttered. "I'm not used to the sand."

"I can kill you now as easily as later," he said in that same whispering voice, and I shivered.

Jesus God, he was going to kill me one way or another, I realized. *Might as well die trying to escape rather than after he's raped and tortured me.* The thought was so matter-of-fact that it surprised me. My mind was very clear, every thought crisp and hard. I had to do something or die; it was as simple as that.

I sped up slowly so he wouldn't notice. To the left of us were the massive, silent beach cottages, closed for the winter. To the right was the ocean, sweeping onto shore in long, narrow waves. I saw the next cross rut coming, big wide tire tracks cutting across the beach. Good. I sped up a little more. My attacker was leaning forward, but he seemed to be concentrating on the dark houses to our left. I pressed the accelerator a little harder.

We hit the rut with bone-jarring force, and the Jeep bounced wildly from side to side. My head hit the ceiling and the kidnapper fell forward, clutching at the dashboard to keep his balance. For that split second, the arm around my shoulders lifted.

I grabbed for the door and tumbled out onto the ground.

"Hey!"

I was already moving, running as fast as I could in the sticky sand, my side hurting before I had gone fifty feet. Ahead of me I saw stairs that led from the beach over the dune, and I called up an extra burst of speed to dive for them. At the top I kept moving, pounding on the wooden sidewalk towards a dark house.

"Help!" I hollered, hoping that someone might be home. "Help!"

No lights came on, and I kept running. Now I was on the rough concrete of the driveway. There! I saw bright lights ahead, and rock and roll music was pounding from inside a small stucco building. Sharkey's!

I stumbled towards the restaurant, fumbling for the kitchen door and falling forward.

"Callie!" I heard someone say. I made it as far as the metal prep table and laid my upper body across the top of it, feeling the coolness of the metal on my cheek. My heart was pounding as I tried to regain my breath. I felt warm hands on my back.

"Callie, you're bleeding!" It was Kyle, and I closed my eyes in relief.

The next couple of hours were a kaleidoscope of lights, noise, and people. After I gasped my story out to Kyle, he called 9-1-1 and requested an ambulance and the police. He found Susan and asked her to stay with me, and then rounded up a posse of men from the bar to go see if the kidnapper was still at my car.

I answered questions about my attacker's appearance and the make of my Jeep as my neck was bandaged, and then I was bundled into an ambulance. At the hospital I received ten stitches in my neck, and while I waited to be released, a detective came by to tell me that my Jeep had been found abandoned on the beach. No kidding. I didn't expect my attacker to sit in the Jeep and wait for the police.

Then the questions began, gentle and probing: my name, my address, my birth date. Did I recognize my attacker? Did I see his face? Did I notice any distinguishing characteristics? Was I sure it was a man? Did he touch me other than with the knife? Where did he jump me? Could I describe him?

The painkillers were kicking in by that time, and I was fuzzily aware that Kyle had come into the room. He held my hand while I answered the detective's questions. I hadn't recognized my attacker, and except for his clothes, I was unable to give much of a physical description.

After a while, the questions stopped, and after a

longer while someone helped me to a car. That was the last thing I remembered.

I woke up in my own bed the next morning, my neck humming with pain. Ah, it hurt. I lay in bed, taking stock of the rest of me. My legs and stomach ached, probably from my frenzied flight across the sand. Jake groaned, and I patted him.

How did I get home?

My neck stinging, I turned over and saw a bottle of Extra Strength Tylenol on the table. A note was propped up next to it, but I grabbed the bottle and swallowed two of the pills before reading it.

Callie-
Here's something for the pain. You're probably hurting pretty bad right about now. Call me when you get a chance.
Kyle

It was almost eleven o'clock by the time I managed to get dressed and go downstairs, Jake and Ice tumbling over my feet. My roommate was on the couch painting her toenails.

"Good, you're up," Kim said, wiggling her toes. "Kyle made me promise I wouldn't wake you up, but I need to go soon."

"Hi," I said, smiling at her out of the corner of my mouth because it hurt to turn my head.

"He also made me promise I wouldn't leave until you woke up, and it kind of put me between a rock and a hard place, you know?" Kim was looking back down at her toenails, her mouth twisted in irritation.

"Sorry," I said, heading gingerly towards the kitchen. *Must have coffee.*

"He went to get you some Tylenol this morning when I couldn't find any. Something up between the two of you?"

I poured myself a cup of coffee so thick it plopped into the bottom of the cup.

"I made that for Kyle three hours ago when I got home from Kenny's. He stayed up all night with you."

I sipped the coffee, unable to process any of this information.

"How are you, by the way?"

I turned my whole body to look at her. "Fine," I said.

She had the decency to look abashed. "I hope you yelled 'fire' when he jumped you, instead of 'rape'. I read somewhere that if you yell 'rape' people are afraid to come help. If you yell 'fire' they will."

"I'll remember that the next time someone tries to rape me."

"Well, Kenny's picking me up soon to go out to lunch," she said. "I'm sorry about what happened to you. That sucks. I've been meaning to talk to you about something, and I know it's not a good time, but I'm moving in with Kenny next week."

A horn sounded. Kim jumped up, slid her feet into a pair of sandals, and grabbed her purse.

"Kim, can I borrow your car?"

She stopped on her way out the door. "I guess so," she said after a minute. "Yeah, sure, knock yourself out. Keys are in it." She slammed the door shut and I was left in peaceful silence. Good old Kim. The only reason she was letting me borrow her car was because she felt sorry for me. I must look like hell, but at least I had some wheels. I had an appointment to keep.

I took Jake for a quick walk. The dark clouds from yesterday lingered through the night and were staining the morning sky the color of smashed violets. I found myself scanning the empty beach, looking for a figure in a dark jacket and ski mask.

I was waking up now, and last night was beginning to sink in. Somebody kidnapped me, probably to rape and kill me. How did that make me feel?

Pretty damn vulnerable.

I was starting to shake. I whistled Jake to my heel and came close to running back to the safety of my house.

I thought about Kyle instead. He stayed with me? I hadn't expected that. I smiled as the animals collapsed on the couch, one on either end.

"You just got up," I scolded, and Jake peeled back one heavy lid to reveal his brown eye and then snapped it closed. Ice yawned and stretched out onto his back.

The detective last night had given me the number of the impound lot at the town garage where my Jeep had been taken. I called, but the police weren't done with it yet.

"They wanted me to tell you your battery's dead," the lady said. "Were you having trouble with it?"

"I don't think so," I said. "I thought it was my starter."

I had just put the phone down, my mind racing, when it rang under my hand.

"Callie! Did you know you were on the radio this morning? The police were out all last night knocking on doors to see if anyone saw your guy. How are you feeling?"

"Hi, Lily," I said. "I'm okay, I guess. A little sore. What are you doing?" I heard the rustle of sheets and she yawned.

"I'm having a lazy morning," she purred, and laughed a throaty, satisfied laugh. I could hear a man's low murmur in the background.

"Oh," I said.

"Anyway, I just wanted to call and see how you were doing. If you need to take some time off, just let me know. By the way, I hired a new banquet manager yesterday."

"Thank God!" I said, with feeling. "Listen, I just realized something about Charlie, the guy who's been staying in the hotel. You said you were having trouble getting him to pay, and I just realized that he doesn't know anything about cars. What owner of a used car business wouldn't know the difference between a faulty starter and a weak battery? I need to call Dale Grain—"

"He knows all about him," Lily interrupted. "Didn't I tell you what happened yesterday?"

Twenty-nine
Snickers Comes Home

"What happened yesterday?"

"I saw Charlie packing his car," Lily continued, "and I went straight to the front desk and found out he still hadn't paid. I marched right out there and confronted him. He confessed everything."

"Everything?" I repeated.

"Yes. You're right, he doesn't own a used car business. In fact, he just got out of prison for burglary. His grandmother died while he was in prison and left him some money, and when he got out he decided he wanted to live high on the hog for a couple of weeks. Some people would have invested the money, but nobody ever accused crooks of being smart. Well, he was starting to run out of money this past week, and it occurred to him that he wasn't going to have any left over if he didn't leave without paying. I marched him right to the front desk and watched while he paid."

"Oh" was all I could think of to say.

"He liked everybody thinking he was a high roller; he got a kick out of it, which is why he told everyone he was looking for a million-dollar vacation home. Pretty sick, huh?"

I agreed.

"Well, he's gone now. I'm going to get back to . . . what I was doing." She laughed, and I heard the man say, "Lily . . ."

She hung up, and I sat, stunned. I wasn't surprised to hear Charlie had been putting us all on. I *was* surprised that I'd recognized the man's voice.

It was Dale Grain.

Shaking my head, I stood up. I agreed to see Valerie today, and I needed to leave. My hands began to shake. I had to go, but I didn't want to go back outside. There were too many places for someone to hide and ambush me. My vision began to tunnel and I shook my head in desperation, unwilling to descend into that pit of fear.

Dammit! I was not going to let that scumbag make me afraid to leave my own house.

I took a deep breath and opened the door.

This early in the morning there are mostly locals on the road, evidenced by the "OBX" prefix on many of the license plates, as well as the "OBL" (Outer Banks Local) stickers.

Five minutes later, I pulled into Margie and Valerie's driveway and headed for the door inside the carport. The flowers in the plant boxes were withering, and the grass in the front yard had grown longer.

I knocked for several minutes before Valerie came

to the door. A large yellow Lab sniffed at me through the barrier of her knee.

"Hey. Come in."

The house was a mess. Clothes were everywhere and ashtrays overflowed onto the coffee table. In the corner, the finches were silent and I double-checked to make sure they weren't dead. They were sleeping, their little heads bowed and eyes closed.

I sat down and the Lab came and put her chin on my knees. I rubbed her head and back and she wiggled in pleasure. She was a big dog, going gray around her muzzle, and she had a lump on her head and scratches across her face and legs.

"What happened to you?" Valerie asked, staring at the bandage on my neck.

"An accident with a knife," I said.

"Someone attacked you?" She looked at me in astonishment. "You know you're supposed to yell 'fire' if someone attacks you."

"I'll have to remember that next time." Why was I the only woman in America who didn't know this?

She stared at me a moment and then shrugged, turning her attention back to the dog who was leaning against my leg.

"You should have seen her when she got home," she said. "What a mess. She had burs all in her fur and blood down one side of her face. And was she thirsty. She must have drunk two whole bowls of water before she would even look at food. Then she passed out on Margie's bed, poor thing."

Valerie was looking rough herself in a dirty T-shirt and a faded pair of shorts. She slid her hand across the side of her face and peered at me with one eye.

"So what did the people who brought her home say?" I asked. I rubbed the dog's chest and she kicked her back leg in ecstasy.

"They told me they saw her when they stopped to walk out on the jetty on the Hatteras side of the Bonner Bridge. She was running back and forth across the road trying to get on the bridge, but cars kept coming and almost hitting her. They got her to come to them, and then they saw our address on her collar. They coaxed her into the car and brought her home. It was real nice of them, to go to all that trouble. Something's wrong, don't you see? Snickers would never leave Margie. I don't know what's happened, but it's something bad. It looks like Snickers ran a long way."

I continued to rub the dog, and she leaned her head up against me trustingly. Her coat was shining and healthy, despite the scratches that crisscrossed it.

"I brushed her. I had to, there was this funny smelling wax all over her fur, a yellow-green wax."

"Wax?" I repeated.

"Yeah. Real strong-smelling stuff. I don't know where she picked it up, but it smelled god-awful." Valerie reached over to the coffee table and shoved a dirty plate aside to pick up a dog brush, the bristles full of golden hair. She smelled it and grimaced.

"See?"

I took the brush and sniffed it. She was right, it did have a strong odor.

"Doesn't it remind you of something?" I asked her.

Valerie scratched at the side of her nose. "I guess. I can't think of what, though."

I smelled the brush again and Snickers butted her head against my thigh, protesting my inattention. I resumed rubbing the loose skin on the side of her head and she closed her eyes in bliss.

"Citronella!" I said. "The stuff you burn to keep away mosquitoes."

Valerie's face brightened for a moment and she even forgot to hide her nose. "Yeah, that's it! I think Margie's got a citronella candle with her camping gear."

She got up and went to the door, and I followed her out to the carport. She yanked a door open and peered into the darkness for a moment, waving her hand back and forth in the air. I had just started to think she'd lost her mind when she found the string hanging from the light bulb above and pulled.

The room was small with shelves along the back. An old coffee table with only three legs leaned against the back corner, and there were two bikes, one rusted with a flat tire, the other brand spanking new. Pots of paint and stenciling patterns were heaped on the coffee table, and old picture frames leaned against the wall.

Valerie was frowning. "It's gone," she said.

"What is?"

She pointed to a blank bit of floor between the old coffee table and two boogie boards. "Her camping stuff. She always kept it here. It's gone."

She stared at me with dawning comprehension. "Do you think she's camping? Is that where she is?"

Thirty

Campgrounds Galore

Can I see a phone book?" I asked, and she led me back inside.

She rifled through some magazines and the classified section of the *Coastland Times* and handed me the small red phone book. I flipped through the pages until I found where the "Campgrounds and Recreational Vehicle Parks" should have been listed. The page wasn't there.

"She must have ripped it out. I wonder why?"

Suddenly, it dawned on me. I put my bag on the counter and started rustling through the contents. Where did I put it? A-ha, there it was.

I pulled out the yellow piece of paper Valerie gave me on my first visit, the one with Margie's scrawled note in the margin. Two cards fluttered to the floor and I picked them up. They were from the roses in Margie's room.

I turned my attention to the yellow page, which, as I suspected, was the same one missing from the telephone book. I could imagine Margie at two in the morning searching for the name and the address of the campground. Had she called to make sure they were open this late in the season, or had she simply not known where she wanted to stay? Once she had it, she must have been in a hurry. When she couldn't find anything to write on, she ripped the page out and wrote a note to Valerie in the margin. Why didn't I look at this earlier?

In my defense, I thought that Margie had gone home to her parents. It was the natural thing for a twenty-three-year-old girl in trouble to do, wasn't it? Then I got caught up in discovering who Margie Sanders really was. I hadn't even thought that she might be close by. Why didn't it occur to me?

I skimmed through the listings of campgrounds. There were over ten on Hatteras Island where Snickers was found, and I picked up the phone and dialed the first number.

The lady was very nice, and I could hear the click of computer keys as she checked the name for me.

"No," she said, "no Margie Sanders."

"Okay," I said. "Thank you for your time."

The next two places I called were also willing to help, though the second one took so long I was afraid the woman had taken a jog around the campground to look for Margie. They both came back with negative answers.

"This isn't going to be easy finding her," I told Valerie, who was lounging back on the couch playing with a strand of hair over her forehead.

"If she's using her real name," she said.

That stopped me. Which name was she using?

Margie Sanders? Sandy Meadows? Some other name? If the campground required an ID to check in (would it? I had no idea.) she would be forced to use Margie Sanders. If not . . .

"Well, I've got to try." I studied the list of campgrounds and picked up the phone again. I tried the next number, and the next. I called all of them with no luck.

"Doug said something about he and Margie camping at a national park campground. I don't see any listed," I said out loud after several minutes of staring at the list. I flipped through the book, but I still couldn't find any. I sighed and stood up. "I guess I'm going to have to go look for her. I really can't imagine she'd use her real name, but I was just hoping. Do you happen to know where the national park campgrounds are located? How many are there?"

Valerie stubbed out her cigarette and continued playing with her lock of hair. "I don't know. I've never been camping."

I headed for the door. It was just ten o'clock and I didn't have to be back at work until six this evening.

"Just find her, okay?" Valerie was pinching the base of her nose, trying not to cry. "She was a really good friend, even if she didn't talk much. She never made fun of me, you know?" She gestured a hand in front of her nose as if she were swatting a fly and then turned away. "She never made fun of anyone."

I nodded and patted her shoulder before going out

the door. I tried not to think about the fact that she was referring to Margie in the past tense.

It wasn't until I was outside that I realized I was driving Kim's Prelude. It didn't seem right to take her car on an unauthorized road trip, but on the other hand, what she didn't know wouldn't hurt her.

My hand went to my throat; the pain wasn't that bad if I didn't turn my head, but it reminded me of last night. I wasn't up to talking to the police today, though they probably wanted to talk to *me*. The thought of getting away, driving far down the coast away from the hotel and men in ski masks was appealing. The appearance of Margie's dog disturbed me, and it seemed important to find her and make sure she was okay.

I drove the car down the Bypass, past the Tanger Outlet Center to the stoplight where I followed the signs towards Hatteras. As I accelerated down the narrow two-lane blacktop of Highway 12, I passed a sign welcoming me into the Cape Hatteras National Seashore. An information center followed. I slammed on the brakes and turned into the parking lot of the Whalebone Junction Information Center.

My questions were easily answered, and a few minutes later I had a map with stars marking the two national park service campgrounds on Hatteras Island. Neither had a phone that could be accessed by the public, which explained why I couldn't find them in the telephone book.

It was a pretty drive, through acres of waving marsh grass turning brown in the autumn sun. Rabbits hopped out onto the median beside the road and stared at Kim's Prelude; tiny birds swooped in front of me as I sped along. The morning clouds retreated northwest in the strong salt breeze as the black-and-white-striped Bodie Island lighthouse rose on my right.

"Bodie Island," I said out loud. Most of the natives pronounced it "Body" Island. I wondered why and resolved to find out when I had the time.

I suddenly realized that the article about me living in the Outer Banks could have come out today. There was so much going on that I had forgotten about it. That was funny. There was a time when something like that would never slip my mind. What would I do if everyone knew who I really was? Could I stand the questions and the appraising glances all over again? I tried so hard to forget what happened in California, but it just wouldn't go away.

The Bonner Bridge rose before me like an old-fashioned roller coaster. It swooped up high above turbulent Oregon Inlet, framed by water-swept sandbars and marsh, and then down and around, depositing me on Pea Island.

In the five months I had been on the Outer Banks, I had been too busy to do much exploring. I remember taking a trip as a kid down to Hatteras to see the lighthouse, the tallest in the United States. We had taken a ferry to Ocracoke, but my memories were clouded by time, and I barely remembered what it looked like. I did remember stopping for saltwater taffy somewhere and managing to smear the sticky blue-green candy all over the back seat. My mom forbade me to say a word for almost two hours, and my grandfather kept winking at me from the front seat. Had Henley and Cindy been there? Funny, I couldn't remember.

I stopped at the parking lot on the other side of the Bonner Bridge, where the dog had been found. There was no sign of Margie's maroon Accord, and I was soon back on Highway 12 headed south. On my left, tall sand dunes covered with sparse grass shielded my view of the ocean. Several cars were pulled off the road in the deep sand as people hiked over the dunes to catch a glimpse of the thousands of migratory birds that hung out on Pea Island. I wished I had time to stop, but time was slipping away. On my right, flat marsh and ponds of rippling water retreated as far as I could see.

My thoughts turned back to my attacker. I had been checking my rearview mirror every two minutes at first, but now I was more relaxed. Was it a random carjacking, or did he kidnap me because I was looking into Angel's murder? Did it have something to do with Margie?

It was hard to shake the feeling that something had been familiar about him. Was it his voice? He had whispered the entire time, so I couldn't be sure.

After a while the windswept dunes gave way to

fantastical cottages with turrets and widow's peaks. I started my search for Margie at campgrounds in the small towns of Rodanthe, Waves, Salvo, and Avon. I stopped at each and asked whoever was at the desk if they had seen a woman fitting Margie's description, then I asked permission to drive through and look for her car. No one questioned my story: I was supposed to be meeting my little sister at a campground on Hatteras but I had lost the address. The Outer Banks are still pretty naïve in a lot of ways, and it helped that I was a presentable young woman. Everyone was friendly, but no one had seen her.

Once past Avon, the only signs of man's existence were the narrow road, constantly threatened by shifting sand, and the power lines standing silent sentry mile after mile.

I was conscious that I was driving farther away from the bridge where Snickers was picked up. How far could the dog have gone in her quest to return home? Was it possible that Margie had dropped her off at the bridge for some reason? Why would she? I decided if I didn't find Margie at one of the campgrounds I would go back and question the people fishing at the bridge. Someone might have seen her.

I saw the diagonal stripes of the Cape Hatteras Lighthouse long before I came to it. The lighthouse garnered national attention when it was moved 2900 feet to save it from the advancing Atlantic; it now stood almost as far away from the ocean as it had in 1870 when it was completed. This little sandbar known as the Outer Banks was never meant to be permanent, and nature had a way of reminding us again and again.

Here, the road twisted through stunted trees, old houses, and shops. Buxton didn't have quite the frenetic tourist feel of the northern towns. It was as if the town said: Come if you want, but I have my own life to lead.

I came to the second national park campground on Hatteras Island. There was a sign on the window of the empty front office indicating that they would soon be closing for the year. The first several sites were sporadically dotted with large RV campers with license plates from Maine, New York, and Canada. I saw a dun park ranger pickup parked in front of the bathrooms, and glimpsed a man in a ranger uniform swinging a bag of trash into the back of the truck. There were a few tents tucked in the bushes, or high on a dune, enjoying the sea-to-sound view.

It was a nice campground, with large, secluded sites. I wasn't surprised when I saw Margie's maroon Accord in one of the parking places. I pulled behind her car and got out, tripping over a brochure flapping in the breeze. I picked it up, noting that it was a Sun Realty brochure listing cottages for rent, and then turned my attention to the car. It had faded, rust-colored paint, North Carolina license plates, and a dancing Grateful

her to get a license and a car registration under an assumed name.

The campsite was up a narrow sandy path leading into a circle of thick bushes. If you stood on your tip-toes you could glimpse the ocean, but I had a feeling that Margie picked the site for the privacy, not the view.

A camp chair sat beside the blue dome tent, and a Sterno stove, a lantern, and a cooler were on the picnic table. There was a pan on the stove.

I called cheerfully, "Margie? Rise and shine." I leaned down to peer in the open tent flap.

An air mattress, a sleeping bag, and a duffel bag of clothes were laid out inside. Next to the bag was a box of cooking utensils and a couple cans of soups and stews. No Margie.

She must have walked to the beach. I sat down on the camp chair and decided to wait for her. Thank God I found her. Hopefully she could explain what happened and maybe even come back with me.

A half-full water bowl and an empty dog dish sat on the ground beside me. A large black bird swooped down, searching the ground for stray nuggets of dog food.

Why did Snickers run away? Did she run all the way from here to the Bonner Bridge? It was a long way, but dogs and even cats had been known to travel farther on their journeys home. But why did she leave Margie?

I looked around the campsite and noticed a couple

of things I'd overlooked when I arrived.

The pan on the stove was full of congealed, burnt Brunswick stew. I opened the cooler and found a packet of hamburger and a tub of butter swimming in lukewarm water. The meat was bad.

I looked around the campsite and noticed something in the bushes at the edge of the clearing next to the tent: a small metal bucket filled with a yellowish-green, strong-smelling wax. It was a citronella candle, the same wax that had been in Snickers's fur.

I crouched down to look at it and noticed splashes of wax on the side of the tent and on the bush.

It was as if the candle had been thrown. Had it been thrown at Snickers? It would have to be lit for the wax to be soft enough to splatter. Who would throw a candle at the dog?

Where did Margie go in such a hurry that she didn't even have a chance to take her dinner off the stove?

Thirty-one

Citronella, Puppies, And Rose Petals

It was possible there was a perfectly logical explanation, but I couldn't think of one as I stared at the overturned citronella candle.

Margie wouldn't have thrown the candle at her dog. I found it hard to believe that she would burn her dinner and just leave the pan on the stove overnight.

What happened?

I straightened up, grimacing as the muscles in my calves pulled from my extended crouch.

Where before the homey atmosphere of Margie's campsite had seemed comfortable and lived in, it now seemed ominous. Where was she? Her car and clothes were still here. Was she at the beach and all my worrying for nothing?

I went to her car; the windows were open and it was unlocked. Canvases, turned inward and tied together in pairs filled the back, and a box of painting supplies was stuffed behind the driver's seat. The front of the car was littered with gold dog hair and a pair of hiking boots.

I heard the pitter-patter of small nails on pavement and looked around to see a young couple walking a golden long-haired puppy. He bounced and cavorted at the end of the leash, and then, catching sight of me, he stood on his hind legs and put his front paws on my thighs. The young woman, tanned and pretty in a green sweatshirt, smiled in my direction. The young man pulled on the dog's leash in an effort to pull him away.

"He's adorable," I said, leaning forward and letting the dog sniff my fingers. He licked them and then lunged for my face to give it a good licking as well. I laughed and straightened. "What is he?"

"A mix," the girl said in a clipped English accent. "Mostly golden retriever and Labrador, but her mother got around quite a bit, you know, so we're not too sure."

I laughed. "I've got a Lab-Setter puppy, though he's almost grown."

The couple beamed like happy parents and the girl leaned over and rubbed the puppy's neck. "They are precious, aren't they?" She stood up and stretched. "What an absolutely gorgeous day."

"It is, at that," I said, and found myself unconsciously mimicking her accent. I hoped she didn't notice and think I was making fun of her.

The man, who hadn't spoken yet, began pulling the puppy towards a tent set up on the other side of the road. The girl waved at me and went after them. She called back over her shoulder, "If you're looking for the girl with the big yellow dog, she isn't here."

"Wait," I said, starting after her. "I *am* looking for her. Do you know were she is?"

The girl stopped and turned to me. The boy continued up the slope and into their campsite. "Lucy," he called, his voice disapproving, and she waved a hand in his direction.

"I don't know where she went. I wondered a little when we didn't see her today." She reached her hand down the back of her jacket and scratched. "The mosquitoes," she explained. "Have you ever tried Skin-So-Soft as a mosquito repellent? It works."

"Really? I'll have to try it. You haven't seen the girl—Margie—today at all?"

"No, or yesterday either. Geoff said it's none of my business." She smiled a little, as if she was used to that.

"How long have ya'll been here?" I asked, forcing myself into a broader Southern accent than I usually had, just so I wouldn't mimic her.

"We came down from Virginia Beach last Sunday. The weather's been wonderful but we have to go back home soon." Her voice was wistful. "We spent the summer working in Virginia Beach. This is the first time I've ever been over here."

"England?" I guessed.

"Windsor, just outside of London." She leaned forward and scratched at a welt on her leg. "I was hoping we'd see the Outer Banks Mermaid before we left . . . I always wanted to be a mermaid when I was a little girl." She smiled impishly.

I smiled back. It was hard not to. "Margie, the girl

who was staying here, did you get a chance to talk to her?"

"Oh, we talked a bit about the dogs. Goldie got loose and ran over to play with her dog, and we chatted a bit. Nothing much. We saw her sketching on the beach, but she looked like she wanted to be by herself so we left her alone." Lucy grimaced, as if perhaps she had wanted to be friendlier but Geoff the boyfriend had discouraged her. "She was here when we got here and she lent us a rubber mallet to pound in our stakes."

Margie had been gone for nine days. Today was Sunday, and she had been here last Sunday when Lucy and Geoff arrived. She left Nags Head Friday night, and it looked as if she may have been here the entire time. I tried to think of what other questions to ask, but Geoff was starting to light the grill and she glanced over her shoulder at him, preparing to go.

"When was the last time you saw her?" I asked.

Lucy turned back to me, her wide hazel eyes guileless. "Let me think. Friday morning I guess, before we left to go to Ocracoke. She was walking the dog when we left. We didn't get back until after midnight—we almost missed the last ferry. Her car was here when we got back, but then we didn't see her at all yesterday or today. I wondered if she might have gone with her friend somewhere while we were in Ocracoke."

"Her friend?" I echoed, trying not to sound as clueless as I felt.

"Oh yes. The young man."

"Uh—what did the man look like?"

"I don't know, really. A bit like a surfer, but not as bad as the ones we had up in Virginia Beach. You know, some of those boys don't take showers? This boy looked clean enough, with a nice smile. He pulled up in an old orange MG, and I remember thinking that maybe she'd been waiting for him, but she didn't look too pleased to see him. He left after a while and never came back."

It was Doug. It had to be. How many clean-cut kids with a nice smile drove an aging orange MG?

"What day did he come?"

Lucy looked over her shoulder at her boyfriend who was standing over the grill watching us. She was beginning to look uncertain, as if, once again, her big mouth had gotten her into trouble.

"Look, I'm a friend," I said, and she turned back to me when she heard the earnestness in my voice. "I think she's in trouble. Her dog showed up about thirty miles from here. I'm really worried about her."

"Thirty miles? My Lord. The poor thing. Why would she . . . ?" I had her attention again, and she turned her back on her boyfriend. "Let me see. He came the morning before we left for Ocracoke, so Friday. He didn't stay long, and he looked kind of upset when he left."

Doug had been hit by a car Friday night. Did he come back sometime Friday and pick Margie up before his accident?

I thought about what Lucy said after she had returned to her boyfriend and the smell of grilling hamburgers wafted over to me from their campsite.

I didn't know what to think. Doug came to visit Margie. Did he find her as I had, or did he know where she was the whole time? Why hadn't he been at work before the accident? Lucy said Margie wasn't happy to see him. What did they talk about? Why did Margie disappear that night, leaving her car and her dog? *How* did she disappear for that matter, without her car? I needed to ask Doug some questions, but he was in the hospital in Norfolk. For the first time, I wondered whether his accident might not have been an accident. I needed to talk to him as soon as possible.

I returned to Margie's tent and searched through her duffel bag. It felt wrong to dig through her clothes, and when I came up empty-handed I felt even worse.

I glanced at my watch. It was almost two, and I needed to be getting back. I looked at Margie's Accord and had another thought: the trunk.

The Accord was one of those models with the trunk latch beside the driver's seat. I popped the trunk and went around back to lift the lid: a bag of dog food; shoes for work; a canvas tarp, neatly folded; and a shoebox.

I pulled out the shoebox and set it on the hood of Kim's Prelude.

On top lay a sheet of paper, blank except for the words, "Dear Daddy-"

I looked at it for a long moment, wondering what had been going on in Margie's head when she wrote those words. Was she planning on writing her father to tell him where she was?

Under the letter were several pictures of Doug, smiling happily on top of a dune, the wide blue ocean behind him. Another picture was of Margie and Doug, their faces squished together as Doug took a self-portrait of them. I would have taken bets that these pictures were taken here at this campground. It would explain how he found her.

I lay the pictures aside and found a letter from Doug. It was written right after Margie broke up with him. It was a painful, awkward letter, and it didn't say anything beyond what I had already guessed. Doug was deeply in love with Margie and hurt by her sudden cold shoulder.

Underneath the letter were various certificates: Employee of the Month for three different months, certificates for training courses she had completed.

Under that was an envelope. At first I thought it was sealed, and then I saw that it had been opened and stuck back together. It took only a moment of thought before I opened it.

Inside were two birth certificates and some pictures of Lee and Hannah Meadows. I looked at the birth certificates. One was for Margie Sanders and one was for Sandra Meadows. Margie must have used the real Margie's birth certificate to apply for the job at the

Holiday House and to get her driver's license. How she got the real Margie Sanders' birth certificate was anybody's guess, but the two girls *had* been roommates at college.

I sighed and put everything back into the box. None of this helped explain where Margie was now.

I was back at square one. Why did I feel such a sense of urgency? There was probably a very rational explanation for the deserted campsite; the most probable was that Margie left with Doug. But why would she leave so suddenly? Why would she leave Snickers?

I needed to talk to Doug, but he was in the hospital. Did the hit and run accident have anything to do with Margie?

Shaking my head in frustration, I started back towards my car. A splash of crimson under my heel caught my eye. At first I thought it was blood, but as I stopped for a closer look I saw that it was a crumpled rose petal.

Thirty-two

Date With Destiny

*A*s I drove north, the sense of urgency in me was growing. I didn't know why, but I just couldn't shake the feeling that Margie was in danger. The crumpled rose petal, so out of place in the deserted campsite, reminded me of the roses in her room. Why didn't I check those out sooner? Why did I disregard her fright the night she dropped the steak? She was afraid of someone, the someone she had talked to at Kelly's the night she disappeared. The same person, I assumed, had sent her flowers. I had been so caught up in finding out about Margie's past I had forgotten her new life on the Outer Banks. The reason she ran may have nothing to do with the fact that she was not really Margie Sanders.

Seaside Florist and Gift Shop was close to the Holiday House Hotel, but off the Bypass in a bright blue building.

"Hi Callie!" Angela called as I entered to the accompaniment of tiny bells. "Did you like that arrangement I sent you last week for the wedding? Weren't those irises glorious?"

"It was beautiful, Angela," I assured her.

Angela was a voluptuous woman in her late thir-

pretty and professional in her hand-woven Indian vest. She smiled at me as she looked up from her ledger book, her pen poised over the next entry.

"What can I do for you?" Her voice was friendly, despite the fact that it was just after five on Sunday—closing time. The Holiday House was a big account for her and she was a businesswoman at heart.

"This is going to sound strange, Angela, but I don't have time to explain everything. Do you know Margie Sanders? She works with me at the Seahorse Café, a dark-haired girl in her early twenties?"

Angela's smile stayed intact as she shook her head. "I'm sure I would know her if I saw her, but . . . "

"Well, to make a long story short, she's disappeared and I'm worried about her. I can't explain all of it, but I found some flowers that were delivered to her house by your shop and I was wondering if you could tell me who sent them."

The smile was slipping now, as she began to shake her head. "I don't know, Callie . . . "

"I'm afraid she might be in trouble, Angela," I said, and something in my tone must have conveyed my urgency.

"Let's see what we can do," she said. "How long ago were they delivered?"

She went to a file cabinet and looked back at me.

"It would have been at least a week ago. I'm not sure exactly. There were two deliveries."

She pulled out a manila file. "These are the driver's

sheets for this month. What's the address?"

I was stumped for a moment. I knew *where* Margie lived, but the exact address? I remembered the directions that Valerie gave me when I first visited the girls' house and fumbled in my purse. With relief, I found the crumpled piece of paper.

"It's 1699 Seminole."

Angela sighed, but flipped back though the sheets in the folder and began to run her finger down the entries.

"I'm going back two weeks." Silence as she turned a page. "Ah, here we go. There was a delivery of a dozen red roses two weeks ago, and . . . two days later the same thing to the same address."

"Can you tell who ordered the roses?"

"No. This is just for delivery. I really can't tell you who ordered them without going back through all the order forms for the day the roses were ordered, which is not necessarily the day the roses were delivered— wait a minute. Here's 1699 Seminole."

She drummed her fingers on the counter. "Hmmm. I seem to remember . . ." She flipped through the pages in the folder and stopped at one, reading it intently. "Right. I knew that address seemed familiar for some reason. See, here." She turned the notebook around and showed me an entry for Friday, October fourteenth.

1699 Seminole/dozen red roses/ card/delivered 3:30 pm- REFUSED

"I remember Scott, my delivery boy, telling me

about this one. He tried to deliver the roses and the girl refused to take them. From what he said, she got a little hysterical about it, told him not to bring any more flowers to her house."

"Do you remember who made the order?" I realized that I was leaning forward across the desk and forced myself to step back. October fourteenth was the day Margie disappeared. She had refused the roses right before she came into work that day.

"It was a phone order, I remember that now. The man called it in the day before. I tried to call him back when the roses were refused—wait a minute." She went into the back and I stood fidgeting, trying not to look at my watch. I was supposed to be at work at six and it was already five-thirty.

Angela returned from the back room with a sheaf of yellow invoices. "These are the orders for October thirteenth." She thumbed through the yellow pages. "Here it is. Dozen red roses to 1699 Seminole. Paid cash. Frank Jones, 441-2000. Hmmm. What's this?"

"He paid cash? So you saw him?"

She was studying a small card. "What? No, it was a phone order. He said he would bring the money by that day, but he must have gotten here after we were closed, because he put the cash in an envelope and put it in the mailbox. Actually, come to think of it, he did that all three times."

Damn.

The phone number, however, was familiar. It was

the main number of the Holiday House Hotel. Angela was holding up a card and squinting at it. "Oh, I see. It's the card that we sent with the roses your girl refused. Mr. Jones told me what he wanted it to say. I must have clipped it to the invoice when I tried to call to tell him they'd been refused. I didn't get hold of him, I remember. The girl said they didn't have anyone by that name staying in the hotel."

She handed me the card and I turned it over with trembling fingers to read what was written in Angela's neat handwriting.

My sweet angel, soon we will be together forever. October 23 is our date with destiny.

Thirty-three

Will The Real Keith Knowling Please Stand Up?

I broke the thirty-five mile speed limit on the Beach Road on my way back to the Holiday House. My mind was churning and I came close to hitting a fisherman in rubber overalls who decided to step out in front of me. A thick fog was rolling in from the ocean, and I forced myself to slow down.

All the pieces were falling into place. The card was proof that Margie was being stalked by none other than Keith Knowling. He called her his "angel" and said October twenty-third was their date with destiny. October twenty-third was the five-year anniversary of Angel's murder.

Today was October twenty-third.

The close resemblance between Margie and Angel must have triggered something in Keith's crazed mind. He had been interested in Margie, but when he got too intense, she become frightened and ran. I was convinced that Keith had somehow tracked her down to the campground and kidnapped her. Why?

Who could predict what a deranged man like Keith Knowling might be thinking? All I knew was that he had killed once and could do it again.

Now that I knew Keith Knowling was involved, I searched my memory for the picture of him the police had shown me. He would be in disguise, of course, but the picture I saw was of a shortish man with dark, receding hair and glasses over muddy, indistinct eyes. How much could he have changed his appearance? Was it someone I knew? The fact that he had given the Holiday House's number proved that he had some connection with the hotel, but was he an employee or a guest?

I squealed tires as I turned into the Holiday House's parking lot. Inside, I picked up the phone and dialed Dale Grain's number, which by now I knew by heart. No one answered, and I left a hurried message on his voice mail explaining what I had discovered. Then I called the main number for the police department and asked for a detective, any detective.

After a moment, a woman answered and identified herself as Sergeant Patricia Huntley. I poured out my story.

There was a deep silence as I finished, and I wondered if Patricia had hung up on me.

"Let me get this straight," she said briskly. "You think you've found evidence that Keith Knowling is, or was, staying in the hotel? You do realize that we've done background checks of almost everyone who is staying there?"

"All I know is that my waitress looks a lot like Angel Knowling. She's disappeared from a campground in Frisco. Roses were sent to her over a week ago and the card that went with them mentions today's date, which is the anniversary of Angel's murder. In the note, this Frank Jones calls Margie his 'sweet Angel.' It's flimsy, I know, but isn't it worth checking out?"

"Yes," Patricia said, and I breathed a sigh of relief. "The coincidence, if it is one, is compelling. I'll try to get hold of Dale and we'll be over ASAP."

I thanked her and hung up, a great burden lifting from my chest. The police were involved. They would see the connection between Margie and Angel Knowling, and they would find Margie and Keith.

I sat back in my chair. Was Keith staying in the hotel? If so, he'd have to have a good fake ID, though it must have been *very* good to fool the police background checks. I thought about Keith Knowling and Margie. He would be what, in his mid-thirties now? A little old for twenty-three-year-old Margie, but it wasn't the first time that a young woman was attracted to an older man. It didn't escape me that Margie was about the same age as Angel was when she was murdered. Who was Keith Knowling? He must be going by a different name now, but which one? Was it someone I knew?

Margie knew him. She said that he *was nice at first but now he just won't leave me alone.* He had been watching her since this summer, that much was clear from the pictures I found. Keith had been aware of Margie for months, though she may not have been aware of him.

I stared out my office window, noticing that as it

grew darker the fog was developing, insidiously sliding across the hoods of cars and wrapping the Holiday House sign in spider webs of white. All of a sudden I remembered that I was supposed to be working. I picked up the phone and called the restaurant.

"Callie? We're dead up here. Oh, good news, by the way," Kate said.

"What?"

"Chef and Leah think the kitchen is ready to be inspected tomorrow. They're convinced we'll get an 'A.'"

"Great," I said with relief. "Listen, if you get busy I'll be down in my office."

"Oh sure, but we're fine."

I hung up and stared out the window some more. Lee said his dog had chased someone over the dune, and then the dog came back and dug up Angel's skull. Had Keith been digging for the skull? That would explain why Lee's dog was able to dig it up so easily after it had been buried for five years.

Trying to figure out why a killer did anything was beyond me. Did he bury Angel's skull in the dune behind the Holiday House because they had come here on vacation? What made Keith decide to dig it up now? Because the fifth anniversary of Angel's death was approaching, or because he found Margie, who looked like his dead wife?

I looked out into the foggy parking lot to see if the detectives had arrived yet.

No sign of them.

I rubbed my eyes and changed angles. If Margie knew Keith Knowling, it was possible it was someone *I* knew. Doug had been dating Margie, but he was too young to be Keith Knowling. Thinking about Doug, I reached for the phone, flipping through papers on my desk until I found the name of the hospital where he was staying. I called, and after several minutes of confusion, was connected with his room. Someone snatched up the phone after the first ring.

"Hello?" The voice was female and tearful.

"Um . . . I was wondering if Doug was able to talk?" I asked, fearing the worst. Maybe he was worse off than we thought. Did he die?

"I'm sorry," the woman said. "Doug isn't here right now."

"Oh." I was at a loss. "Is he expected back soon?" The words were dumb, but I wasn't sure what else to say. Had he gone for X-rays or surgery?

"No, I'm afraid Doug has . . . checked out."

My heart thumped. "Checked out?" I repeated stupidly. Was that a euphemism for death?

"No, no," the woman said. "Who is this, anyway? This is Doug's mother."

"I'm Callie," I said. "I work with your son. I was just calling . . . to see how he was doing."

"He's recovering. In fact, he left the hospital this afternoon. I went to get coffee. I've been with him the whole time . . . " The words were defensive, as if I had accused her of neglect. "When I came back he was gone. I don't know where he is. His father is driving to North Carolina to look for him, but I'm supposed to stay here in case he comes back."

I mouthed the expected platitudes, *I'm sure he's fine, he'll be back soon,* but I hung up the phone feeling worried. What was so important that Doug felt the need to leave the hospital with a broken arm and a concussion? I thought of the articles about Angel Knowling that Kyle and I found in his room. Why had he kept them all these years? Granted, he was a journalism major and maybe he did a project on her, but was there some other reason? As far as I knew, Doug was the only one who knew where Margie had been hiding. Did he kidnap her, get hit by a car, and then leave the hospital to come back for her?

I got up and began to pace, three feet one way, three feet back in the narrow confines of the office. I glanced out the window. It was getting dark, and I tapped my foot in frustration. Where were the police?

I decided to go wait for the detectives in the lobby.

"Get a load of this fog, Callie!" Dowell said when he saw me. "I heard over my police scanner that there have been accidents all over the beach."

"Hi, Dowell," I said, looking impatiently out the front doors.

"Did you hear about Doug? He left the hospital this morning without telling anyone. His parents are frantic with worry. They don't know where he went."

"Yes, I heard." I tapped my nails on the counter.

"Did you hear about the kids who broke into the banquet rooms and stole the Halloween display?"

I was engrossed in thoughts of Keith Knowling.

"Did I tell you about the guy who wanted to move to 328 so bad that he offered to pay a housekeeper twenty bucks if she'd clean it right away? As if 328 is such a hot room. Jeez, 327's got a Jacuzzi, and 330's got a widescreen TV. But you can't talk reason to some of these—"

Something clicked inside my brain. "What room?"

"Room 328," Dowell said, puzzled by my tone. "Anyway, like I was saying . . . "

Wasn't 328 the room old Jonathan told me Angel had stayed in?

"What guy?" I interrupted.

"What guy what?"

"What guy wanted to stay in 328?"

"It was that reporter guy, Mark Holloway."

Thirty-four
Thump

I stared at Dowell, trying to process the name. Mark Holloway, the guy we all assumed was a reporter. The same man who kept asking all the questions about Angel, the one who thought I looked familiar. What if he wasn't a reporter? Was it possible that he was Keith Knowling? I hadn't paid enough attention to him because I had been so busy avoiding him. Hindsight is twenty-twenty, as my grandfather always said.

"What exactly did he say?" I pressed Dowell.

He frowned, clearly unsettled by the intensity of my tone. "What's the big deal, Callie? He said he wanted to move to 328, I told him the room wasn't clean yet, so he offered to pay Micki twenty bucks to clean it."

"Did he say anything else?"

Dowell pursed his lips. "Well, I *did* ask him if he was a reporter and winked at him, because of course we all know that he is. I guess he was kind of stunned that we knew, because he looked surprised and hemmed and hawed. I asked him what paper he was with and he said the *Daily Press.* He didn't sound like he wanted to tell me, but what was he going to do, lie?"

"The *Daily Press,* huh? Hand me the phone, will you?"

Dowell put the phone on the counter and I called information for Hampton, Virginia, the city where I knew the paper was based. It was a Hampton Roads paper, one that I was familiar with from when I was growing up in Virginia Beach. It was also, coincidentally, the newspaper that served the area where Angel had lived.

It only took a few minutes to get the *Daily Press* operator on the phone, and only a few minutes more to confirm what I had already guessed. Mark Holloway was not one of their reporters.

I ran back to my office and dug through the pile of newspapers on my desk until I found the picture of Keith Knowling. I stared at it, comparing it to Mark Holloway. They didn't look the same, but I forced myself to consider that Keith Knowling had to be in disguise. Mark Holloway was about the right age, in his mid-thirties, maybe a little taller than the five-eight listed in the article, but not by much. Mark didn't wear glasses, but his eyes were brown. The main difference was his weight. Mark Holloway was reed thin, his face lean and angular, his whole body as trim as a greyhound's. Keith Knowling was a hefty five-eight, beefy in his face and body. Keith would have to lose a good forty pounds to be as thin as Mark Holloway. Was it possible? I stared at the picture. If Keith were to return to the scene of his crime, he would change his appearance dramatically, wouldn't he? There were more subtle differences: Keith's receding hairline where Mark's hair was full and dark; Keith's expression was open and friendly and Mark was more intense. All that could be changed couldn't it?

It was possible.

Mark was asking about room 328. He wanted to stay in the same room in which Angel and Keith had stayed. That was too much of a coincidence. How else could Mark know what room Angel stayed in if he *wasn't* Keith Knowling? Jonathan was the only one who remembered the room number, and while he did tell the police, it had not been publicized.

And Mark thought he recognized me. Did he realize who I was later and then send the press releases about me to the papers?

If he was really a reporter, why would he lie about what paper he was with?

But I could almost swear that I had never seen Mark Holloway until the day he checked into the hotel—the day after the police announced that the skull was Angel Knowling's. How was that for a coincidence? Mark would've had to be in the area before he checked in if Lee's dog chased him off the dune the night the skull was found. Also, Mark would have to be around to woo Margie, send her flowers, and meet her at Kelly's. Just because he didn't stay at the hotel didn't mean he wasn't around. What about the phone number from the florist? The Holiday House phone number was given the day *before* the skull was found. Why would he do that? Then again, he couldn't give his real number.

I jumped up, went back out to the front desk, and glanced out the door, hoping that I would see a police car pulling in. All I saw was the fog, writhing and rolling outside the glass.

"Look at his registration," I said. "Where does it say he's from?"

Dowell went to the computer and the keys clicked as he typed.

"Hampton, Virginia," he said.

Hampton was the city adjoining Newport News, where Angel was killed. Was it that simple? Had Keith Knowling been in Hampton all these years? He changed his name, changed his appearance, but he didn't go far.

"Oh jeez, *there he is*," Dowell whispered. "Hi, Mr. Holloway," he called cheerfully. I closed my eyes. It could not have been more obvious that we were talking about him.

Mark Holloway headed for the front doors wearing a dark green jacket. He hesitated when he saw me, but then just lifted a hand in greeting and continued out into the fog.

"Jesus," I hissed. Was it a black jacket that I saw that night on my attacker? It *could* have been dark green. "Call the police, Dowell, and tell them I think Mark Holloway is Keith Knowling. I'm going to follow him to see where he's going. Once I know I'll call them. I think he's got Margie hidden someplace close!"

I said this in a rush over my shoulder as I headed

for my office, where I grabbed my purse and the keys to the Prelude. I looked down at them. Even better. He would be expecting me to drive the Jeep. I headed to the loading dock, colliding with someone as I ran through the door.

"Ooof," I said. "Sorry—Kyle!" The cut on my neck screamed with pain.

"Callie. I've been calling you all day at home, and when I called the restaurant they said you were in your office. I wanted to see how you were—"

"Come on," I said, grabbing his arm and hustling him out the door. "Let's go! I'll explain on the way."

Looking stunned, Kyle allowed himself to be dragged outside into the thick wet fog. I was so relieved to see him that I could have kissed him—*wanted* to kiss him, but that would have to wait until later.

Kyle's Dodge pickup was parked at the loading dock and I climbed into the passenger seat, already looking around for Mark Holloway. Where did he go? I could barely see five feet in this fog, but I saw brake lights at the road, and then a dark car turned right out of the parking lot. Kyle, bless his heart, didn't ask any questions. He got into the driver's seat and looked at me.

"Go, go," I said. "He just took a right."

"Who did?" he asked, but he started the engine.

"I think it's Keith Knowling. Take a right."

I explained as he accelerated, trying to catch up to the rear taillights we could see in the distance.

"So you think this Mark Holloway person is Keith Knowling? Why do you think he's got Margie?"

I explained about finding Margie's campsite, going to the florist, and the note that led me to believe that Keith was the one who kidnapped her.

"I think he's hiding her someplace close since he's staying in the hotel. He would want her close to him. It was obvious that Dowell and I were talking about him, so I'm afraid he might take Margie and run. I figure we follow him to wherever he's going and then call the police."

Kyle was shaking his head. "If I hadn't come along you would have followed him by yourself?"

"Sure. Can you go any faster? I see the taillights right up there."

"You would have followed a dangerous killer all by yourself."

I turned and saw for the first time that Kyle was angry. His jaw clenched as he took his eyes off the road to stare at me. "Do you know how dangerous that is? How stupid?"

I had to smile. It had been a long time since anyone worried about me. "I was afraid that he was going to take Margie and run," I said patiently. "I was going to call the police, already have in fact. We'll call when we see where he's going. There he goes!"

Ahead of us, the taillights turned into a restaurant parking lot. We slowed as we drove by and I saw with disbelief that the car we had been following was a blue SUV, not the dark sedan Mark was driving.

"We lost him!" I cried in despair. The fog pressed against the windshield, softening and smudging everything around us.

"He couldn't have gone far. He either turned off or this car pulled out behind him," Kyle said, accelerating again. There were more taillights ahead and we roared down the Beach Road at an unsafe fifty-miles-an-hour. These taillights belonged to a pickup truck. By now we were past Sharkey's, and ahead of the pickup truck was only empty road.

"We lost him," I said again, a panicky feeling crawling through my stomach. What if he was going to pick up Margie and make a run for it? What if he was going to kill her?

"He must have turned off. We'll find him." Kyle turned around and drove back the way we had come. We were looking in every driveway and every parking lot we came across, and the fog had lifted a bit so we could see. We saw no sign of the dark sedan. Just past Sharkey's I saw a light-colored Taurus under a dark cottage—still no sedan. We continued on, but something was nagging at me.

I found a Sun Realty rental brochure at Margie's campsite. If you had to hide someone where would you go? Certainly not to a hotel room, where people were in the next room and a maid came every day. A house would be best, but if you didn't own a house on the Outer Banks what would you do? You would find one of the thousands of empty rental cottages that dotted the beach this time of year. You would call and ask about renting it this week, and find out if it was going to be empty. You would make sure it was close and convenient to the Holiday House Hotel.

He said a blue Taurus was following him . . .

"He must have turned down a side road and gone to the Bypass—"

"Turn around," I said. "I think I know where he's keeping her."

I explained about the rental brochure as we drove back towards Sharkey's. As I talked, I remembered something else. "I'm thinking about when I was carjacked. I'm almost positive that it was Keith Knowling. That type of thing is so rare around here it's almost too much of a coincidence. If it *was* him, he was looking very intently at the cottages right before I escaped. That's probably why I was able to take him by surprise when I hit the rut. I ran to Sharkey's, so it wasn't very far away from there. I think I saw—yes, there! Pull into the next driveway."

The fog was back, wrapping around the car as we pulled up the driveway and under the dark cottage. It was one of the big ones, probably six or seven bedrooms with matching bathrooms and a pool and elevator for all I knew. It was a twin to the cottage next door, separated from it by a narrow line of pampas grass.

"What did you see?" Kyle doused the lights and turned to look at me.

"I think I saw a blue Taurus parked under that house." I pointed to the mammoth cottage beside us. "A blue Taurus. Remember what Doug's roommate said? Doug thought he was being followed by a blue Taurus? It occurred to me that Keith might have two cars, one that he drove to the hotel, and another rental car that he used to follow Doug. Maybe he planned to make his escape in it. We lost the other car right around here, and I wouldn't be surprised if it's not parked someplace close by. You can put one car under an empty cottage and not be able to see it from the road, but two cars might attract notice."

"You think he might be hiding Margie in there?" Kyle craned his neck and looked up at the cottage to the right of us.

"It would make a perfect hiding place, wouldn't it?"

Kyle nodded thoughtfully. "Stay here," he said, and got out of the truck before I could say anything. "Take the car and go to Sharkey's if I don't come back," he said, and closed the door.

I swiveled in my seat and watched as he walked towards the other house, keeping close to the pampas grass so that if someone happened to be looking out the window they wouldn't see him. He ducked under the house. I opened my door and got out, shivering and straining to hear something.

The fog muffled all sound, even the sound of the breakers on the beach behind the houses. My heart was pounding and I clutched the trellis that wrapped around the pilings, wondering where Kyle went. I could see the outline of the car under the other house, but I couldn't see its make or color from here. Suddenly, a light flashed and my heart leapt.

It was only the soft glow of the car's inside light, and I could hear the faint pinging of the open-door buzzer. After a moment, the light went out and I expected Kyle to come back across. He didn't.

"Damn, damn," I muttered. Where did he go? How could he leave me here when, for all I knew, he was being attacked or even killed? Keith Knowling was a dangerous, deranged man. There was no telling what he would do if he caught Kyle sneaking around.

Minutes passed, and I strained to see through the fog.

Nothing.

Suddenly, I heard a muffled "Hey!" and then a sickening thump.

fear

I ran to the other house, ducking through the pampas grass to the exterior stairs that led up to the massive decks on the first level. I climbed the stairs, trying to be quiet.

The fog muffled and distorted the sound I'd heard, so I wasn't sure which direction it came from. I welcomed the fog now as I flattened myself against the wooden siding and slid along until I came to a window. I stopped and then peeked around the edge, but all I could see was a curtain.

I heard another thump from the back and I slid past the dark window and ran down the deck. The sound had come from somewhere up ahead and I slowed as I came to another window. This one was also curtained, but a faint light glowed inside.

I ducked and crawled underneath the sill and then hugged the wall when I reached the edge of the house. Across from me was a stairway going up to a second level of decking.

I listened.

Silence, and then I heard something being dragged. Taking a deep breath, I poked my head out just in time to see Kyle's legs and feet disappear inside the house. The door closed with a heavy thud.

Oh Jesus, oh Lord, Keith has Kyle. Keith must have caught him unawares and either stabbed him or hit him—I would have heard a gunshot—and now he had Kyle inside.

I needed to get the police. I needed to get the police *now*. I couldn't bear the thought of leaving Kyle to bleed to death in the hands of Keith Knowling, but I couldn't face him without a weapon. I had turned to go back the way I came when I heard a door opening.

Keith was coming back out.

I looked around desperately and threw myself at the stairway. I raced up them, conscious of the footsteps that were approaching where I'd just been hiding. At the top, I dove for the side of the house where I crouched, panting and striving to hear. Had he seen me? Heard me? The footsteps receded down the deck. If I had run for it, he would have seen me.

I moved lightly towards the back of the house, praying for a set of stairs leading down to the ground and safety. There were two sliding glass doors but no stairs, except for the ones I had just come up. The footsteps were coming back now, and I froze. Someone was coming up.

I looked around for a weapon. Nothing. I rushed over to the railing, but it was a three-story drop to the concrete below.

Turning, I ran back to the sliding doors and tried

the first one I came to. It was locked. The footsteps had almost reached the top of the stairs.

I lunged for the second door, dodging around a chair and tripping over a full ashtray. The sound of the ashtray spinning across the deck sounded horrendously loud. I tried the door and almost wept with relief when it slid open. I slammed it behind me, fumbling with the lock as I heard the footsteps pounding around the side of the house.

I ran for the door, banging my shin on the edge of something wooden and very hard. I dashed out into the hall just as I heard Keith hit the glass door behind me, shaking and kicking it so hard I was afraid he was going to come crashing right through.

I glanced around the wide landing overlooking the cathedral foyer. The stairs were right there, but I hesitated. Margie might be in one of the bedrooms. Acutely conscious of the sound of the glass door being battered, I ran down the hall throwing open the doors. All I saw were massive bedrooms and opulent bathrooms.

There was sudden silence.

Was Keith inside?

I needed to go *down.* I scrambled down the polished wooden steps into a foyer. The impressive front doors were to my right and a hall leading to the back of the house was on my left. I turned towards the doors, undecided, and then headed for the back of the house—towards Kyle. If Keith was upstairs, I might have just enough time to find Kyle and get us both out of here.

When I burst into the living room I tripped over a sectional couch and landed on my back. I heard someone groaning close to my head and I scrambled to my hands and knees, already crawling backwards as fast as I could before I focused on Kyle. His eyes were glazed and he was clutching his head.

"Kyle!" I sobbed, grabbing him by the shirt and trying to pull him to his feet. I looked around, trying to watch all the entrances as I struggled to pull him off the floor. He was disoriented, and I winced as I saw blood dripping from the back of his head. I got him part way up, and then he slumped back to the floor, grasping feebly at the edge of the couch.

Where was Keith? If he were inside he would be here by now. He must have been forced to look for another entrance, which meant he could be anywhere. I jumped to my feet and ran to the back door and locked it. I looked around, but that was the only outside entrance I saw. Outside, the fog swirled thickly against the window, but there was no sign of Keith. Where did he go? I had no way of knowing how many other entrances the house had. "It's okay, it's okay," I said to Kyle who was crouched by the sofa.

"Call the police," he muttered. "God, I'm going to *kill* that bastard."

Of course! There had to be a telephone. I ran over to the counter that separated the large gourmet kitchen from the living room. Where was it? I saw the jack, but there was no phone attached to it. Did Keith hide the phone for some reason? I started opening drawers and cabinets. Out of the corner of my eye, I saw someone come around the side of the house. Cursing, I ran back to Kyle.

"You have to get up, Kyle, come on, get *up*," I coaxed, grabbing him by the back of the shirt and helping him to his feet. He leaned on me heavily, and I didn't like how dilated his pupils were. Staggering, we made it down the hall to the front door and I pulled on the handle, trying to figure out the lock with one hand.

"Dead bolt," Kyle said, and I realized with horror that he was right. The door was bolted, with no sign of a key. Behind us we heard the sound of breaking glass.

"Now what?" I cried, turning around in a circle and looking for someplace to go. I was heading for the stairs again, not sure how I was going to get Kyle to climb them, when I heard someone say my name. At first I thought it was Kyle, but I looked up to see that someone was standing at the end of the hall.

"Callie," he said again, moving towards us.

This wasn't Keith Knowling. Couldn't be Keith Knowling.

"Who . . . ? How . . . ?"

"Surprise." He smiled at me as if he didn't have a care in the world. With a shiver, I realized he held a large, serrated fillet knife—the same knife that had been held at my throat last night

Thirty-six

The Mermaid

I shook my head. I just didn't understand.

"Why? Why are you here, Charlie? You're not Keith." It was an inane statement, but I was so intent on thinking that Mark Holloway was Keith Knowling. Yet here was blond, handsome Charlie standing with a knife in his hand. Charlie, who had been lying about who he was and why he was on the Outer Banks.

"I'm Lucas Charles Lewis, at your service," he said, and gave a slight, mocking bow.

It clicked: the name, who he was, everything. I realized that I had made a very wrong assumption. I should have listened to old Jonathan when he said he remembered Angel, but had never seen her husband. Angel didn't come to the hotel with her husband. She came with her lover.

"You're Betty's son," I said. "You were Angel's lover. *You* killed Angel, and you've been stalking Margie since this summer. Where's Margie?"

He smiled and took a step forward.

"Why this summer?" I said quickly, trying to distract him. What were we going to do? Where was Margie? "Why didn't you come back earlier? Was it because you were in jail?" This, as I remembered what Lily told me this morning.

"Yes, I was in jail," he said. "You must have talked to Lily. *That* was a stellar performance, if I do say so myself. I had her eating out of my hand. I knew the game was almost over and I didn't see the point in giving any more of my father's hard-earned money to the Holiday House Hotel.

"I was in jail, but not for burglary. Some stupid girl said I raped her out in California. All women are liars. You lied, Margie lied." He smiled, horribly. "She's my Angel, you know. I believe that people can come back from the dead. My Angel is living in that girl's body."

He laughed at my obvious confusion. "Oh, I don't expect you to understand. No one does. I know it's true. Even Angel's brother knows it's true, or why would he show up here to see Margie? I didn't know who he was at first, but once I heard his name I knew."

"Angel's brother?"

"Mark Holloway. You didn't believe that he was a reporter, did you? I'm sure he didn't want to deal with all the publicity, so he came up with that story so everybody would leave him alone."

Ah. Well, that explained Mark. He had probably found out about room 328 from the police. What did he hope to gain from seeing the room? Did he see it as a link to his sister, as a way to come to terms with her death?

"How did you find out Margie was really Sandra Meadows? Why did you call her parents?" I needed to keep him talking while I thought of a plan. My back was aching from supporting Kyle, and I shifted his weight a little, his head lolling against my shoulder.

"I found that other birth certificate, the one that said her name was Sandra Meadows born in Hammets Hill, Massachusetts, so I called her parents. Surprise, surprise! They didn't know where their dear daughter was. But I knew, oh, I knew."

"You threatened to tell her parents where she was that night at Kelly's. You told her you would tell them where she was if she didn't—what? What did you want her to do? Sleep with you?"

I was finding it hard to believe that this man, this golden man as friendly as a bumbling puppy, had killed one woman and kidnapped another. Where was Margie? Kyle mumbled something against my neck.

"I got him good, didn't I?" Charlie said, glancing at Kyle. "No, I didn't ask her to *sleep* with me. What kind of person do you think I am?"

I didn't answer that one.

"I merely asked that she go out with me on one or two dates, to continue what we had been doing for the last several weeks—before she told me she *didn't want to see me anymore.*" His voice twisted into a falsetto. "I thought we were just friends, Charlie. Can't we just stay friends?" Hearing Margie's words coming out of this man's mouth was terrifying. What had he done with her? Was she already dead? Kyle mumbled something against my neck again.

"How did you find Margie, Charlie? How did you know she was at the campground?"

"Her little buddy, Doug," Charlie said. "I followed him in my rental car, the Taurus. I figured he would know where she was, and I was right. I didn't expect it to take so long, but eventually he led me to the campground. I waited until that night and then I went back and persuaded her to come with me. I asked her *nicely,* brought flowers and everything, and she turned me down. So I convinced her otherwise."

I cringed at his casual use of the word "convinced" when the reality must have been much more brutal. "And then you ran down Doug that night," I said.

Charlie laughed. "That's what he gets for messing with my girl. Ask Keith Knowling. He's still running after I set it up to look like he killed Angel. Not much use, is he?" Charlie said, hearing Kyle's muttering. "You need to find a man who can take care of you. Of course, Laurie McKinley, you still have a husband, don't you? What do you think he would say if I told him you were playing around with another man?"

"How did you find out who I was?" I watched as the knife waved back and forth. His eyes shifted to something behind me, but I was afraid to turn and look. He had moved closer now, and I had absolutely no plan of action other than dropping Kyle and running, which I couldn't do. Or could I? Most likely he would follow me and leave Kyle alone, but what then? Where would I go? I eyed the stairs.

"There's nowhere for you to go, Callie. Let me see, how did I know who you were? I recognized you. I had all the time in the world while I was in jail to watch the news. I knew all about you."

"You sent the press releases, and when that didn't work, you tried to kidnap me. You were going to bring me here." Kyle muttered something else. This time I caught some of it.

"Keep him talking," he said in my ear.

Huh? I almost looked down at him I was so surprised to hear the clear, concise words. He was conscious, planning something. I forced myself to look back at Charlie. "Why did you send the press release? Why was I a threat?"

"*You talked to my mother,*" Charlie hissed. "She's the only one who knew about me and Angel. My mother was Angel's only friend. When she contacted the media after Angel was killed, I talked her into staying quiet. I told her we didn't want to ruin poor little Angel's reputation, now did we?"

"Your poor mother. She loves you so much, you know. How you must have disappointed her."

"My mother believes what she wants to believe, like most women. God, you are all so weak! She wanted so much to believe that I was doing well out in Hollywood, and when I told her the rape conviction was a silly mistake she wanted to believe that too. When I told her I had come home to make a new life for myself, she gave me Dad's money to get started. She wouldn't touch it anyway. She hated him."

That was how he could afford to stay in the hotel and convince us all he was a successful businessman. It also explained his facile lying—he was an actor at heart and it must not have taken much effort to impersonate a wealthy car salesman.

"What about Keith?" I asked. I had to keep him talking. "How did you set him up for Angel's murder?"

"Actually, it just all worked out. I knew he'd come home that night and find her. I figured he'd call the police and that they would suspect him right off the bat. His running was just luck. The police never even knew I existed. I was careful to wipe my prints away after I killed her, and then Keith came along right behind me and got his prints everywhere. I wonder what he thought when he came home and saw his wife lying in the backyard?"

"Callie, when I tell you to, run," Kyle whispered in my ear. "There's a door behind the stairs. Run for help. Break out the window if you have to."

"He thought he would be blamed for her murder," I said, conscious of Kyle's weight lifting as he shifted his feet. What was he planning? Again Charlie's gaze moved to something behind me. I had a feeling he was looking at the same door that Kyle mentioned and that I couldn't see. What if the door led to a bathroom with no windows? I glanced at the stairs again. It seemed safest to run up those, but Kyle said to go for the door. Indecision flickered through me as I felt him shift his weight again.

"You were fine letting him take the blame. Where is he, anyway? Did you kill him too?"

"It was so much nicer for him to be blamed for Angel's murder," Charlie said, stepping closer—much closer and he would be right on top of us. My eyes went to the stairs again and Charlie saw me and grinned. "I have no idea where Keith is. All I know is that he's living in hell, and that's all I care about."

"Why did you kill her?" I asked softly. Kyle tensed.

"She told me it was over, that she just wanted to be friends. I loved her so much, I loved her before any other man even noticed she existed. She was mine. And then she said *she never loved me*—"

"Run," Kyle whispered, cutting through Charlie's anguish and rage.

Kyle dropped to the floor and I looked at the stairs—so close!—and then took a leap of faith. I turned and rushed towards the door.

Behind me, Charlie screamed something and then sprang down the hall, but I was already to the door, pushing it open and going through it. I glanced over my shoulder just in time to see Kyle grab Charlie's foot as he came down the hall, pulling him off balance.

"Run, now!" Kyle shouted, and Charlie swung at him with the knife. "RUN!"

I ran.

Slamming the door behind me, I locked it, trying to ignore the struggle I heard in the hall. I turned and saw in shock that Margie was lying on the bed, her hands tied to the bedposts, her eyes closed. I rushed over just long enough to put a hand on her face and discover that she was breathing, though it was a slow, drugged exhalation. If I could entice Charlie to follow me, it was unlikely that he would stop to harm Margie. After all, she was still alive after two days in his care.

"I'm going for the police, Charlie!" I shouted at the top of my lungs, hoping he would hear, hoping he would leave Kyle and come after me. I looked around for a phone. There was a jack, but the phone in here was also missing.

I suited action to words and ran for the window that Kyle must have seen.

The window was locked, and outside I could see fog swirling over the deck. Behind me, I heard Charlie hit the door. I turned long enough to see that it wasn't going to withstand his attack much longer, and then turned back to the window, fumbling with the lock. What happened to Kyle? There was no time to wonder; I had to get out, go for help.

The door crashed open and I struggled to lift the heavy storm window high enough to climb through. I strained—just another inch—and then I was crashing through the screen, my head and shoulders outside and my legs still inside as I tried to wriggle through the small space. Behind me, Charlie got a hold of my foot. I kicked desperately, catching him someplace soft and obviously painful judging from his cry. For a moment, the hold on my foot was gone and I scrambled out the window, landing on my stomach on the deck outside. I crawled forward and then got up and ran, pounding along the deck towards the back of the house. Why, oh why hadn't I gone towards the road? It was too late now, and I skidded around the side of the house as I heard Charlie clambering out the window to come after me.

There were stairs leading down to the ground and I dove for them, sliding down the last three or four on my butt and landing on the hard concrete by the covered pool. Then I was up and running.

"Fire, help, fire!" I screamed, but my words were lost in the thick fog. There was a fence surrounding the pool and I ran in the only direction I could, towards the beach. In front of me was a gate, and I crashed into it, my fingers working the metal latch. I risked a glance over my shoulder and saw Charlie about fifty feet away. *Oh my God.* I got the gate open and ran up the walkway and down a set of stairs onto the beach. Behind me, Charlie had reached the top and was pounding downward. Should I go left or right at the bottom? Sharkey's was close, just a few houses down to the left.

"Fire, help, fire!" I hit the soft sand and turned left. Except for the wet hiss of the ocean, there was only silence around me; not even a bird answered my desperate call.

I ran as fast as I could through the sliding, heavy sand. I could hear Charlie's breathing and I knew he was gaining on me. He grabbed my arm and I tore out of his grasp, lashing out with my leg and catching him in the shin. I ran, veering towards the hard sand right beside the waves.

"Help!"

Charlie was right behind me. My lungs felt as if they would burst and I knew I couldn't go on much longer. He grabbed my shirt as I gained the hard sand and I twisted away, pulling so hard that when his hold broke I flew backwards into the foaming water. I felt a heavy weight hit me and I went under as Charlie came crashing down on top of me. We rolled over and over in the water and he yanked on my hair, keeping my head under. In desperation, I gulped for air and choked on a mouthful of briny seawater. A wave broke over our heads and Charlie's grip was broken. The foaming wave tumbled me end over end until I came to a stop on the hard, shell-embedded sand. I lay there, unable to move as I coughed up what seemed like a gallon of seawater. I began to crawl up the beach towards the dunes, looking over my shoulder to try and see where Charlie was.

He was staring at the fog-shrouded ocean. He seemed to have forgotten about me.

"Angel?" he called. "Baby? Is that you?"

Fog coalesced over the foaming water, shimmering silver in the diffused light of the moon. Was that a woman's head I saw? Was there someone *out* there?

Charlie stood waist deep in the rolling, washing waves. "I didn't mean to do it, baby, but you made me so mad. Why did you have to run away from me? Even when I watched you walk down the aisle with that bastard, I knew you would be mine someday."

I scooted up the beach away from Charlie, but he was so engrossed he didn't even notice me. The fog swirled and shifted and I blinked, trying to focus my gaze. There was something out there, that was for sure, and Charlie thought it was Angel. The hair on my neck prickled in fear and I slowly began to crawl backwards, trying not to draw attention to myself.

"I know I hit you, but you deserved it. You made me do it. I loved you so much, you knew that, but you left me, and you made me look like a *fool*. Why'd you have to do that? We would have been together forever if you hadn't run away." He put his arms out to brace himself against an approaching wave and then started wading deeper into the water.

"Wait! Where are you going?" he shouted.

I caught an impression of long, moonlight-streaked hair framing an oval face, and then it was gone. Or was it just a reflection of light off the water?

Charlie dove into the next wave, and when I saw him again he was swimming straight out to sea. He disappeared into the mist.

Though I continued to watch, until pounding feet on the walkway and Kyle's voice brought me back to myself, Charlie did not return.

Neither did the mermaid.

Thirty-seven
Happiness Wanted

The sun was low on the horizon, bathing the ocean in silver-gold as the sky lightened to a pale blue. It was chilly this morning, but at least there was no trace of fog.

"Raow," Ice commented, leaning against my leg and slitting his eyes against the light.

"It is a pretty day, isn't it? Enjoy it while you can, soon it'll be winter."

On the beach, Jake ran around to his favorite watering spots, carrying the orange volleyball in his mouth. Seagulls circled him, calling down raucous insults from on high.

It had been two weeks since Charles Lucas Lewis disappeared into the waves. His body washed up on shore down by Oregon Inlet a couple days after he tried to kill me.

I stroked Ice's back and he stretched under my fingers. "Nasty man," I said, and Ice purred in agreement.

I glanced at my watch and saw that I had about an hour before I was due in to work. There was just enough time to stop by and check on Kyle who was at home recovering from a bad concussion and knife wounds in his arm and side. He would be fine with some rest, but I still felt guilty. If it weren't for me, he never would have been hurt. I knew I would carry that guilt for the rest of my life.

"If you're being nice to me just because you feel guilty, get over it," Kyle had snapped at me the other day. He was not a pleasant patient.

It wasn't just guilt, and he knew it as well as I did.

Jake barked at a pelican that was floating on the waves out of his reach. I shook my head as he plunged into the cold water in an attempt to reach the bird. I'd have to give him yet another bath.

I had taken a few days off work, but I was back in time to make sure the new menu was up and running by November first. I had less to do now that Lily had hired a new banquet manager, but therein lay a new problem. She hired Stacy, Kyle's ex-wife. Talk about a sticky situation.

Margie, or Sandy, as she was going by these days, wasn't back to work yet. She had told me that she would be back soon when I visited her. She wanted to stay on the Outer Banks and paint, and she would work at the Holiday House until she could support herself by painting alone.

Doug, surprisingly enough, *had* quit the hotel. He got a job at one of the local papers as a journalist. He wanted to ask Sandy to marry him, he told me; now he had a reason to do more than surf and skate along at minimum wage. He had been at Sandy's side for the past two weeks as she healed.

Doug was the first to see the resemblance between Sandy and Angel, mainly because he'd done a project on the "Murdered Mermaid" while he was in school. On the day we found Sandy in the cottage by the ocean, Doug had shown up at the police station demanding that they find her. When he left the hospital, he drove to Hatteras where he found her deserted camp, and he'd known that she didn't leave voluntarily.

Sandy still hadn't spoken much about her ordeal, but I knew Charlie kept her, drugged, at the house in Nags Head for two days. No one knew exactly what he had planned for her that Sunday, but I could guess. I still shivered at how close we'd come to losing her.

Lee Meadows hadn't changed much. He and Hannah had been staying in the hotel for the past two weeks while Sandy healed, and Lee had managed to piss off about everybody who worked there. He had accepted that his daughter would not be returning to medical school, and that if he wanted to have any contact with her he was going to have to accept her decision to remain on the Outer Banks. Hannah and Doug were getting along famously, and I thought that everything might be all right with Sandy.

Jake romped up the dune with his volleyball and flopped down next to me, exhausted and happy. The newspaper beside me fluttered in the breeze and Ice reached out a paw to pat at it.

Keith Knowling had surfaced in Montana, where he had been hiding for the last five years. He'd been living in fear of arrest and came forward when he learned that his wife's killer had been found.

I stretched and stood up, feeling the cool November sun on my face. I leaned down to pick up the newspaper and looked at my face on the front cover.

I had not gotten away unscathed. Though the press release Lucas sent to the papers was never printed, I hadn't been able to hide from the publicity generated by his death. My identity was discovered and splashed over every newspaper from here to California. Everyone knew that Laurie McKinley was hiding on the Outer Banks.

My instinct was to run, and run as far and as fast as possible.

But I realized that I had learned a lot about myself this fall, a lot about the self-reliance of women. Happiness is a fleeting rainbow; it disappears when you get too close. The only thing that keeps us going is that there's always another one on the horizon.

Running was not going to bring me happiness.

So I was staying and sticking it out. It was one of the hardest decisions I had ever made, and time would tell if it was the right one.

I looked out over the blue ocean, rising and falling in gentle, splashing breaths. Was that a woman's head I saw just past the breakers? No, it was just the pelican again, bobbing among the waves.

I still wasn't sure what happened the night Charlie Lewis died. I told the police that he had seen something in the waves—something he thought was Angel

Knowling's ghost. I told them that he swam out into the ocean after her. He swam so far that he couldn't make it back.

They never asked me what I saw.

I'm not sure what I would have said. Would I have told them I saw a mermaid?

I shook my head and laughed. Ice reached up a paw to bat at my leg and I leaned down to stroke him.

I saw something that night. But was it a pelican, like the one floating on the waves out there right now? Was it a dolphin?

Or was it a mermaid?

I laughed again, and Jake perked up his ears.

"Only on the Outer Banks," I said to him.

I took one last look at the ocean and turned to head back home. It was another beautiful fall day on the Outer Banks, and I was looking forward to tomorrow.

And the next day.

About The Author

Wendy Howell Mills, like her book's heroine, is a restaurant manager on the beautiful Outer Banks of North Carolina. She has been in the restaurant business for over eleven years, and enjoys using her experience to write unique mysteries involving restaurant settings. She loves the Outer Banks, and only a *very* large hurricane pries the author, her husband, and their menagerie of animals away from the beach.

Wendy is also the author of *Callie & the Dealer & a Dog Named Jake,* winner of the Dark Oak Mystery Award, and the first book in the Callie McKinley Outer Banks Mystery series.